THE NEW PROPHECY
WARRIORS
STARLIGHT

WARRIORS

WARRIORS:
THE NEW PROPHECY

THE NEW PROPHECY

WARRIORS

STARLIGHT

ERIN
HUNTER

HARPERCOLLINS*PUBLISHERS*

Starlight
Copyright © 2006 by Working Partners Limited
Series created by Working Partners Limited
For information address HarperCollins
Children's Books, a division of HarperCollins Publishers,
195 Broadway, New York, NY 10007.
www.harperchildrens.com

Library of Congress Cataloging-in-Publication Data
Hunter, Erin.
Starlight / by Erin Hunter.— 1st ed.
p.   cm. — (Warriors, the new prophecy ; bk. four)
Summary: The warrior cat Clans arrive at their new home and set
about exploring and fighting over the unfamiliar territory.
ISBN-10: 0-06-082758-0 (trade bdg.)
ISBN-13: 978-0-06-082758-8 (trade bdg.)
ISBN-10: 0-06-082760-2 (lib. bdg.)
ISBN-13: 978-0-06-082760-1 (lib. bdg.)
[1. Cats—Fiction. 2. Fantasy.] I. Title.
PZ7.H916625Sta 2006   2005020600
[Fic]—dc22   CIP
                                                              AC

Typography by Karin Paprocki
17 18 19 20 PC/LSCH 20 19 18 17 16 15 14
❖
First Edition

Special thanks to Cherith Baldry

ALLEGIANCES

THUNDERCLAN

LEADER   **FIRESTAR**—ginger tom with a flame-colored pelt

DEPUTY   **GRAYSTRIPE**—long-haired gray tom

MEDICINE CAT   **CINDERPELT**—dark gray she-cat
APPRENTICE, LEAFPAW

WARRIORS   (toms, and she-cats without kits)

DUSTPELT—dark brown tabby tom
APPRENTICE, SQUIRRELPAW

SANDSTORM—pale ginger she-cat

CLOUDTAIL—long-haired white tom
APPRENTICE, SPIDERPAW

BRACKENFUR—golden brown tabby tom
APPRENTICE, WHITEPAW

THORNCLAW—golden brown tabby tom

BRIGHTHEART—white she-cat with ginger patches

BRAMBLECLAW—dark brown tabby tom with amber eyes

ASHFUR—pale gray (with darker flecks) tom, dark blue eyes

RAINWHISKER—dark gray tom with blue eyes

SOOTFUR—lighter gray tom with amber eyes

SORRELTAIL—tortoiseshell and white she-cat with amber eyes

APPRENTICES (more than six moons old, in training to become warriors)

SQUIRRELPAW—dark ginger she-cat with green eyes

LEAFPAW—light brown tabby she-cat with amber eyes

WHITEPAW—white she-cat with green eyes

SPIDERPAW—long-limbed black tom with brown underbelly and amber eyes

QUEENS (she-cats expecting or nursing kits)

FERNCLOUD—pale gray (with darker flecks) she-cat with green eyes

ELDERS (former warriors and queens, now retired)

GOLDENFLOWER—pale ginger coat

LONGTAIL—pale tabby tom with dark black stripes, retired early due to failing sight

MOUSEFUR—small dusky brown she-cat

SHADOWCLAN

LEADER BLACKSTAR—large white tom with huge jet black paws

DEPUTY RUSSETFUR—dark ginger she-cat

MEDICINE CAT LITTLECLOUD—very small tabby tom

WARRIORS (toms, and she-cats without kits)

OAKFUR—small brown tom
APPRENTICE, SMOKEPAW

CEDARHEART—dark gray tom

ROWANCLAW—ginger tom
APPRENTICE, TALONPAW

TAWNYPELT—tortoiseshell she-cat with green eyes

QUEENS (she-cats expecting or nursing kits)

TALLPOPPY—long-legged light brown tabby she-cat

ELDERS (former warriors and queens, now retired)

RUNNINGNOSE—small gray and white tom, formerly the medicine cat

BOULDER—skinny gray tom

WINDCLAN

LEADER **TALLSTAR**—elderly black and white tom with a very long tail

DEPUTY **MUDCLAW**—mottled dark brown tom

MEDICINE CAT **BARKFACE**—short-tailed brown tom

WARRIORS (toms, and she-cats without kits)

TORNEAR—tabby tom
APPRENTICE, OWLPAW

WEBFOOT—dark gray tabby tom
APPRENTICE, WEASELPAW

ONEWHISKER—brown tabby tom

CROWFEATHER—dark gray, almost black tom with blue eyes

ASHFOOT—gray she-cat

QUEENS (she-cats expecting or nursing kits)

WHITETAIL—small white she-cat

ELDERS	(former warriors and queens, now retired)
	MORNINGFLOWER—tortoiseshell she-cat
	RUSHTAIL—light brown tom

RIVERCLAN

LEADER	**LEOPARDSTAR**—unusually spotted golden tabby she-cat
DEPUTY	**MISTYFOOT**—gray she-cat with blue eyes
MEDICINE CAT	**MOTHWING**—dappled golden she-cat
WARRIORS	(toms, and she-cats without kits)
	BLACKCLAW—smoky black tom **APPRENTICE, VOLEPAW**
	HEAVYSTEP—thickset tabby tom **APPRENTICE, STONEPAW**
	HAWKFROST—dark brown tom with a white underbelly and ice-blue eyes.
	SWALLOWTAIL—dark tabby she-cat
QUEENS	(she-cats expecting or nursing kits)
	MOSSPELT—tortoiseshell she-cat
	DAWNFLOWER—pale gray she-cat

CATS OUTSIDE CLANS

SMOKY—muscular gray and white tom who lives in a barn near the horseplace

DAISY—she-cat with long creamy brown fur who lives with Smoky

FLOSS—small gray and white she-cat who lives with Smoky and Daisy

TWOLEG
NEST

TWOLEG PATH

CLEARING

TWOLEG PATH

SHADOWCLAN
CAMP

HALFBRIDGE

SMALL
THUNDERPATH

GREENLEAF
TWOLEGPLACE

HALFBRIDGE

STREAM

ISLAND

RIVERCLAN
CAMP

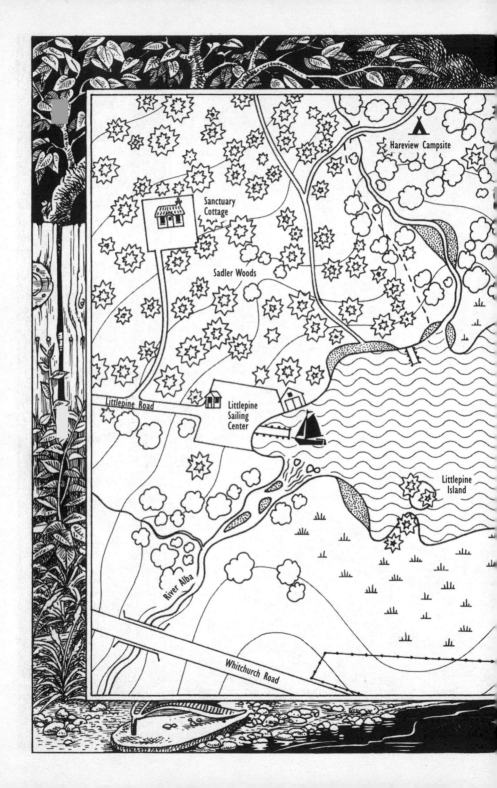

PROLOGUE

Moonlight washed over the hillside, casting heavy shadows around a thick wall of thornbushes. The bushes surrounded a hollow with rocky sides that sloped down steeply to a pool in the shape of a full moon. Halfway up the side of the hollow, a trickle of water bubbled up between two moss-covered stones, glimmering like liquid starshine as it fell into the pool below.

The branches rustled and parted as cats emerged at the top of the hollow and began to pick their way down to the water's edge. Their pelts shone with a soft, pale light, and their pawsteps left a frosty glitter on the moss behind them.

A tortoiseshell she-cat was the first to reach the pool. She looked around with glowing eyes. "Yes," she purred. "*This* is the place."

"You're right, Spottedleaf. When we chose the four cats to lead the Clans out of the forest, we chose well." The reply came from a blue-gray warrior who was approaching from the other side of the hollow. She leaped down from a jutting rock to face the tortoiseshell across the moonlit water. "But the Clans still have a hard task ahead of them."

Spottedleaf dipped her head in agreement. "Yes, Bluestar. Their courage and faith will be tried to their limits. But they have come this far—they will not give up."

More starry warriors joined them, clustering around the water until the hollow was lined with their sleek, shining shapes.

"Our journey was hard, too," one cat meowed.

"We felt the pain of leaving the paths we had walked for so long," added another.

"Now we must learn to walk in new skies." Spottedleaf's voice was full of confidence. She sat on a rock near the tumbling stream and wrapped her tail around her paws. "We must guide our Clans to this new meeting place, where we can speak to the leaders and medicine cats. Then this will truly be home for all five Clans."

A murmur of agreement rose, and a gleam of hope shone in the eyes of the cats around her.

"They will catch fish from the lake," one cat meowed.

"And prey is running in the hills and beside the water," another put in. "All the Clans will find food, even in leaf-bare."

The blue-gray warrior still seemed uneasy. "There's more to life than fresh-kill," she mewed.

A bracken-colored tom thrust his way to the front of the crowd. "They're not kits," he pointed out impatiently. "They know how to avoid Twolegs and their dogs. Foxes and badgers, too."

"Not all trouble comes from Twolegs," Bluestar snapped.

She swiveled her head to glare into the tom's eyes. "And not from foxes or badgers either, Oakheart. You know that as well as I do. The Clans bring trouble within themselves."

The warriors glanced uneasily at one another, but Oakheart dipped his head. "Of course. And they always will. That is part of what it means to be a warrior."

"Trouble from within greatest danger brings." A new voice spoke, deep and gravelly.

Bluestar whipped around, her neck fur rising, and stared at the newcomer standing at the top of the hollow. It was too big and solid to be a cat. Instead, it seemed as if a clot of darkness had entered the circle of thornbushes, in which the watching cats could just make out broad, muscular limbs and the gleam of small, bright eyes.

After a few heartbeats Bluestar relaxed. "Welcome, friend," she meowed. "StarClan owes you thanks. You have done well."

"By me is little done," the newcomer replied. "These cats their destiny have faced with courage."

"The Clans have traveled far and suffered a great deal of sadness that we were powerless to ease," Spottedleaf agreed. "They kept going even when we lost sight and hearing of them among the mountains, when they walked the paths of a different Tribe. Now they must learn to be four Clans again." She looked solemn. "There will be much pain, especially for those who traveled together to the sun-drown-water. They won't find it easy to forget their friendship."

"They must mark out their new territories as soon as they

can." Oakheart's voice rumbled in his throat. "There'll be trouble there."

"Every loyal warrior will want the best for their Clan," meowed Bluestar.

"So long as it is their Clan that they fight for," returned Oakheart, "and not themselves."

"That's where the danger lies," murmured an anxious voice. A tomcat with a glossy black coat was gazing down into the silvery water as if he could see danger rising to the surface like a giant fish. "I see one cat, hungry for power that is not deserved. . . ."

"Not deserved?" A lean tom with a crooked jaw sprang to his paws on the other side of the pool, the fur on his shoulders bristling in fury. "Nightstar, how dare you say 'not deserved'?"

The black tom's pelt rippled in the moonlight as he looked up. "Very well, Crookedstar, not deserved *yet*," he meowed. "This cat needs to learn the virtue of patience. Power is not a piece of prey to be grabbed before it escapes."

The cat with the crooked jaw sat down again, though the anger stayed in his eyes. "Would you have all our warriors as timid as mice?" he muttered.

Nightstar's eyes narrowed and his tail-tip twitched, but before he could spit out a reply another cat padded forward: a thick-furred gray she-cat with a broad face and a fierce gleam in her eyes. She stood beside Spottedleaf at the mossy edge of the pool and gazed down into the water. After a few moments, ripples began to spread in circles from the middle of the pool and wash against the bank.

The gray she-cat lifted her head. "I have seen what will come," she growled. "There are dark times ahead."

A stir of anxiety passed through the cats like wind rippling through reeds, but no cat dared to question her out loud.

"Well?" Bluestar demanded when the silence had stretched out for several heartbeats. "Tell us what you mean, Yellowfang."

The gray she-cat hesitated. "I am not certain what I have seen," she rasped at last. "And you won't like what I have to tell you." She closed her eyes, and when she spoke her voice was deeper and quieter than before, so that every cat had to strain to listen: "*'Before there is peace, blood will spill blood, and the lake will run red.'*"

Bluestar stiffened, and she bent her head to look into the water. A red stain was spreading across the surface, rippling outward until the water flamed scarlet. It seemed to reflect the fire of sunset, yet above the hollow the moon still floated in thin drifts of cloud.

A gasp of horror rose from the cats. Spottedleaf padded forward, trembling, and stared desperately into the water as if she were searching for something that would challenge Yellowfang's ominous words.

"Are you trying to find out what will happen to Firestar?" Bluestar asked her gently. "Don't search too hard, Spottedleaf. You of all cats should know that sometimes there is nothing we can do."

Spottedleaf raised her head, and there was a fiercely

determined light in her eyes. "I would do *anything* to help Firestar," she hissed. "I will protect him with all the power of StarClan."

"But even that may not be enough," Bluestar warned her.

Around them, the warriors of StarClan began to pad away from the pool, climbing the slope and slipping back through the thornbushes until the shimmer of their pelts vanished and the only light in the hollow came from the reflection of the moon in the water.

The creature in the shadows remained a moment longer, watching in silence until the last cat had gone. Then she stirred, and a shaft of moonlight struck her powerful shoulders.

"Midnight, this not your place," she growled to herself. "Is no more to do." She paused and added, "Once more, maybe, with Clans I will meet. Clouded is time to come."

As she turned to push her way back through the thorns, the moonlight caught the broad white stripe down the badger's head; then Midnight was gone, and the hollow was left empty.

CHAPTER 1

Brambleclaw stood at the top of the slope, gazing at the clawpricks of silver fire reflected in the lake below. The Clans had finally found their new home, just as Midnight had promised. StarClan was waiting for them, and they were safe from the Twoleg monsters at last.

Around him warriors from all four Clans murmured to each other, staring uneasily at the dark, unfamiliar space at the foot of the hill.

"It's impossible to tell what's down there in this light." Brightheart, a ginger-and-white ThunderClan warrior, swung around so that her one good eye could take in the whole of the landscape.

Her mate, Cloudtail, twitched his tail. "How bad can it be? Think what we've come through to get here. We can fight off anything on four legs."

"And what about Twolegs?" demanded Russetfur, the ShadowClan deputy.

"The journey has left us all tired and weak," Blackclaw of WindClan added. "Foxes and badgers could track us down easily when we're all out in the open like this."

For a moment Brambleclaw felt a tremor of fear. Then he braced his shoulders. StarClan would not have brought them here if they did not believe the Clans could survive in their new territories.

"What are we waiting for?" a new voice spoke up. "Are we going to stand here all night?"

Stifling a *mrrow* of laughter, Brambleclaw turned to see his Clanmate Squirrelpaw standing behind him. The ginger apprentice was tearing the tough, springy grass with her front paws, her green eyes glowing with anticipation.

"Brambleclaw, look!" she purred. "We did it! We found our new home!"

She tucked her hindlegs under her, ready to dash down the hill, but before she could take off, Firestar pushed through the cats and stood in her way.

"Wait." The ThunderClan leader touched his daughter's shoulder affectionately with the tip of his tail. "We'll go together, and keep a sharp lookout for trouble. This may be the place that StarClan wished us to find, but they would not expect us to leave our wits in the forest."

Squirrelpaw dipped her head respectfully and stepped back, but when she shot a sideways glance at Brambleclaw, he saw that her eyes still gleamed with excitement. For Squirrelpaw, their journey's end could not possibly be scary.

Firestar padded over to join Blackstar and Leopardstar, the leaders of ShadowClan and RiverClan. "I suggest we send a patrol ahead," he meowed. "Just a couple of cats, to find out what it's like down there."

"Good idea—but we can't just stand here and wait for them to return," Leopardstar objected. "It's much too exposed."

Blackstar grunted in agreement. "If a fox came along now, it could pick off the weaker cats with no trouble at all."

"But we need to rest." Mudclaw of WindClan came up to join the discussion. His leader, Tallstar, lay on the ground a little way off, with the medicine cat Barkface crouching over him. "Tallstar can't go much farther."

"Then let's send the patrol right away," Firestar suggested, "and the rest of us will follow more slowly until we find somewhere more sheltered. Yes, Mudclaw," he added, as the WindClan deputy opened his mouth to argue, "we're all tired, but we'll sleep more easily if we're not stuck out on the open hillside like this."

Blackstar called Russetfur over to him, while Leopardstar signaled with her tail for her deputy, Mistyfoot.

"I want you to go as far as the lake, then come straight back," Leopardstar ordered. "Find out what you can, but be quick, and stay out of sight."

The two cats flicked their ears, then whirled and raced away, loping along with their bellies close to the ground; within a couple of heartbeats they had vanished into the darkness.

Firestar watched them go before letting out a yowl to call the rest of the cats around him. Mudclaw went back to Tallstar and nudged the old leader to his paws. Their Clans clustered together behind the leaders of ThunderClan,

RiverClan, and ShadowClan and began to follow them down the slope toward the lake.

"What's the matter?" Squirrelpaw demanded, noticing that Brambleclaw wasn't moving. "Why are you standing there like a frozen rabbit?"

"I want . . ." Brambleclaw glanced around and spotted his sister Tawnypelt padding past a little way off; he summoned her with a jerk of his head. "I want all of us to go down together," he explained when the tortoiseshell she-cat joined them. "All the cats who made the first journey."

Four cats remained from the six who had left the forest in search of a new home many moons ago. They had gained something very precious on that journey, as well as a safe place for their Clans to live: a strong bond of friendship had been forged between them, stronger than rock and deeper than the endless water that washed against the cliffs where Midnight the badger lived.

Now Brambleclaw wanted to travel with his friends one more time before their duties to their separate Clans forced them apart.

Tawnypelt let out a purr of approval. Meeting her green gaze, Brambleclaw knew that, like him, she understood they would soon be rivals again; that the next time they met could be in battle. The pain of parting swelled in his heart, and he pressed his muzzle to his sister's, feeling her breath warm against his whiskers.

"Where's Crowfeather?" she asked.

Brambleclaw looked up and spotted the young WindClan

warrior a few tail-lengths away, anxiously pacing beside Tall-star. The WindClan leader looked so exhausted he could hardly put one paw in front of the other; his long tail dragged on the ground and he was leaning heavily on the brown tabby warrior Onewhisker. The WindClan medicine cat, Barkface, walked close behind, a worried look on his face.

"Hey, Crowfeather!" Squirrelpaw called.

The WindClan cat bounded across. "What do you want?"

Brambleclaw ignored his unwelcoming tone. Crow-feather's tongue was sharp enough to slice your ears off, but if danger threatened he would fight to his last breath to defend his friends.

"Travel down to the lake with us," he urged. "I want us to finish the journey how we started—together."

Crowfeather bowed his head. "There's no point," he murmured. "We'll never be together again. Stormfur lives in the mountains now, and Feathertail is dead."

Brambleclaw ran his tail lightly over the young warrior's shoulder. He shared his grief for the beautiful RiverClan cat who had sacrificed her life to save Crowfeather and the Tribe cats from the terrible lion-cat known as Sharptooth. Then Feathertail's brother Stormfur had stayed with the Tribe of Rushing Water because of his love for the prey-hunter Brook. Brambleclaw missed him bitterly, but knew that pain was nothing compared to the agony Crowfeather felt over Feathertail's death.

"Feathertail is with us now," Squirrelpaw insisted, coming to join them. Her eyes shone with the strength of her belief.

"If you don't know that, Crowfeather, you're even more mousebrained than I thought. And we'll see Stormfur again, I'm sure. We're closer to the mountains here than we were in the forest."

Crowfeather let out a long sigh. "Okay," he meowed. "Let's go."

Most of the cats had gone past them already, moving cautiously across the unfamiliar territory, keeping close to each other as they had done throughout the long and dangerous journey to get here. A little way ahead, Brambleclaw saw Mothwing, the RiverClan medicine cat, walking beside a group of apprentices from all four Clans. On the far side of a patch of gorse, the ground fell away into a grassy hollow. Tallpoppy, a ShadowClan queen, was struggling to guide her kits down the steep slope; Cloudtail and Brightheart from ThunderClan darted over to help, each picking up a kit in their jaws. Farther down the slope, Cedarheart, a gray ShadowClan tom, prowled along the edge of a thorn thicket, his gaze flicking back and forth as he kept watch for foxes and badgers that might be looking for easy prey.

If he had not known these cats all his life, Brambleclaw would not have been able to distinguish one Clan from another; they walked side by side, helping one another. He wondered grimly how long it would be before they were divided again, and how painful that separation would be.

At an impatient exclamation from Squirrelpaw—"Come on, Brambleclaw, or we'll leave you to make a den for yourself here!"—he headed down the slope, pausing every so often to draw in the night air. The scent of cat was strongest, but beneath it he could detect the scents of mouse and vole and rabbit. He couldn't remember when he had last eaten; surely the leaders would allow them to hunt soon?

He was imagining the delicious taste of fresh-kill when he was startled by a hiss from Tawnypelt, who was a couple of tail-lengths ahead of him. "Look at that," spat the Shadow-Clan warrior, pointing with her tail.

Brambleclaw's ears pricked when he saw the thin mesh of a Twoleg fence shining like a huge cobweb in the pale dawn light. Two or three of the other cats had paused to stare apprehensively at it as well.

"I knew we'd come across Twolegs sooner or later!" Squirrelpaw meowed with a disgusted twitch of her tail.

Brambleclaw tasted the air again. He could pick up the scent of Twolegs, but it was faint and stale. There was another, less familiar scent too, and he had to think hard before he remembered what it was.

"Horses." Crowfeather confirmed his guess. "There's one over there."

He gestured with his tail, and Brambleclaw noticed a large, dark shape standing under a clump of trees some way inside the fence. He thought there was another one beside it, though it was hard to tell in the shadows cast by the branches.

"What are horses?" Whitepaw mewed worriedly as she peered through the fence.

"Nothing to worry about," Tornear from WindClan reassured her, touching the apprentice's shoulder with the tip of his tail. "They used to run across our territory sometimes, with Twolegs on their backs."

Whitetail blinked as if she couldn't quite believe him.

"We saw some of them on our journey to the sun-drown-water," Brambleclaw added. "They didn't take any notice of us when we crossed their field. It's the Twolegs looking after them that we need to watch out for."

"I can't see any Twoleg nests," Tawnypelt pointed out. "Maybe these horse things look after themselves."

"Let's hope so," meowed Brambleclaw. "Horses alone shouldn't bother us."

"Provided we stay away from their clumsy feet," added Squirrelpaw.

The cats followed the Twoleg fence until they came to a thicket of trees where the other cats were gathering. Glancing around, Brambleclaw spotted Cinderpelt, the ThunderClan medicine cat, and her apprentice, Leafpaw, Squirrelpaw's sister.

"What's going on?" Squirrelpaw demanded. "Why are we stopping?"

"The patrol the leaders sent has just come back," Cinderpelt explained.

Following her gaze, Brambleclaw saw the leaders of the four Clans and the WindClan deputy, Mudclaw, standing close together beside a tree stump. Mistyfoot and Russetfur, who had been sent on the patrol, faced them. The other cats had sunk down on the short, springy grass around the tree stump, glad of the chance to rest.

With the others behind him, Brambleclaw weaved through the cats until he was close enough to hear what the Clan leaders were saying.

Mistyfoot was just giving her report: "The ground's very boggy by the lake. There's no point going any farther until daylight. We don't want to lose any cats in the mud."

"ShadowClan is used to wet ground underpaw," Blackstar reminded her, before any of the other leaders could comment. "But we'll stay with the rest of you if that's what you want." There was an edge to his tone, as if ShadowClan were granting them a huge favor by not going ahead to explore on their own.

Brambleclaw narrowed his eyes. It seemed too soon for the Clans to begin competing with one another over who claimed which part of the new territory. He had grown used to having all four Clans around him, ignoring the differences that had kept them apart for more seasons than any cat could remember. He was also afraid that some cats were weaker and more exhausted than others, which might make any clashes more damaging than they needed to be.

He hoped the leaders would decide to stay where they were for the rest of the night. The hills were still close enough to cut down the force of the wind, and the trees provided even more welcome shelter. A strong scent of prey drifted from the shadows, and his paws itched to hunt.

"I think we should stay here," Firestar meowed, to Brambleclaw's relief. "We all need to rest, and it sounds pretty uncomfortable by the lake."

Leopardstar murmured agreement. Before Firestar had finished speaking, Tallstar collapsed onto his side and lay there panting, as if he couldn't manage a single pawstep more. Mudclaw stalked up to him, sniffed him briefly, and spoke a word or two in his ear.

"Tallstar looks exhausted," Brambleclaw murmured to Crowfeather. "This is his last life, isn't it?"

Crowfeather nodded, his face somber. "He'll be fine now that we're here," he meowed, though Brambleclaw suspected that he was trying to convince himself as much as any other cat.

Blackstar leaped up to the top of the tree stump. The powerful white tom stood with tail held high, his huge black paws planted on the rough wood. He let out a commanding yowl, and the faces of all the cats turned toward him to listen.

"Cats of all Clans!" he called as the last stragglers came up. "We have reached the place StarClan meant us to find, but we are all tired and hungry. We will make camp here until we have rested."

"Who asked him to speak for the leaders?" Squirrelpaw muttered. Her green eyes flashed indignantly as Brambleclaw, spotting a couple of ShadowClan warriors within earshot, silenced her with a flick of his tail across her mouth.

"What about fresh-kill?" a cat called from the back.

"We will wait until sunrise," Blackstar replied. "Then the prey will be running and there'll be enough for us all."

"Meanwhile we ought to keep watch," Firestar added,

leaping up beside Blackstar so that the ShadowClan leader had to step back a pace. "Deputies, find two or three warriors who can stay awake for a while longer. We don't want foxes sneaking up on us while we're asleep."

Mudclaw, who seemed to be speaking for WindClan since Tallstar was so weak, meowed his agreement, followed by the RiverClan leader, Leopardstar. The brief meeting broke up and the cats began looking for places to sleep. Barkface nudged Tallstar to his feet and helped him to a clump of long grass, where the frail WindClan leader lay down again, trembling from nose to tail. Onewhisker sat close to him and began to lick his fur gently.

"I guess I'll be needed," Crowfeather mewed, and he loped away to join the other WindClan cats.

Tawnypelt touched noses with her brother. "I'd better check in with Russetfur," she meowed. "See you later, Brambleclaw." Whisking around, she headed for a group of her Clanmates who were clustered around the ShadowClan deputy.

Brambleclaw wondered if he ought to volunteer to keep watch. Even though he had been a warrior for fewer than four seasons, ThunderClan needed every cat to help feed and protect their Clanmates—especially since they had lost their deputy just before leaving the forest. Shivering, Brambleclaw remembered how Graystripe had been trapped by Twolegs and carried away inside a Twoleg monster. He glanced at Firestar to see his leader giving orders to Sorreltail and Brackenfur. He guessed he wouldn't be needed right away, so he looked around to see if any of the other ThunderClan cats could use his help.

Dustpelt stood in the shadows beneath the trees with his mate, Ferncloud, and their son Birchkit, the only one of their latest litter to survive the lack of prey back in the forest. Ferncloud was crouched over Longtail, nosing him anxiously as he lay in the grass. Longtail was not many seasons older than Dustpelt, but he had been forced to join the elders when his eyesight failed; the journey from the forest had been particularly hard for him. Goldenflower, Brambleclaw's mother, lay close to his flank on the other side. She was the oldest ThunderClan queen, and Brambleclaw realized with a pang of sympathy that she looked too weary to do anything more than press her warm fur against Longtail.

Dustpelt nudged the pale tabby tom's shoulder. "Come on, Longtail," he meowed. "Not far now."

As Squirrelpaw bounded over to help, Brambleclaw spotted a sheltered place where the ground fell away a couple of tail-lengths beyond the clump of trees; grass grew thickly there, and a few bushes with low-growing branches.

"What about making a den over there?" he suggested, pointing with his tail.

"Good idea," meowed Dustpelt. He nosed Longtail again. "It's all right, Longtail; you can sleep as long as you want once we get you to a more sheltered place."

Longtail heaved himself to his paws; Squirrelpaw padded beside him with her tail curled around his neck to guide him. Brambleclaw let Goldenflower lean on his shoulder, while

Ferncloud encouraged Birchkit to follow.

"This had better be the place we're looking for," Dustpelt remarked, looking around at the exhausted cats. "None of us have the strength to travel any farther."

Brambleclaw didn't reply. He knew Dustpelt was right— but he couldn't tell him for sure that this was the place StarClan had meant them to find. He watched the others slide between the branches and settle into the piles of dry leaves under the bushes. Catching a glimpse of Leafpaw padding past with a mouthful of moss for bedding, he recalled the medicine cat apprentice's unquestioning faith that their warrior ancestors had made the journey with them. He wished he could feel the same certainty. All along he had clung to the belief that their troubles would be over when they reached their new territory. Now, daunted by the strangeness of everything around him, he could see they were only just beginning.

Squirrelpaw's voice broke into his thoughts. "Dustpelt, do you want us to hunt for you?"

Her mentor flicked her ear with his tail. "No, we'll all hunt later. Look at you; you're asleep on your paws. Go with Brambleclaw and get some rest."

"Okay." Squirrelpaw's jaws split into an enormous yawn.

"What about under that gorse bush?" Brambleclaw led the way to the spot he had pointed out a few tail-lengths up the slope, and crawled under the lowest boughs.

Squirrelpaw followed him and curled into a tight ball with her tail over her nose. "Good night," she murmured indistinctly.

Brambleclaw scrabbled in the debris underneath the bush until he had made a comfortable nest. Curling up close to Squirrelpaw, he breathed in her warm, familiar scent. He was glad that they had not made a proper camp yet, where warriors and apprentices would have their separate dens. He would miss sleeping next to Squirrelpaw, he realized with the last flicker of conscious thought. Then sleep covered him like the lapping of a soft black wave.

Brambleclaw's dreams were dark and confused. He was searching for something in the middle of a thick forest, but he could not remember what he was looking for, and every path he took ended abruptly in tangles of briar or impassable walls of thorn. In desperation, he tried to force his way through, but a branch poked him painfully in the side.

"Wake up, Brambleclaw! You've been asleep forever—what do you think you are, a hedgehog?"

Brambleclaw's eyes flew open to see Squirrelpaw prodding him with her forepaw. Watery yellow daylight was seeping through the branches of the gorse bush.

"It's morning," Squirrelpaw went on. "Let's go and see if we can hunt. If you can stop hibernating, that is."

Blinking sleep from his eyes, Brambleclaw staggered to his paws, shook scraps of dead leaves from his pelt, and followed Squirrelpaw into the open.

The confusion of his dream slipped away when he remembered where he was. But it was replaced with a renewed feeling of anxiety as he looked at the landscape in daylight for the first time. He wondered if this vast, unfamiliar place would ever seem like home.

A cold breeze blew, ridging the surface of the lake and rattling through the reeds that edged the shore. The shining gray water stretched in front of Brambleclaw for almost as far as he could see; above the hills that rose on one side, a glow in the sky showed where the sun would shortly rise. Back the way they had come, the land sloped up more gently to bare moorland. The Twoleg fence stretched across it, and in the growing light Brambleclaw could just make out a couple of Twoleg nests in the distance. He let out a faint sound of approval; such small nests couldn't hold many Twolegs, and being so far away they were unlikely to interfere with the Clans.

Farther around the lake, below the hills, was a smudge that looked like gray-green mist; Brambleclaw realized it was a mass of leafless branches, stretching along the shore and up to the crest of the ridge. His heart lifted to think that soon he could be underneath trees again, however strange they might be.

At the far end of the lake the gray smudge of trees darkened, and Brambleclaw guessed that they were pines, still green in the depths of leaf-bare. They covered the ground like a gently rippling pelt as the wind stirred them.

The glow on the horizon grew too bright to look at as the sun edged up; the last stars were fading, and the sky was a clear, pale blue.

"Time to hunt," Brambleclaw meowed to Squirrelpaw, who was standing beside him.

He looked around for Firestar or one of the senior warriors, to find out if any patrols were being sent out. His leader was emerging from a nearby gorse thicket with Leopardstar, Blackstar, and Mudclaw. The leaders must have been holding a meeting, Brambleclaw guessed, and he felt a twinge of apprehension to see Mudclaw in Tallstar's place, representing WindClan.

"I wonder if Tallstar went to join StarClan during the night," he muttered, his belly clenching with grief at the thought.

Squirrelpaw shook her head. "I don't think so," she mewed. "Or they would have brought his body out so his Clan could pay their respects."

Brambleclaw hoped she was right. Before he could say anything else, Firestar leaped onto the tree stump where the leaders had addressed the Clans yesterday. Blackstar jumped up beside him, and Mudclaw scrambled up on the other side. There was barely room for all three cats to stand together on the flat top of the stump, so Leopardstar did not try to join them, but sat on a twisted root at the base.

"We'll need a new place to hold Gatherings," Squirrelpaw remarked.

Firestar's yowl, calling the Clans together, interrupted her. Stems of grass and fern parted, and the branches of bushes shook as the cats emerged from their sleeping places. They all looked thin and worn, easy prey for any hostile creatures the territory might conceal, and they glanced around nervously, as if they could feel hungry eyes burning into their pelts on every side.

Brambleclaw bounded down the slope toward the stump, with Squirrelpaw close behind. Halfway down he spotted Tallstar's black-and-white shape curled in the grass where he had gone to sleep the night before. The WindClan medicine cat, Barkface, was sitting beside him, sniffing anxiously at his fur. Neither cat made any attempt to join the others gathered around the tree stump; it was obvious Tallstar wasn't well enough to take part in the meeting.

"Cats of all Clans," Firestar was announcing as Brambleclaw reached his Clanmates. "Today there are decisions to be made and tasks to be carried out—"

"Hunting patrols will go out right away," Mudclaw interrupted, shouldering Firestar aside. "WindClan will take the hills and RiverClan can fish in the lake. ThunderClan_"

His Clanmate Onewhisker sprang to his paws with a hiss of anger. "Mudclaw, what are you doing, giving orders like this?" he growled. "The last time I looked, Tallstar was still leader of WindClan."

"Not for much longer."

Brambleclaw blinked in surprise at the deputy's cold voice. He hoped Tallstar hadn't heard, and, craning his neck, he was relieved to see that the old cat was still asleep in his grassy nest with Barkface beside him.

"Some cat has to take charge," Mudclaw went on. "Or do you want the other Clans to divide the territory among themselves and leave WindClan out?"

"As if we would!" Squirrelpaw mewed indignantly.

Onewhisker glared at Mudclaw, his fur bristling and his

eyes blazing with fury. "Show a bit of respect!" he spat. "Tallstar was the leader of our Clan when you were a kit mewling in the nursery."

"I'm not a kit now," Mudclaw retorted. "I'm the deputy. And Tallstar hasn't done much to lead us since we left the forest."

"That's enough." Firestar silenced the WindClan deputy with a wave of his tail. "Onewhisker, I know you're worried about Tallstar. Mudclaw is only doing his duty."

"He needn't act like he's leader already," Onewhisker growled. He sat down with a sharp glance from side to side, as if he were challenging any other cat to make a comment.

"Onewhisker has a fair point," Firestar went on to Mudclaw. "It's difficult for a deputy to stand in for their leader—difficult for the rest of the Clan as well as for the deputy."

Mudclaw, who had raised his head arrogantly when Firestar seemed to be backing him up, looked furious. His jaws parted, but before he could speak he was forestalled by Blackstar.

"If WindClan has a problem over their leadership, let them discuss it in private. We're wasting time."

Mudclaw let out an angry hiss and pointedly turned his back. Brambleclaw flexed his claws, ready to spring if the WindClan deputy caused more trouble. Mudclaw was one of the most aggressive cats in all four Clans, and he had never liked Firestar or ThunderClan. Brambleclaw could foresee trouble when he became WindClan's leader, especially now, when new Clan boundaries had to be established.

Firestar's voice interrupted his troubled thoughts. "I would like to start ThunderClan's life here by honoring a new warrior. Squirrelpaw, where are you?"

"What? Me!" In her astonishment, Squirrelpaw squeaked like a kit. She sprang to her paws, her ears pricked and her tail standing straight up.

"Yes, you." Brambleclaw saw a gleam of amusement in Firestar's eyes as he beckoned to his daughter. "ThunderClan owes you more than I can say for making the journey to sun-drown-place, and helping lead the Clans to this new home. Dustpelt and I agree that if ever an apprentice deserved her warrior name, you do."

Brambleclaw stretched out and gently touched his muzzle against the tip of Squirrelpaw's ear. "Go on," he murmured. "Firestar is right. You deserve to become a warrior after everything you've done for the Clan."

She blinked at him, too shocked to speak, then turned and picked her way to the tree stump where Firestar was waiting. Before she reached it, her mother, Sandstorm, stepped forward. Squirrelpaw stopped in front of her. Sandstorm's eyes glowed with pride as she gave her daughter a few swift licks to smooth her fur. Brambleclaw watched Leafpaw come over as well to press her muzzle against her sister's side.

Squirrelpaw's mentor, Dustpelt, padded up to lead her the rest of the way to the stump, and he stood beside her as they waited for Firestar to speak.

Firestar leaped down and blinked encouragingly at

Squirrelpaw before lifting his head to address the gathered cats. "This is the first time any cat has spoken these words in our new home," he began. "I Firestar, leader of ThunderClan, call upon my warrior ancestors to look down on this apprentice. She has trained hard to understand the ways of your noble code, and I commend her to you as a warrior in her turn."

There was a burning intensity in his eyes, and Brambleclaw understood how much this moment meant to Firestar, not just for ThunderClan but for all four Clans that had journeyed here from their home far away. By calling upon StarClan to make a new warrior, they were claiming this unfamiliar place as their own. There had been many, many times on the journey when they had feared they had left their warrior ancestors behind, but Firestar addressed them now as confidently as if their starry spirits glowed overhead. Brambleclaw felt his fur prickle with guilt, wishing he could be so certain that StarClan had made the journey with them. Still, he told himself, they had reached somewhere that looked as if it would make a safe home for the Clans; perhaps his leader was right to feel confident. He shook his head, forcing his concerns away, and listened to the warrior ceremony.

"Squirrelpaw," the ThunderClan leader was saying, "do you promise to uphold the warrior code and to protect and defend your Clan, even at the cost of your life?"

Squirrelpaw's reply rang out clearly. "I do."

"Then by the powers of StarClan I give you your warrior

name. Squirrelpaw, from this moment you will be known as Squirrelflight. StarClan honors your courage and your determination, and we welcome you as a full warrior of ThunderClan."

Firestar rested his muzzle on Squirrelflight's head, and she gave his shoulder a respectful lick. Determination was an unusual virtue to mention in the warrior ceremony; in Squirrelflight, it sometimes showed as stubbornness, and had led her close to trouble more than once. Brambleclaw wondered if father and daughter were remembering all the times they had clashed, when Squirrelflight's fierce independence had brought her into conflict with her leader and the warrior code. But then, Brambleclaw reflected, there had been times on their journey when her determination and will to succeed had put fresh heart into all her companions. Pride flooded him as he remembered her tireless courage, her refusal to think they would ever fail to reach their journey's end.

When she stepped away from Firestar, Leafpaw bounded up to her, greeting her by her new name. "Squirrelflight! Squirrelflight!"

Her call was taken up by the cats around them. Squirrelflight looked around, her green eyes shining with pride. All four Clans seemed pleased that she had been given her warrior name—but then, all four Clans had had plenty of opportunity to see how much she deserved it. As Brambleclaw thrust his way to her side he saw Tawnypelt and Crowfeather heading toward her, too. Those who had made the journey to Midnight's cave would always have the most special bond with Squirrelflight.

"Congratulations," Tawnypelt meowed, while Crowfeather nodded and rested his tail-tip on her shoulder for a moment.

Brambleclaw pressed his muzzle to hers. "Well done, Squirrelflight," he murmured. "Mind you," he added teasingly, "you'll still have to pay attention to senior warriors."

Squirrelflight's eyes gleamed with wicked amusement. "You can't order me around now—I'm not an apprentice anymore!"

"I can't see that it will make much difference," Dustpelt put in, overhearing her. "You never did as you were told anyway."

Squirrelflight let out a *mrrow* of laughter and affectionately butted her former mentor on his shoulder. "I must have listened to something," she meowed. She blinked, and added, "Really, thanks for everything, Dustpelt."

The meows of welcome died down as Blackstar stepped forward and signaled with his tail for silence. "This is all very touching, but now we must find out about this new place so that we can start establishing our new territories. We're going to send a patrol with one cat from each Clan to explore the lakeshore and the land around it."

Brambleclaw's ears pricked, and he felt Squirrelflight tense beside him, her pelt just brushing his. He caught Tawnypelt's eye, and saw an answering gleam of anticipation.

"We decided to send three of the cats who made the first journey together," Firestar went on. "Brambleclaw from

ThunderClan, Crowfeather from WindClan, and Tawnypelt from ShadowClan."

Excitement thrilled through Brambleclaw from ears to tail-tip. It felt right that the cats who had made the first journey should be chosen.

Blackstar curled his lip as Firestar named each cat, but didn't argue.

"Huh!" Tawnypelt muttered. "It's the first time he's ever let me represent ShadowClan."

Brambleclaw swept his tail soothingly over her shoulder. He knew that Blackstar was unlikely to forget that Tawnypelt had been born in ThunderClan, however hard she tried to prove she was a loyal warrior of ShadowClan.

"Mistyfoot will go for RiverClan," meowed Leopardstar, speaking for the first time, and reminding Brambleclaw painfully that neither of the RiverClan cats who had made the journey was still with their Clan. A hollow place yawned inside him as he thought of Feathertail and Stormfur.

"But what about *me?*" Squirrelflight protested. "I went on the journey too. Why can't I go on the patrol?"

"Because that would make two cats from ThunderClan," Blackstar replied crushingly. Brambleclaw knew the ShadowClan leader was wrong if he thought that would silence Squirrelflight.

"A patrol of four cats isn't enough to go into unknown territory," she objected.

Blackstar opened his mouth to disagree, but Firestar spoke first. "She could be right," he pointed out. "I think we should let her go. It could be her first warrior task. She can't sit vigil tonight like other new warriors, as we have no proper camp."

Blackstar glanced at Leopardstar, who twitched her tail, giving nothing away, and then at Mudclaw, who dipped his head. "WindClan has no objection," he meowed.

"Very well," Blackstar growled. "But don't think for one moment that will give ThunderClan any extra rights over the territory."

Brambleclaw exchanged an exasperated glance with Crowfeather. Trust Blackclaw to think that other Clans were trying to steal an advantage before the new territories had been divided up!

"Of course not," Firestar replied evenly. "Squirrelflight, you may go with the patrol."

Squirrelflight's tail curled up in delight.

"Go all the way around the lake, and explore as much of the surrounding land as you can," Firestar instructed. "We need to know what kind of territory it is, and where the best hunting places will be. Think about the different sorts of hunting each Clan will require, because it might help with setting boundaries later on. It would be good to get an idea of how the territory could be split up, and where might be good places for camps. And keep a close watch for Twolegs, or anything else that might be dangerous."

"Is that all?" Crowfeather muttered.

"I reckon you'll need two days to travel all the way around the lake," Firestar went on. He lifted his head and narrowed his eyes as he peered across the water, trying to judge the distance. "Try not to spend too much time exploring. We're exposed to danger while we stay here, so we need to get all the Clans settled as soon as we can."

"We'll do our best, Firestar," a new voice called out. Brambleclaw glanced over his shoulder to see Mistyfoot, the RiverClan deputy, padding over to join them.

"Hi, there," he mewed, moving up to make room for her. Mistyfoot looked wary about joining the close band of cats that had made the first journey.

"Good luck," called Leopardstar, and Firestar added, "May StarClan go with you all."

By now the sun had risen well above the hills. His paws itching to be off, Brambleclaw dipped his head toward Firestar and the other leaders, and raised his tail to signal the others to follow him. Out of the corner of his eye he saw Tawnypelt wince, and he heard a hissing intake of breath from Crowfeather. His fur prickled with embarrassment as he realized that Mistyfoot ought to be in charge of the patrol, since she was the deputy of her Clan. He stopped and took a pace back; Mistyfoot gave him a long, cool look, then nodded briefly to him as she took the lead.

"Mousebrain!" Squirrelflight whispered.

They headed for the edge of the lake, with Blackstar's voice drifting behind them on the breeze as he began to arrange the hunting patrols.

"Squirrelflight! Wait!" Brambleclaw looked back to see Leafpaw bounding after her sister. "Be careful, won't you?" she begged.

Squirrelflight touched noses with the young medicine cat. "Don't worry about us," she meowed. "We can look after ourselves."

"But you're as tired as the rest of us from the journey," Leafpaw warned. "Hunt as soon as you can, and don't stray too far from the lake or you might get lost."

Squirrelflight brushed her tail across Leafpaw's mouth to stop her. "We'll be fine," she insisted. She lifted her head and pointed with her nose to the gleaming stretch of water below them. "Look, you can see exactly where we're going. We'll be back before you know it." She paused for a moment, then added quietly, "Have you had a sign from StarClan? Is that why you're so worried?"

Leafpaw shook her head. "No, nothing like that, I promise. It's just hard to let you go again. It feels too much like the first time you left, when you went to sun-drown-place."

Brambleclaw went over and rested his muzzle against Leafpaw's shoulder to comfort her. "And we came safely home, didn't we? Trust me, Leafpaw, I'll look after her."

Squirrelflight jerked away in mock indignation. "I don't need looking after! It's more likely to be me watching out for your battered old fur!"

Leafpaw gave a purr of amusement, letting them lighten the mood. "Well, just take care, all of you. And if you have a chance to look out for any herbs, that would be great. Our medicine supplies will need refilling very soon."

Squirrelflight licked her ear. "Sure. I'll keep my eyes

open—when I'm not looking for foxes, badgers, Twolegs, Thunderpaths. . . ."

"Are we going or not?" growled Crowfeather. "We don't have much daylight, and we need to get at least halfway around the lake before nightfall."

Leafpaw ignored him. "StarClan go with you," she murmured to Squirrelflight, before whisking around and bounding back up the slope.

Brambleclaw tasted the air and listened to the lapping of waves on the shore. The gray water was flooded with color as the sun rose higher over the hills. It stretched ahead so far that the trees on the distant shore were nothing more than a greenish blur, and curved hungrily around the marshy land in front of them. Something about the stillness of the water, the silence that hung over it like mist, told Brambleclaw that it was much, much deeper than the river in the forest, even when it flooded. He gave Mistyfoot a swift sidelong glance. She looked daunted too, though like all RiverClan cats she was an excellent swimmer.

As if aware that his eyes were on her, the RiverClan deputy gave herself a shake. "Right," she meowed, gazing around at the patrol. "This is it. Let's see where StarClan has brought us."

CHAPTER 2

Leafpaw stopped halfway up the slope and turned to watch her sister and the rest of the patrol make their way down to the lake. From the tingling of her own fur, she could tell how excited Squirrelflight was, not just at the prospect of exploring the new territory, but because she was with the friends she had made on the journey to sun-drown-place once more. For a few heartbeats Leafpaw felt almost breathless with envy, wishing that she could have a bond that strong, based on that depth of trust and that many shared experiences, with another cat.

Her gaze was drawn to the lean, gray-black shape of Crowfeather. Of all the others, he was the hardest to understand. Leafpaw wished she knew him better. He seemed the least willing to trust cats from another Clan, yet during the long journey through the mountains she had seen him put himself in danger over and over to help cats who weren't from WindClan. Leafpaw's pelt prickled, making her shiver from nose to tail. Something told her Crowfeather had an important path laid out by StarClan, but she had no idea where it might lead—nor was there any reason for StarClan to let her know the destiny of a cat from another Clan.

She jumped as something brushed against her shoulder, and turned to see Cinderpelt gazing at her with wise blue eyes.

"Do you wish you were going with them?" the medicine cat asked.

Leafpaw hesitated. She was a medicine cat, not a warrior—her duties lay with her weak and exhausted Clan. So why did she feel a tug in her paws to follow the little patrol that was padding away along the line of the shore? Her mind flooded with an image of bounding after them to walk alongside Crowfeather, who was bringing up the rear; she drew in her breath sharply, almost able to feel his dark gray pelt brush against hers as they picked their way over the tufts of boggy grass.

"Are you all right?" mewed Cinderpelt, looking at her closely.

Leafpaw blinked. "Yes, I'm fine. Of course I don't want to go with the patrol. There's enough work for me here."

"That's true," Cinderpelt meowed. "We have four Clans of exhausted cats to look after, and our stock of healing herbs barely amounts to a couple of leaves and a pawful of crushed berries."

Leafpaw gulped, suddenly wondering if she should have gone with the patrol after all to look for new supplies of medicine.

"We're going to meet with the other medicine cats," Cinderpelt went on. "We need to discuss what to do about finding new herbs, and how we are going to share tongues with our warrior ancestors when we are so far from Highstones." She gazed up at the sky, where the half-moon drifted behind wisps of cloud, and her voice dropped to barely a whisper. "I hope we find another Moonstone place soon."

She gestured with her tail, and Leafpaw saw her friend Mothwing, the RiverClan medicine cat, sitting in the shelter of a bramble thicket with Littlecloud, the medicine cat from ShadowClan. Around them, warriors and apprentices from all four Clans were dividing into groups as the hunting patrols prepared to leave.

Cinderpelt waited until most of the patrols had gone before joining the other medicine cats. Leafpaw bounded over to touch noses with Mothwing.

Mothwing blinked nervously at her. "I feel so helpless!" she murmured into Leafpaw's ear. "I have no supplies, and the cats are so tired and weak."

Leafpaw wasn't surprised that her friend was anxious. Although Mothwing had trained as a warrior and received her warrior name several seasons ago, she had not been a medicine cat apprentice for as long as Leafpaw. The death of Mudfur before they left the forest meant that she had to take on all the responsibilities of a medicine cat before she had finished her training. Leafpaw felt a wave of gratitude that Cinderpelt was still alive, and young and strong enough to live for many, many more moons. She was in no hurry to lose her mentor, and she didn't envy Mothwing at all. But she reminded herself that Mothwing had been taught well, and she would be able to ask the other medicine cats for advice if she needed to. Besides, in this new place they would all have things to learn.

She gave Mothwing's ear a quick lick. "You'll be fine," she promised. "We'll all help you."

Cinderpelt glanced around. "Where's Barkface?"

"Still with Tallstar, I guess," Littlecloud replied. He let out a sigh. "I'm not sure there's much any cat can do for him now."

Leafpaw flinched. It didn't seem fair that StarClan should summon the WindClan leader to join them when he hadn't even seen his Clan's new home.

"Here he comes now." Cinderpelt twitched her ears to where Barkface was approaching with his head bowed and his tail trailing.

"How is Tallstar?" Littlecloud demanded.

Barkface heaved a sigh from the depths of his belly as he flopped down under the brambles beside the other medicine cats. "Sleeping," he replied. "He is very weak. The journey has been too much for him, and it is clear that StarClan is waiting for him to join them."

"Isn't there anything you can do?" Leafpaw meowed.

Barkface shook his head. "We may have traveled all the way from the forest, but Tallstar has a longer journey than all of us ahead of him. He has been a noble leader, but he cannot go on forever."

"All the Clans will honor him," Cinderpelt murmured. She

bowed her head for a moment and then straightened up, giving her fur a shake. "Meanwhile there are tasks that we must do."

"We need to look for herbs," Mothwing meowed. "Disease could spread easily when we're all tired and hungry."

"True," replied Cinderpelt. "Soon we'll go and search, and hope that StarClan leads us to what we need. But before that. . . ." Her voice trailed off, and she scratched at the ground with her forepaw before she went on. "There may be a patrol out looking for new camps for each Clan, but we need more than that if this is to be our home. Where are the Clans going to gather at full moon? What about the Moonstone? It's many days' journey from here to Mothermouth."

Leafpaw's paws ached at the thought of retracing her steps along all the weary paths they had followed since they left Highstones. Surely it would be impossible to travel there every half moon to meet with StarClan? But where would new leaders go now to receive their names and their nine lives?

There was a long pause. None of the cats had the answer— or knew where to suggest looking.

"Are we *sure* this is the right place?" Littlecloud mewed at last. "Without the Moonstone, the only way we can reach StarClan is through dreams and signs, and I've seen nothing to reassure me that this is where we are supposed to be."

"It *must* be right," Leafpaw pleaded. She struggled to think how she could make the other medicine cats believe her, when they were so much more experienced than she was. "Stoneteller met with his Tribe's warrior ancestors in the

Cave of Pointed Stones," she added, remembering their visit to the Tribe of Rushing Water. "So maybe there are other places like the Moonstone."

"I believe that StarClan sent us a sign when we saw their reflections shining in the lake," Cinderpelt mewed, and Leafpaw felt the fur on her shoulders lie down in her relief. "But we still need a place where we can share tongues with them."

"Maybe they'll send us a sign to tell us where we can find another Moonstone," Barkface suggested.

"Maybe." Littlecloud sounded dubious. "I just hope it's soon, that's all."

"But does it really matter?" Mothwing asked. "I mean, there's nothing to stop us from finding the right herbs, and. . . ."

Her voice died away as the other medicine cats stared at her in astonishment. Leafpaw winced; how *could* Mothwing believe that the only task of a medicine cat was to heal?

Mothwing's gaze flicked from one cat to the next, uncertainty and embarrassment in her eyes.

"Mothwing means we can carry on looking after our Clanmates while we wait for StarClan to speak to us," Leafpaw meowed helpfully.

Mothwing turned to her in relief. "Yes—yes, that's right."

Cinderpelt's ears twitched.

"I suppose we could start restocking our supplies," meowed Littlecloud.

Barkface heaved himself to his paws. "If you don't mind, I

ought to stay with Tallstar. But I'd be grateful for some colts-foot, if you can find it. He's having trouble breathing."

"There'll be no coltsfoot leaves until newleaf," Mothwing pointed out anxiously. "Would juniper berries do as well?"

Barkface nodded. "Quite right. Thanks, Mothwing."

"We'll bring you some," Cinderpelt promised.

With a brief grunt of thanks, Barkface padded to the clump of grass where Tallstar lay, an unmoving heap of black and white fur. Leafpaw saw him exchange a word or two with Onewhisker, who was keeping vigil beside his dying leader. Then he settled down with his flank touching Tallstar's, letting the old cat know that he would not be alone as he began his long, dark journey.

"Well done, Mothwing!" Leafpaw mewed. "I didn't think of using juniper berries instead."

Mothwing turned her head to give Leafpaw's ear a quick lick. "Where shall we go first?"

Cinderpelt stood up stiffly, favoring the leg she had injured long ago on the Thunderpath. "If we go that way," she began, gesturing with her tail, "we'll end up in the Twoleg horseplace. I think we should head the opposite way, closer to the lake."

"Firestar says it's boggy there," Leafpaw reminded her.

"There's all sorts of good stuff growing in bogs," meowed Mothwing. She gave Leafpaw a gentle flick around the ear with her tail. "If you were a RiverClan cat, you wouldn't mind getting your paws wet!"

"And I wouldn't mind catching a frog or a toad to eat,"

mewed Littlecloud. When the other cats glanced at him in surprise, he added defensively, "They don't taste that bad! There were always plenty in ShadowClan's territory, even when the rest of the prey was scarce."

As they drew nearer to the lake the tough moorland grass gave way to sedge and moss. The ground was spongy, and water oozed up around Leafpaw's paws at every step.

"I hope it's not all like this," she muttered to herself, pausing to shake droplets of water from each paw. Looking ahead, she saw that although this stretch of marshland reached right down to the lake, trees were growing on the bank farther around, and in the distance a wooded tongue of land stretched out into the water. *That might be a good place for a camp*, she thought.

She broke into a run to catch up the others, and found them standing beside a large clump of horsetail; farther away were more clumps of the big, healthy plants. Leafpaw's spirits rose.

"This is excellent," Cinderpelt meowed. "It never grew as well as this in our old territory. We'll collect some on our way back. Leafpaw, what is it used for?"

Leafpaw wasn't sure she liked being questioned in front of the other medicine cats as if she had barely started her training, but at least she knew the answer. "Infected wounds," she answered promptly.

"That's right," meowed Littlecloud. "And we're going to need it. The cats have picked up all kinds of scratches and scrapes on the journey."

Cinderpelt nodded. "We must remember where to find it."

She set off again, and the other cats followed. Leafpaw was pleased when she was the first to spot a clump of water mint, one of the best cures for bellyache.

"But we're never going to find Barkface's juniper berries down here," Mothwing pointed out, leaping over a tiny stream. "It's much too wet."

"Why don't you and Leafpaw head away from the shore?" Cinderpelt suggested. "I can see bushes over there. Some of them might be juniper."

"Sure." Mothwing swerved away from the water, heading toward the ridge they had crossed on the previous night. Leafpaw followed close behind, relieved to feel drier, harder ground under her paws.

When they reached the higher ground, they pushed their way into a sheltered thicket of trees. Leafpaw quickly recognized the spiky dark leaves and purple berries of juniper bushes among the undergrowth.

"Just what we need," she mewed happily, beginning to bite off some of the stems.

When they had collected as much juniper as they could carry, they turned back toward the lake. Emerging from the trees, Leafpaw spotted the tiny, indistinct figures of Cinderpelt and Littlecloud in the distance, following the water's edge. From up here, she realized that what she had thought was a wooded spur of land stretching out into the lake was actually an island, separated from the shore by a narrow channel of water.

"Look!" she meowed to Mothwing. "There's an island in the lake."

The young medicine cat's eyes shone. "That would make a great place for a Gathering!" she exclaimed. "It's big enough for all the Clans, and nothing would disturb us there. Let's go down and tell the others." Snatching up her collection of juniper stems, she bounded off toward Cinderpelt and Littlecloud.

Leafpaw picked up her own stems and followed more slowly. Mothwing hadn't given her the chance to point out that only RiverClan cats felt confident about swimming, and none of the other Clans would be able to reach the island. It was a pity, because Mothwing was right: the island would be a perfect place for all the Clans to meet, safe from predators and Twolegs.

When she reached the others, Mothwing was excitedly telling them about the island. All four cats padded down to the edge of the lake to have a closer look. The ground was drier here, falling away into a rocky shore with a few tough thorns rooted in cracks.

"It looks safe enough," meowed Cinderpelt, "but how would we get there? Do you fancy telling the elders that they have to swim every time they want to go to a Gathering?"

Littlecloud gave a snort of amusement, and Mothwing looked wounded.

"Maybe it's shallow enough to wade," Leafpaw suggested diplomatically, though she wasn't keen on finding out.

"I could swim over there and have a look," Mothwing offered.

Cinderpelt nodded. "If you want to."

Mothwing didn't need any more encouragement to launch herself down the rocks toward the water.

"Be careful!" Leafpaw called after her.

Her friend waved her tail in acknowledgment before wading out into the lake. Soon the water reached her belly fur and she had to swim, pushing through the water with strong, confident strokes. So it wasn't possible to wade all the way to the island, Leafpaw thought. She narrowed her eyes against the sunlight reflected in the water as she tracked the small dark head bobbing through the waves.

Behind her Littlecloud meowed, "Why don't we hunt while we're waiting? I'm so hungry I could eat a badger!"

His words made Leafpaw conscious of her own grumbling belly, but she did not move until she had seen Mothwing reach the shore of the island; she pulled herself out of the water and waved her tail cheerfully at Leafpaw before vanishing among the bushes.

Leafpaw turned away just in time to see Littlecloud pounce on a vole and crouch down to devour it in swift bites. She couldn't help feeling relieved that he hadn't found a frog or a toad after all, in case he had offered her some. It would have been rude to say no, but Leafpaw didn't think she was quite hungry enough to eat something that looked so tough and unappetizing.

A little way off, Cinderpelt was stalking something in the long grass that grew at the foot of the rocks. A heartbeat later she made her kill and beckoned to Leafpaw with her tail.

"Come on. Mothwing will be fine. There's plenty of prey over there."

Leafpaw cast another glance back at the island, but there was no sign of the RiverClan medicine cat, and nothing Leafpaw could do to help her. Padding softly up to the nearest tumble of rocks, she heard the scuffling of a tiny creature and froze. A grass stem twitched aside to reveal another vole scrabbling among the fallen seeds underneath. Leafpaw crept forward, hardly lifting her paws from the rough ground. Once she was in range she leaped, and dispatched her prey with one swift bite to the neck.

Leafpaw couldn't remember when she had last seen such a plump vole. The prey that remained in the forest after the Twolegs started to tear it up had been scrawny and terrified, and opportunities for hunting on the journey here had been limited.

She was just finishing the last, satisfying bite when Littlecloud called, "Mothwing's coming back!"

Leafpaw swallowed her mouthful and dashed down to the water's edge. Mothwing was swimming strongly toward the shore, and soon she waded out to stand on dry ground and shake the water from her pelt.

"Well?" Cinderpelt demanded. "What did you find?"

Mothwing let out a gusty sigh. "It's perfect! Trees and bushes grow all around the edge, but in the middle there's an open stretch of grass. There'd be room for all the Clans to gather there."

Littlecloud shook his head. "RiverClan maybe, but you'd

never get the other three Clans to join you." His tone was worried as he added, "Some cats with more courage than sense would drown if they tried."

"And right in the middle of the open space," Mothwing went on enthusiastically, as if Littlecloud hadn't spoken, "there's this huge oak tree. As big as the oaks at Fourtrees, but it has low-growing branches, so the leaders could climb up there to address the Clans." Her blue eyes shone. "I wish we could use it!"

"Well, we can't," Cinderpelt said regretfully. "Although you're right, Mothwing; it sounds ideal. Thanks for checking it out."

"There's prey, too." Mothwing swiped her tongue over her jaws.

Leafpaw wanted to ask Mothwing if she had noticed anything unusual about the island, like a strange-shaped rock or a twisted tree, anything that would suggest the presence of StarClan. Perhaps the island wasn't meant for Gatherings, but there might be a new Moonstone there.

But once it was clear that the other medicine cats wouldn't agree that the island could be used for Gatherings, Mothwing had turned away. She was padding up the beach with her tail drooping, tired out from her swim. Leafpaw decided she would ask her another time about the possibility of a Moonstone on the island.

The rest of the medicine cats began to make their way back to the temporary camp as well. Leafpaw followed last of all, with a regretful glance over her shoulder at the island.

The Clans needed a place to gather and a new Moonstone as much as they needed safe, sheltered camps with plenty of prey. The gathering place and the Moonstone would be the home of the fifth Clan that had been forced to leave the for-est—StarClan.

Leafpaw shivered, even though reeds sheltered her from the cold breeze coming off the lake. Unless they found these places quickly, the Clans' future in their new territory was filled with shadows of doubt.

CHAPTER 3

Mistyfoot led the patrol across the marshy shore at a steady trot. Brambleclaw breathed deeply, tasting the prey-scented air and basking in the warmth of the pale winter sun on his fur. His paws itched to bound ahead, but he forced himself to keep to the pace Mistyfoot had set, knowing they had a long way to go.

"This is no good," Squirrelflight grumbled as she slipped into yet another boggy hollow. She stopped and flicked water from her hindpaw with a disgusted expression on her face. "We'll all end up with webbed feet if we live here."

"It might not be so bad for RiverClan," Mistyfoot replied. "But there won't be much prey on ground like this, so it wouldn't be much use."

"We don't have to use *all* the territory around the lake," Tawnypelt pointed out. "There's plenty of space, so it doesn't matter if no cat wants this bit."

"As long as there's something better up ahead," Crowfeather added.

Brambleclaw paused to scan the land around them. On one side the land rose steeply to a ridge of hills. The Twoleg fence and the horses were behind them now, and beyond that the grassland sloped up until it vanished beneath a thick growth of gorse and other bushes. Ahead, the swampy ground stretched along the lakeshore. In the distance Brambleclaw could see a wooded spur of ground jutting out into the lake, and more trees right ahead.

"It looks as if we'll be out of the marshes soon," he meowed.

"Can't we climb the hill, Brambleclaw?" Squirrelflight asked. "*Please.* I'm sick of wet feet."

"There'll be prey up there, too," Tawnypelt mewed longingly. "What do you say, Brambleclaw? We need to hunt."

"We're supposed to be patrolling the lake," Brambleclaw replied.

"And the territory around it," Crowfeather reminded him.

"I suppose we could make a few forays away from the lake," Brambleclaw meowed thoughtfully. "We won't learn much if we stick to the shore the whole time. Let's start by heading up to the ridge. We'll hunt on the way, and—"

A quiet cough interrupted him, and Brambleclaw felt his fur prickle as he met Mistyfoot's level stare. "S-sorry, Mistyfoot," he stammered. "I mean, if that's okay with you."

Amusement glimmered in the RiverClan deputy's eyes. "Look, Brambleclaw, maybe it's best if you lead. These cats are obviously used to taking orders from you."

"I wouldn't say that." Brambleclaw felt even more embarrassed. "We discussed things, mostly, when we were on our journey."

"He means we argued," Tawnypelt meowed dryly. "At least, *some* of us argued." She gave a hard look at Squirrelflight and Crowfeather.

"What, us?" Squirrelflight's eyes opened wide and her tail curled up. "Never!"

Stifling a *mrrow* of laughter, Brambleclaw led the way up the slope to the drier ground. He thanked StarClan that Mistyfoot understood that they had fallen into a habit of organizing themselves on their journey, without the typical Clan hierarchy of leaders and deputies and senior warriors. It felt good to be traveling with his friends again, though he felt Stormfur's absence like a thorn pricking his flank. He wondered what it would be like when the Clans separated and he lost his easy friendship with Crowfeather and Tawnypelt. Would the empty place inside him go on growing forever?

There was prey among the bushes farther up the slope, and it did not take long for all five cats to hunt successfully and settle down to a good meal.

"Mmm . . ." Squirrelflight murmured, lying on her side and splaying out her paws in a luxurious stretch. "That was the tastiest mouse I've eaten in moons. Now I could do with a good, long sleep."

"Oh, no, you don't!" Brambleclaw prodded her with his paw. "We've got a long way to go, and we need to get as far around the lake as we can in daylight."

"All right, keep your fur on." Squirrelflight scrambled up, her green eyes teasing. "You're such a bossy old furball. Don't forget I'm a warrior now!" She whisked around him, flicking him with her tail.

"You don't give me the chance to forget," Brambleclaw retorted, though he couldn't keep the laughter out of his voice. How long had it been, he asked himself, since any of them had had the time or the strength to play?

He gathered the others together—Mistyfoot watched him give the order without saying anything, the expression in her blue eyes impossible to read—and they set off once more, taking a slanting route down to the lake. As he looked back toward the temporary camp, Brambleclaw saw that the spur of land he had spotted earlier was actually an island; three tiny, fuzzy shapes were standing on the shore looking out at it.

"There's Leafpaw!" Squirrelflight meowed.

Brambleclaw didn't ask how she could recognize her sister from so far away; he knew there was some sort of special connection between them, so that each of them always had a good idea where the other one was and how she was feeling. A flicker of jealousy stirred within him, but he pushed it away.

They headed down from the ridge toward a point on the lakeshore farther along from the island. To Brambleclaw's relief, the marshy places and small reed-fringed pools thinned out; instead the ground was covered with long grass that felt cool and comfortable under his pads.

"This is more like it!" muttered Crowfeather. WindClan cats were the least used to wet ground, coming from the well-drained sandy moorland above the woods where the other Clans had lived.

Sunhigh came and went as the five cats traveled along the edge of the lake. A stretch of smooth round pebbles ran down to the water, reminding Brambleclaw of the banks of the river in the forest. A little way from the shore, he spotted the spreading ripples where a fish had just risen.

"Plenty of prey for RiverClan," he pointed out to Mistyfoot.

She nodded. "Mind you," she meowed, "we might need to work out new ways of fishing. We're used to standing on the bank or on stepping stones and scooping them out with our paws. What would we do if all the fish went to hide in the middle of the lake?"

There was an amused snort from Squirrelflight, but Brambleclaw silenced her with a glare. Mistyfoot hadn't been joking—her Clan could starve next to a lake full of prey if they didn't have the right hunting techniques. He narrowed his eyes and stared across the lake to the greenish smudge that might be the sort of trees ThunderClan had lived among before. Surely hunting mice and squirrels would be the same here as it had been in the forest?

The pebbles beneath their paws grew larger and more slippery, and they slowed down to pick their way carefully, without getting their feet trapped between the stones. The lake bulged into the land ahead of them, and Brambleclaw stopped to look at the opposite shore. Pine trees surrounded a grassy area at the edge of the water, where a wooden structure stuck out into the lake. It looked a bit like the Twoleg bridge in the old territory, but it didn't seem to lead anywhere.

"What's that?" Brambleclaw asked, signaling with his tail.

"Some Twoleg thing." Crowfeather was disdainful.

"I hope that doesn't mean Twolegs swarming all over the place," meowed Tawnypelt.

"I don't think so," Mistyfoot replied. "I can't see any Twolegs there now. Maybe they come only in greenleaf, like they used to in our old territory. Their kits like to play in the water."

"I always thought Twolegs were mousebrained." Crowfeather sniffed.

Squirrelflight was staring across at the bridge thing, her jaws parted to drink in any scent carried on the breeze. "I can't smell anything but forest scents and prey," she reported at last.

"We're too far away to pick up all the scent trails," Brambleclaw meowed. "We'll check it out when we get over there. Like Mistyfoot said, there aren't any Twolegs around now."

He signaled for the patrol to move on again. They walked in silence, as if the Twoleg half-bridge had reminded them of their old enemies, and made them warier. Before long Brambleclaw heard another sound above the gentle lapping of waves on the shore: the gurgle of running water. The ground underpaw grew wetter, and just ahead he could see a thick line of reeds winding away from the lake.

"A stream!" Mistyfoot exclaimed, bounding forward.

The rest of the patrol picked up their pace until they joined her on the bank. Pushing through the reeds, Brambleclaw saw that the stream flowed out of the lake; it was wider than the streams they had crossed previously, too broad to jump across, with deep channels curving around pebbly shallows and small, stony islands. The water looked green and cool, shaded by reeds and the occasional tree that grew along the banks. Clumps of brown, dry bracken all around promised more lush vegetation in greenleaf.

Mistyfoot looked around, the tip of her tail twitching. "RiverClan would like a place like this."

Brambleclaw noticed that she did not make an instant claim to this territory on behalf of her Clan, but he saw the longing in her eyes as she surveyed the stream. He agreed it would be a good place for RiverClan, but it wasn't their decision to make. Their duty was to report back to the rest of the cats when they had explored all the land around the lake, and the leaders would decide how to divide it up.

"Hey!" Squirrelflight mewed. "I just saw a fish!"

A heartbeat later Brambleclaw spotted one, too, a silver flash that sent ripples spiraling out as it touched the surface of the water.

"Perfect!" mewed Mistyfoot. "Shall I catch some for us?"

"We know how to catch our own, you know." Tawnypelt spoke politely, but with an edge to her voice.

Mistyfoot gave her a curious look. "Where did you learn that?"

"On our journey," Crowfeather meowed abruptly.

"Feathertail taught us." He turned away and stalked a few paces downstream, where he sat close to the water, staring into the depths with one paw raised, ready to strike.

Brambleclaw's heart ached for him. None of them would ever forget the brave and gentle RiverClan cat who had done so much to help Crowfeather feel at ease in the group, and in the end had given her life to save him from Sharptooth. Brambleclaw wondered whether Crowfeather's pain would ever be healed. Sometimes he seemed as prickly and self-contained as he had been at the start of their journey, before he had learned to trust his companions, and before he had fallen in love with Feathertail.

Mistyfoot gave a sympathetic murmur; Brambleclaw saw grief in her eyes too, and remembered that she had been Feathertail's mentor. But the RiverClan deputy didn't attempt to go over to the WindClan warrior and comfort him. Perhaps she knew he wouldn't welcome any cat intruding on his sad memories. Instead she crouched down where she was to wait for a fish. Tawnypelt and Squirrelflight joined her, but Brambleclaw stayed close to the reeds, all his senses alert for danger. They still didn't know what this new territory might conceal, and four cats intent on hunting would make easy prey for a hungry fox.

There was no scent of predators or Twolegs, and by the time his friends had hooked several fish out of the stream there had been no sound to disturb them.

"Aren't you hungry, Brambleclaw?" Squirrelflight asked, padding up to him and setting down the plump silver fish she carried in her jaws. "Or have you forgotten how to fish?"

"I was keeping watch," he protested. He broke off when he spotted the gleam in her green eyes.

"Mousebrain," she purred, patting the fish toward him with one forepaw. "I know exactly what you were doing, and I caught enough for both of us. Come and share."

Tawnypelt shot Brambleclaw a look from narrowed eyes as he sat down beside Squirrelflight. "You seem pretty close," she remarked quietly. "No need to ask StarClan what your future holds!"

Brambleclaw squirmed in embarrassment, uncomfortable at the thought of other cats gossiping about who he chose to spend time with. Then he relaxed. He had no reason to be secretive about his feelings for Squirrelflight, especially with his own sister. "Then that makes one less thing for StarClan to worry about," he retorted lightly.

When the meal was over, he stood up, swiping his tongue around his jaws. "Where now?" he asked. "Back to the lake, or shall we have a look downstream?"

"I'd like to explore downstream," meowed Mistyfoot. "We could see if there are any good places for a camp."

Brambleclaw nodded, and the cats padded in single file along the bank of the stream, away from the lake. Brambleclaw let Mistyfoot take the lead, because she had the best idea of what she'd be looking out for to make a good RiverClan camp. As far as he could see, there were plenty of places where her Clanmates would feel at home: reed beds, clumps of bramble thickets for fresh-kill that wasn't fish, with the gurgling of the stream always in their ears. Before very long, they came to a small trickle of water that fell down a slope thickly covered with fern and moss to join the main stream. The land between the two streams was sheltered by clumps of hazel and brambles.

"That's perfect!" Mistyfoot's eyes shone; she crossed the main stream, leaping from one pebbly island to the next, then paused as if she had almost forgotten that they needed to watch out for danger. She lifted her head to taste the air before vanishing into the undergrowth.

"It looks as if RiverClan are settled," Tawnypelt commented.

"Nothing is settled," Crowfeather reminded her sharply. "It's for the leaders to decide how the territories are divided up."

"Well, don't tell me WindClan want to live by a stream, because I won't believe you," Squirrelflight retorted.

"Crowfeather's right, but there's no need to argue." Brambleclaw tried to sound neutral, but he couldn't help feeling a twinge of envy. This place was perfect for RiverClan, but it would suit ThunderClan very well, too. Okay, so they had never hunted for fish back in the forest, but they could learn, and there were enough trees growing here to provide them with fur-clad prey as well. Brambleclaw wasn't going to say anything now because it might upset Mistyfoot, but no final decisions could be made before they had seen everything. "With any luck, we'll find somewhere right for all of us," he meowed firmly.

Mistyfoot soon came back, her tail in the air and her eyes

gleaming with satisfaction. "I've seen enough for now," she mewed. "We could definitely make a camp here. Let's keep going, and see if we can find somewhere for your Clans, too."

Trying not to feel irritated by the trace of smugness in her tone, as if she was doing them a big favor by accompanying them when RiverClan seemed to have found their perfect home, Brambleclaw led the way to join her on the other side of the main stream. They headed back toward the lake, past the place where they had stopped to fish, and emerged from the trees into an open space stretching down to the shore. Not far ahead was the Twoleg half-bridge, and now that they were closer, Brambleclaw caught a faint but familiar tang in the air.

"There's a Thunderpath nearby!" he hissed. The hair on his shoulders lifted and his blood turned to ice as he remembered the Twoleg monsters gouging through the forest, ripping the trees out of the ground and leaving an unrecognizable landscape of mud and ruts. Would Twolegs and their monsters drive them away from this place too?

Beside him, Squirrelflight stood with her paws braced against the ground and her fur fluffed up, as if she too was watching their home being destroyed all over again.

"I haven't heard any monsters," Mistyfoot meowed calmly. "Let's go and look."

She took a pace forward, glancing back when she realized that none of the others had followed her. "Look," she went on, "we lived near the old Thunderpaths for seasons and seasons, and they never did any cat any harm, so long as we were careful. This one is quieter already—we haven't heard a single monster today. There's no need to lose your fur over it. Now come on."

Brambleclaw gave himself a shake. He felt a bit cross that he had frozen at the first hint of danger, leaving Mistyfoot to take charge of the patrol. He padded forward warily with the others bunched around him. The scent of the Thunderpath strengthened and soon he spotted the hard, black surface, winding through the grass like a flattened snake. It was much narrower than the old Thunderpath, and as Mistyfoot had pointed out there were no monsters charging back and forth on it.

"What's it for?" Crowfeather wondered, walking right up to the edge. "Look—it just goes down to the lake and stops."

Brambleclaw realized he was right. The Thunderpath ended beside the lake in a wide area covered with the same hard, black stuff. At one side was a small Twoleg nest made of wood.

"The Twoleg scent is faint and stale," Tawnypelt remarked. "I'd guess they haven't been here for moons."

"Look what I've found!"

Brambleclaw spun around and froze when he saw that Squirrelflight had ventured right out onto the half-bridge, and was gazing down into the water.

"Be careful!" he called, bounding over to her. His paws made a soft thudding sound on the planks of wood, and every few paces one of them rattled ominously. He tried not to think what it would feel like to plunge through into the icy gray water.

"Look!" Squirrelflight leaned over the edge and pricked her ears.

Following where she pointed, Brambleclaw saw another Twoleg object floating on the water. It looked like an upturned leaf, but it was much bigger and was made of wood. It was partly hidden by the half-bridge, so they hadn't seen it from the shore.

"What is it?"

"Twolegs call it a boat," Mistyfoot told them, padding up. Her fur lay flat on her shoulders, and she obviously wasn't bothered by the rattling half-bridge. "They used to bring them onto our river sometimes—did you never see one? Sometimes they used them for fishing."

Brambleclaw tried to picture a Twoleg crouching in this this *boat*, waiting to hook out a fish with its big clumsy paws. He found it hard to believe they'd be quick enough to catch anything, but if Mistyfoot said so, it must be true.

"I think this must be a place where the Twolegs come in greenleaf, like the river," Mistyfoot went on. "That means we don't have to worry about them now."

"We'll need to worry in greenleaf, though," Squirrelflight meowed.

Mistyfoot shrugged. "We'll think about that when the time comes. There'll be thicker growth everywhere by then. We can keep out of the Twolegs' way, just as we did before." She lifted her head to look squarely at Brambleclaw and Squirrelflight, and her gaze took in Crowfeather and Tawnypelt, who were waiting anxiously where the half-bridge joined with the shore. "Of course there will be dangers in our new home, wherever we end up," she meowed, "but we mustn't forget that we had enemies back in the forest, even before the Twolegs brought their monsters. If StarClan brought us here, it was not because there were no dangers here at all, but because we could learn to live among them, just as we did before."

Squirrelflight nodded, chastened, but Brambleclaw curled his lip. He didn't like the way Mistyfoot was treating them all like anxious apprentices. She had no idea of the dangers they had faced on the first journey to sun-drown-place! More Thunderpaths than she had crossed in her entire life, as well as dogs, hostile kittypets, Twolegs who wanted to trap them, hungry foxes . . .

"Are you going to stay here forever?" Squirrelflight had padded past him and was looking over her shoulder with her tail raised questioningly. Mistyfoot was already back on the shore with the others.

"No, I'm coming," Brambleclaw muttered. He followed Squirrelflight off the half-bridge and tried not to feel mutinous when Mistyfoot led the way out of the clearing, away from the Thunderpath.

"She's the deputy of her Clan," Squirrelflight murmured, dropping back to walk close beside him. "You can't blame her for having more experience than us."

Brambleclaw was about to reply fiercely that their journey to sun-drown-place made them more experienced than any other forest cat when he saw that Squirrelflight was looking at him with sympathy in her green eyes. It wasn't fair to take out his temper on her. If he was honest with himself, he was mostly feeling embarrassed because he had frozen with fear at the sight of the Thunderpath, afraid that what had driven them out of the forest was going to happen all over again.

He stretched his head forward to lick Squirrelflight's ear. "I know," he meowed. "And everything she says is true. Come on, let's not get left behind."

They broke into a run, and Brambleclaw felt a jolt of relief as they left the Twolegplace and the half-bridge behind and headed into the next part of the territory.

They were approaching the dark green smudge that he had seen across the lake from their temporary camp. As he had guessed, it was a pinewood, like the part of the forest in ThunderClan's old territory that had surrounded Treecutplace. He sniffed the air, but there was no sign of the bitter stench left by tree-cutting monsters, and the ground was smooth and flat, unscarred by the ruts that monsters left behind.

The sun had started to go down, and a red light shone through the trees, casting dark shadows across their path. Tawnypelt's tortoiseshell fur smoldered as the light glanced across her shoulders, and her eyes gleamed.

Brambleclaw realized that it wasn't just the woods around Treecutplace that were like this; ShadowClan's old territory had also had lots of pine trees, giving way to sticky, marshy ground where only a few stunted trees grew.

"Do you think ShadowClan would like to settle here?" he asked his sister.

"Maybe." Tawnypelt's tail twitched. "But back in the forest there were more trees with lower branches. We'd have trouble climbing most of these."

Brambleclaw saw that she was right. The pines around them grew straight up, with smooth, slippery trunks, and the lowest branches began well above a cat's head. An energetic warrior could claw his way up the trunk, but elders or queens and their kits would have trouble. If foxes or badgers attacked, the weakest cats in the Clan would find it hard to escape.

"But you won't camp in the trees," Crowfeather meowed. "If you make this your territory, you'll need somewhere easy to defend for your camp."

Tawnypelt nodded and looked around. The old ShadowClan camp had been in the shelter of a clump of bramble bushes, dense enough to keep the cats hidden and prickly enough to discourage even the most curious foxes. "I can't see anywhere here," she commented.

The ground sloped gently upward from the lake, which was just visible through the trees as a glimmer of silver. As far as Brambleclaw could see the forest floor was smooth and clear, with little undergrowth where prey might be found. When he tasted the air, the strongest scent except for their own was squirrel—but a Clan could not survive by waiting for squirrels to come down from the trees.

A pang of sympathy for his sister tore through him like a claw. In the forest they had left, ShadowClan's territory had been dreary and unwelcoming: partly bog, partly scrubby forest with few tall trees. He had always wondered if the darkness in the hearts of some of the ShadowClan cats came from their gloomy surroundings. This wasn't quite as forbidding, but it still wasn't right for cats.

"It might be different farther on," he mewed encouragingly. "Let's head away from the lake."

Tawnypelt took the lead as they moved warily up the slope. The thick covering of brittle pine needles muffled their pawsteps; everything was so quiet that their meows sounded too loud, and gradually every cat fell silent. Brambleclaw nearly jumped out of his fur when a bird shot up with a loud alarm call.

Squirrelflight sniffed at a clump of yellowish fungi and drew back with her lip curled in disgust. "I wouldn't want to live here," she muttered to Brambleclaw. "Do you think there's any point in going farther?"

"It's up to Tawnypelt," he replied. "This is more like ShadowClan territory than anything we've seen so far."

They padded on, but before they had gone many more pawsteps Mistyfoot stopped. "This is no good," she meowed. "We're getting farther and farther away from the lake, and it's going to get dark soon."

"I need to find somewhere for a ShadowClan camp," Tawnypelt insisted stubbornly.

"But the Clans sent us to patrol the whole lake." Mistyfoot's tail twitched. "We can't waste time exploring one place more than anywhere else. You've already said that these trees remind you of your old home, so maybe this should be ShadowClan territory."

"And what do you think I'm going to say to Blackstar about where we'll actually live?" Tawnypelt's voice had grown sharper, and her neck fur began to rise. "You needn't think ShadowClan are going to take the worst territory. If there's nowhere to camp, then forget it!"

Mistyfoot's neck fur bristled too. "Trust ShadowClan to be difficult!"

"It's all right for you, isn't it? RiverClan's got everything sorted out. You were pretty quick to stake a claim when we found that stream!"

Mistyfoot let out a furious hiss, unsheathing her claws, and Brambleclaw quickly stepped forward to push himself between the quarreling she-cats. Much as he sympathized with Tawnypelt, it would be a disaster if she got into a fight with the RiverClan deputy. There was no way they could deal with injuries out here, with no medicine cats and no healing herbs; and how would they ever finish their mission if they were quarreling among themselves?

"Stop! Tawnypelt, no cat will force ShadowClan to settle in a place they don't want."

"Huh!" Tawnypelt shot a last glare at Mistyfoot before turning away.

"I think we should go on a bit farther," Brambleclaw mewed to Mistyfoot. "We need to find somewhere to spend the night."

"I know." Mistyfoot still sounded out of temper. "I just think we should head back to the lake."

"But—" Brambleclaw broke off. A faint breeze had sprung up, bringing with it an unexpected scent. He tasted the air, just to be sure. "More cats!" he exclaimed.

"What?" Squirrelflight bounded over. "Where?"

Brambleclaw angled his ears in the direction they had been going. "Up ahead."

"They must be rogues or loners." Crowfeather sounded concerned. "Or maybe some other Clan has already staked a claim here."

The suggestion worried Brambleclaw for a moment; then he comforted himself with the memory of stars shining in the lake. If StarClan had brought them here, then there could be no other warrior ancestors watching over this territory. StarClan had been silent and invisible while the Clans traveled through the mountains, where the Tribe of Endless Hunting watched over their former home.

"Maybe they're just passing through," he meowed. "But we ought to check it out."

"I don't think it's important now." Mistyfoot waved her tail as Brambleclaw opened his jaws to protest. "All right, all right. But you can tell the leaders why it took us so long to get back."

"Fine," Brambleclaw agreed, before heading through the trees in the direction of the scent. Soon they came to a low wall of rough gray stone with a Twoleg nest beyond it.

"Twolegs!" Tawnypelt sounded disgusted. "Those must be kittypets we can smell."

Squirrelflight rolled her eyes. "All this fuss about kitty-pets!"

"You stay here," Brambleclaw mewed softly. "I'm going to take a closer look."

"What for?" Mistyfoot's tail twitched impatiently, but she didn't say anything else when Brambleclaw crept forward.

With his belly close to the ground, he got as close to the wall as he could before leaping to the top. The sunlight was almost gone by now, and shadows were gathering in the Twoleg garden. Nothing stirred. Brambleclaw was about to jump down for a closer look when he heard the sound of claws on the stone beside him, and Squirrelflight's voice exclaimed, "Catmint!"

"I thought I told you to stay back there," Brambleclaw hissed.

Squirrelflight gave him an innocent look. "Did you? Sorry. Anyway, the medicine cats will be interested to hear that we've found a supply of catmint."

"That was well scented," Brambleclaw admitted grudgingly. "Now if you must come, stay with me, and for StarClan's sake keep quiet!"

He dropped into the garden behind a clump of whiskery Twoleg plants. Squirrelflight landed softly beside him, and together they crept closer to the Twoleg nest. The scent of kittypets was very strong: two of them, Brambleclaw thought. He was about to suggest going back when a light flashed on in the nest and he found himself blinking in the yellow glow. Instinctively he slid to one side, back into the shadows, and watched as a Twoleg appeared and began to pull pelts across to hide the light.

"Squirrelflight?" he whispered. "Where are you? Let's get out of here."

Squirrelflight's voice came from the other side of the patch of light. "Er . . . Brambleclaw, you might want to rethink that."

At first Brambleclaw couldn't see her in the fast-gathering darkness. Then as the Twoleg hid the last of the light he spotted her, close to the wall of the nest. Her back was arched and her fur fluffed out so she looked almost twice her size. Two angry kittypets faced her, trapping her against the wall.

Brambleclaw stared in disbelief. In spite of their hostile encounter with a kittypet at the start of their journey, he still expected most kittypets to be small and soft—no danger to a trained warrior. But these two looked lean and dangerous, their muscles sharply etched beneath sleek pelts. The nearest to him, a big black-and-white tom, had one ear that was torn jaggedly, proving he was no stranger to fights.

In the moment that Brambleclaw stood frozen, the tom lashed out at Squirrelflight. She shrank back with a furious hiss. "Leave me alone, kittypet!"

With a yowl of rage, Brambleclaw launched himself across the garden, straight at the black-and-white kittypet. Barreling into him, he swept the tom off his paws and tried to pin him down. The tomcat writhed under him, clawing at his face and pummeling his belly with his hindlegs. Brambleclaw heard Squirrelflight let out a screech and caught a glimpse of her rolling over, locked together with the other kittypet, a light brown tabby.

Fear crashed over him like an icy wave. The journey had left them both thin and tired, and they were no match for strong, well-fed, battle-hungry cats.

He fought to sink his teeth into the kittypet's throat, but the black-and-white tom heaved his shoulders and flipped Brambleclaw over before he could close his jaws on fur or flesh. Brambleclaw felt his weight land on top of him, and saw sharp white teeth snapping at his ear. He felt claws rake over his side, and battered vainly at his opponent's belly with his hindpaws.

Suddenly the kittypet's weight vanished. Brambleclaw scrambled up, panting, to see Mistyfoot swipe her claws down the black-and-white tom's shoulder. She sprang out of reach before he had a chance to jump around and face her. While he was still unbalanced, she leaped onto his back and sank her teeth into the scruff of his neck.

Just beyond, the tabby broke away from Squirrelflight and raced around the side of the nest, yowling. Brambleclaw saw Tawnypelt and Crowfeather pelting across the garden, but before they reached the fight the door of the nest was flung open. A Twoleg stood in the doorway, letting out a loud screech. It flung something that skimmed over Brambleclaw's head and landed with a crash in the bushes. The noise distracted Mistyfoot, and the black-and-white tom wrenched itself from under her paws and fled into the nest. The Twoleg advanced into the garden, casting a long, menacing shadow into the light shed through the doorway.

"Run!" hissed Mistyfoot.

Making sure that Squirrelflight was on her paws, Bramble-claw dashed for the wall. Something else slammed into the ground behind him, and there was another yowl from the Twoleg. Then he was leaping up, claws scrabbling on the rough stone, and landing hard on the other side. The others kept pace with him as he fled for the trees, and they didn't stop until the Twoleg nest was out of sight.

"Well!" panted Mistyfoot. "Maybe you'll listen to me next time, Brambleclaw, and think about just how far we need to explore."

Brambleclaw bowed his head, shame scorching him from ears to tail-tip. It had been stupid to go so close to the nest. He had been showing off, trying to prove what a good leader he could be. "Sorry, Mistyfoot," he mumbled.

"So you should be. You could have been badly injured, or trapped by Twolegs." The RiverClan deputy's voice was tart. Glancing around, she added, "Do you have any idea where we are now?"

Brambleclaw realized that they hadn't fled from the nest in the same direction they had come. Tall pine trees stood all around them, with not a hint of where the lake might be. It was almost completely dark.

"No, I thought not," Mistyfoot went on caustically. "Lost in strange woods, and it's getting dark. We'd better look for somewhere to spend the night, and hope we can find our way back to the lake in the morning."

This time she took the lead, stalking through the trees

with her tail held high. Tawnypelt and Crowfeather followed; Tawnypelt gave her brother a sympathetic glance and murmured, "I know you were trying to help."

Brambleclaw shrugged. He couldn't defend his actions—it was only thanks to Mistyfoot that he had escaped from the kittypets with his fur intact. He kept to the rear of the group, his tail drooping, and hardly looked up when Squirrelpaw dropped back to give him an affectionate nuzzle.

"Cheer up!" she mewed. "It's not that bad. We found out something that ShadowClan will need to be warned about if they decide to settle here."

"Blackstar won't want those two kittypets in his territory," Brambleclaw muttered.

"Oh, I don't know." Squirrelflight's eyes glimmered; she glanced at the others to make sure that Tawnypelt was out of earshot before adding, "They'd make pretty good recruits for ShadowClan, if you ask me."

Brambleclaw let out a purr of amusement. "Come on; we don't want to get left behind." They bounded after the others, their pelts brushing as they swerved through the close-growing trees. The ground started to slope more steeply, with rocks jutting out here and there; Brambleclaw slowed down after snagging his claws painfully on a lump of stone. Tussocks of grass and small bushes were rooted in the gaps between the rocks, and the scent of prey grew stronger.

Tawnypelt reached the top first. Halting on a flattened boulder, she called back, "Come and see this!"

Mistyfoot and Crowfeather sprang up beside her, with

Brambleclaw and Squirrelflight just behind. Even though the last of the sun had gone and shadows were gathering, Brambleclaw could make out a wide, shallow dip in the ground, half-hidden under dense brambles. The half-moon, shining through thin cloud, cast watery beams of light onto the trees that surrounded the hollow, their gnarled branches almost sweeping the ground.

Squirrelflight rasped her tongue over Tawnypelt's ear. "A camp for ShadowClan!" she whispered. "We'd never have found it if Brambleclaw hadn't gone looking for those kitty-pets."

Mistyfoot shot her a glance that was half-annoyed, half-amused.

"Maybe it would make a good camp." Tawnypelt was trying to sound calm, though Brambleclaw could tell that she was excited. "But that will be for Blackstar to decide, if ShadowClan moves into this territory."

"At least it's possible," meowed Mistyfoot. "You might find even better places, once you've had the chance to explore properly."

"But it's too late to go any farther tonight," Crowfeather pointed out.

"You're right," Squirrelflight agreed. "My paws are dropping off! Where are we going to sleep?"

Brambleclaw thought it would be a good idea to shelter under the bushes in the hollow, but there was water at the bottom of the slope they had just climbed, and he was thirsty.

He picked his way carefully down again, and the others followed.

As Mistyfoot crouched beside him to lap at the tiny pool, she asked, "Do you want to hunt? Or shall we leave it till morning?"

"Morning," Squirrelflight replied, though the question hadn't been addressed to her. She gave a huge yawn. "I'm so tired I couldn't catch a mouse if it sat on my paws. Besides, we've eaten enough today to feed a whole Clan!"

Brambleclaw realized she was right. Back in the forest there had been many days when the Clan hadn't found as much fresh-kill as they had caught since they left on their patrol.

When all the cats had taken their turn to drink, they settled down to sleep among the grass at the foot of the slope. Mistyfoot organized sentries, and Crowfeather took first watch. As Brambleclaw curled up comfortably beside Squirrelflight, he could just see the WindClan warrior's pricked ears outlined against the darkness of the forest.

It's been a good day, he thought, closing his eyes. *We have found possible homes for two of the Clans. But what about ThunderClan? What if there's nowhere for us?*

CHAPTER 4

Clouds covered the sun the next morning as the patrol set off to find their way back to the lake. Heading in what they thought was the right direction, Brambleclaw stopped short when he smelled scent markers, and spotted the walls of the Twoleg nest through the trees.

"Yuck!" Squirrelflight's lip curled. "That's worse than fox dung. Those kittypets must have marked their territory."

The patrol skirted the markers warily; to Brambleclaw's relief there was no sign of the hostile kittypets. With the nest in view, he could remember which way they had approached it the night before, and it was not long before they crossed their earlier scent trail.

"This way!" Brambleclaw meowed.

A chill wind shook the tops of the pines, and as they reached the shore the cats felt the full force of it. Brambleclaw turned to face it, the cold blast flattening his fur against his sides. He guessed they had traveled about halfway around the lake. Looking back the way they had come, he could see the dark smudge of the island against a background of pale green hills. The surface of the lake was gray and choppy, under clouds that bulged with rain.

"Just what we need!" Tawnypelt grumbled, tucking her nose into her chest.

Waving his tail for the rest to follow him, Brambleclaw retraced his steps into the trees. "I think we should stay under cover," he suggested. "It's more sheltered here."

"Just as long as we don't get lost again," Mistyfoot warned. "Let's stay where we can see the lake."

The others were all happy to get out of the icy wind. They moved off, keeping the lake in sight through the outlying trees but not venturing onto the open shore.

They had not gone far before Crowfeather let out a muffled grunt and streaked off with his tail streaming behind him. Staring after him, Brambleclaw scented squirrel before he spotted the gray-furred creature nibbling a pinecone at the foot of one of the trees. Its ears flicked up in alarm as Crowfeather raced toward it. Dropping the pinecone, it sprang for the safety of the tree. But Crowfeather was faster. With a mighty leap he grabbed the squirrel's tail and pulled it back to the ground. He padded back with the limp body dangling from his jaws.

"Good catch!" Squirrelflight meowed.

Crowfeather nodded as he dropped the fresh-kill in front of them. "Come on; let's eat."

Crouching beside the others to eat his share, Brambleclaw itched with impatience to get moving again. The leaders expected them home by nightfall to report what they had discovered, and they still had a lot of territory to explore—and two Clans still needed homes.

"Let's go," he meowed as soon as they had finished. To his relief, Mistyfoot didn't protest, just swiped her tongue around her jaws and kept pace with him as he set off through the trees at a steady trot.

Brambleclaw's paws tingled with excitement. This could be the day when they found ThunderClan's new home! RiverClan and ShadowClan had already found good places, and he guessed that the ridge of hills across the lake would suit WindClan. But deep down, finding somewhere for his Clanmates to live and hunt safely was what he wanted most of all. Their home in the forest had suited them so well, in spite of being close to the Thunderpath and Twolegplace. Would they find anywhere nearly as good here?

As if she could read his thoughts, his sister, Tawnypelt, padded up beside him and touched her muzzle briefly to his side. "Worried about something?" she mewed.

"I'm okay," he told her, trying hard to convince himself. "I'll just be happier when we've found some territory for ThunderClan."

"There's a long way to go yet," Tawnypelt mewed encouragingly.

Soon they came to a wide path winding through the trees. The pine-needle cover gave way to short grass; regular dents in it had filled with water to form small pools.

"Horses have been along here," Crowfeather mewed, lapping at one of the puddles.

Tawnypelt tasted the air. "Twolegs, too. But there's no sign of them now."

Mistyfoot was gazing up at a tree close to the edge of the path. "That's a Twoleg thing," she reported, flicking her tail at something above her head.

Brambleclaw looked where she was pointing. A round shape made of something hard and shiny had been fastened to the tree. It was bright blue, the same glittering color as some of the monsters on the Thunderpath.

"What do you think it's for?" Squirrelflight asked.

"Maybe it's like a Twoleg scent marking," Brambleclaw suggested. "This path could be a boundary between two territories."

There seemed nothing dangerous about the mark, but all the cats looked around warily as they crossed the path. Brambleclaw reminded himself crossly that he never used to be this scared of Twolegs. Not until they brought their monsters to the forest and shut up all the cats they could catch in small Twoleg dens. Now he wondered whether he would ever feel safe around Twolegs again, and he let out a sigh of relief when they reached the shelter of the trees on the other side.

Gradually the pine trees began to thin out. Cold rain began to fall, billowing over the cats as the wind rattled the branches above them, sending a prickly shower of pine needles onto their heads.

"I'd give anything for a nice warm den!" Squirrelflight grumbled, flicking raindrops from her ears.

Heads down, they plodded on until the trees stopped altogether, giving way to a broad, straight-edged grassy clearing. At the edge of the wood they crossed another Twoleg path, narrower than the first, the grass worn away by many feet. By now everything was so wet that no cat could pick up a scent; all Brambleclaw could be sure of was that no Twolegs were there now.

"There's another one of those half-bridges," he mewed, pricking his ears toward the wooden structure that jutted out into the lake. Squirrelflight didn't seem keen on venturing onto it when billows of icy rain scudded across the surface of the lake and rattled against the wood.

They cautiously crossed the exposed space beyond the trees, crouching down until the short grass brushed their belly-fur. For a while there was no sound except for the falling rain and the trees clattering in the wind. They had a clear view of the lake from here, and Brambleclaw realized that they were about to enter the last stretch of trees before the bare ridge of hills; beyond that was the place where the horses were, and then the copse of trees where all four Clans waited to hear about their new homes. If WindClan was going to take the hills, which seemed logical, this was ThunderClan's last chance to find somewhere to live.

Brambleclaw's ears twitched as he picked up the sound of running water. Could it be a place where his Clanmates could make camp, with somewhere to drink close by?

"It must be another stream," Crowfeather meowed, hearing it too.

Beneath their paws, the ground sloped down and the grass gave way to pebbles, which in turn disappeared beneath a broad, fast-flowing stream. Unlike the stream they had found in the place where RiverClan might make their camp, there were no stepping stones or islands to help the cats across.

"We'll have to wade," Tawnypelt decided. "It doesn't look too deep."

She padded down to the edge of the water and dipped in her paw, drawing it out again with a hiss; the water was obviously icy cold. Then she shook herself and walked into the water, placing each paw carefully on the slippery pebbles. There were fewer reeds here than in the first stream where they had stopped to fish the day before, and hardly any shrubs or other undergrowth. A pang of disappointment bit through Brambleclaw. This would be no place for a camp, especially not with traces of Twolegs so close by.

"Watch out when you get to the middle," Mistyfoot called. "Sometimes there are hollows that you can't see above the water, and it could suddenly get deeper."

The water almost reached Tawnypelt's belly fur by now. She paused and nodded without looking back, then went on more cautiously. Brambleclaw and the others followed; Crowfeather let out a startled meow as he slipped on a loose stone, but found his balance again after some rather undignified splashing, and managed to keep his head above the surface of the water.

Tawnypelt jumped out and shook herself from nose to tail, scattering drops of water around her. "You'll be fine," she called to the others. "I didn't have to swim at all."

Cold, wet, and with his belly fur clinging uncomfortably to his skin, Brambleclaw wasn't sure that was much of a benefit right now. Beside him, Mistyfoot padded confidently through the water as if she were on dry land; Brambleclaw noticed her keeping one eye on Squirrelflight, who had the shortest legs of all of them, and had to tip back her head to stop the water from lapping at her muzzle.

There was another stretch of open grass on the far side of the stream, with more trees beyond. Soaked to his ears by the time he scrambled up the opposite bank, Brambleclaw made a dash for cover, but the branches here had shed their leaves, and didn't offer much shelter from the rain.

He crouched beneath a tree while he waited for the others to catch up, trying to imagine what it would be like in green-leaf, with thicker grass and ferns and a canopy of leaves rustling above him. Right now the ground was unpleasantly soggy, and he couldn't see any thickets of bramble or hazel like the ones in their old territory.

At least these trees were oak and beech, not pines like the forest they had just left. They would provide good shelter for the mice and birds ThunderClan was used to hunting. Brambleclaw's spirits began to lift, but he was still uneasy about all the signs of Twoleg activity—the paths, the brightly colored mark on a tree, the half-bridges. He wondered if it was just his nerves telling him there were more signs of Twolegs here than in their old territory, and he shook himself to clear his head.

"What do you think?" Mistyfoot prompted, joining him.

Before Brambleclaw could reply, Squirrelflight bounded up and began scuffling with one forepaw among the discarded beech shells lying in the grass.

"With all these nuts around there should be plenty of squirrels," she meowed.

Mistyfoot narrowed her eyes at Brambleclaw, and he tried not to look as if he were beginning to give up all hope of finding somewhere for ThunderClan to live. "Why don't we rest for a bit?" she suggested. "Find somewhere out of the rain and hope it stops soon."

"Hope catches no prey," Crowfeather commented dryly as he and Tawnypelt came up, flicking droplets of water from their ears.

"That's a good idea, Mistyfoot," Brambleclaw meowed.

"If we can *find* any shelter," Tawnypelt added.

"Let's go farther into the woods," Mistyfoot decided. "The wind will be colder blowing off the water."

They padded into the trees on a slanting course that led away from the lake. When they could still make out the silver sheen of water behind them, they came to a huge, ancient oak standing among the beech trees. The ground had fallen away around the twisting roots, and there was a faint, stale scent of rabbit, as if this had once been used as a burrow. There was room for all the cats to creep in among the roots, where they were sheltered from the wind, though rain still trickled in.

Brambleclaw huddled close to Squirrelflight and began to lick drops of rain from the fur around her neck and shoulders.

"This feels way harder than anything we had to do on the journey," she murmured after a while. "All that way—all the danger we faced getting here, the times we nearly didn't make it—and now we have to decide where the Clan is going to make its new home. It doesn't feel as if StarClan is going to lead us straight to a nice, safe camp. What if we make the wrong decision?"

She had come so close to the heart of his fears that Brambleclaw paused to gaze into her forest-green eyes. "I thought it would be easier than this too," he admitted.

Squirrelflight peered out of their shelter, blinking raindrops off her eyelashes. "These are the right sort of trees, but it's so open here compared with the old territory. ThunderClan won't feel safe if there isn't enough cover."

"Or if the territory's full of Twolegs," Brambleclaw pointed out.

"Come on!" Tawnypelt stopped licking her chest fur and looked up to face him. "There were plenty of Twolegs back in the forest. It wasn't a problem then, and it won't be a problem now."

She was talking sense, but more than anything else, Brambleclaw knew that he wanted to feel safe in his new home, and he didn't feel safe here, at least not yet.

"It'll look better in newleaf," Mistyfoot meowed encouragingly. "Everywhere does."

"Hmm. . . ." Squirrelflight shifted so that she could lick the damp fur at the base of her tail. "We still have to find a camp, though."

"You've hardly set paw in the territory yet," Crowfeather pointed out.

"I know." Brambleclaw made a determined effort to stop worrying and concentrated on giving Squirrelflight a few more vigorous licks.

Her jaws gaped in an enormous yawn. "This rain doesn't help. If it goes on much longer it'll wash my fur off."

Brambleclaw stopped and let his muzzle rest against Squirrelflight's warm flank. He was just dozing off when he felt her give a wriggle and heard her say, "I think it's easing off."

Lifting his head, Brambleclaw realized that the steady pattering of the rain on the grass outside their shelter had faded away into uneven, short-lived bursts. The wind had dropped, and a watery beam of sunlight glinted on the drops that hung from every branch and twig.

Tawnypelt meowed, "The clouds are breaking up."

Brambleclaw scrambled out from the roots and glanced up to see that it was almost sunhigh. The rest of the patrol emerged behind him. Mistyfoot scented the air, while Crowfeather groomed the ruffled fur on his gray-black shoulder.

"Any chance of hunting?" Squirrelflight meowed, stretching each hindleg in turn.

"Sure," Brambleclaw replied. "Let's look for something on the way." It would be a chance to see how well the woodland could feed hungry cats.

The five cats spread out among the trees. Brambleclaw kept his ears pricked for the sound of prey, and he paused every few steps to taste the air. At first all he could smell were wet leaves and dripping branches, and he felt his spirits sink. Were there so many Twolegs here that all the prey had fled? But at least the ground was becoming more uneven, with bushes and clumps of dead bracken where little creatures might hide.

Suddenly he picked up a tiny scuffling sound among the leaves at the foot of a tree. Squirrelflight heard it at the same moment, and streaked toward it. Her paws thudded on the ground, and the prey—a vole—shot out and vanished into a clump of brambles. Squirrelflight raced after it with her nose stretched out. Brambleclaw groaned—she should have known better than to chase something so noisily in the quiet forest.

"She won't catch it now," Crowfeather commented.

They watched Squirrelflight plunge into the bushes. For a heartbeat her dark ginger fur was visible among the waving branches before it disappeared. A fading yowl came out of the bushes, and then all was still.

"What happened?" exclaimed Tawnypelt.

Brambleclaw dashed toward the brambles, the vole forgotten. "Squirrelflight!" he yowled. "Squirrelflight, where are you?"

He pushed his way into the thorny branches.

"Careful!" he heard Mistyfoot warn him from behind.

Brambleclaw scarcely heard her. Springy twigs slapped him across the face, and he felt a thorn sink into his pad. "Squirrelflight!" he called again.

"I'm down here!" The faint reply came from somewhere below.

Brambleclaw looked down and gasped. A tail-length in front of him the ground fell away sharply; another couple of pawsteps and he would have slipped over too.

Glancing back over his shoulder he saw Tawnypelt pressing up close behind him. "Stay back," he warned. "There's some sort of cliff here. Let me have a look first."

Keeping his belly close to the ground, he crept forward until he could look over the edge. Remembering the gorge in the mountains where Smokepaw had fallen, he braced himself to see Squirrelflight's broken body lying on stones far below. Instead she was standing in a clump of brambles no more than three or four fox-lengths beneath him, staring up at him with wide green eyes.

"Squirrelflight!" He gasped. "Are you all right?"

"No, I'm not!" Squirrelflight meowed crossly. "I've got so many thorns in me I feel like a hedgehog. And I never caught that wretched vole. But I've found something amazing! Come and see."

"Will we be able to get out again?"

Squirrelflight sighed. "Honestly, Brambleclaw, are you a mouse? Get down here. You've got to see this."

Brambleclaw felt his fur prickle with excitement. He glanced back at the other members of the patrol. Tawnypelt was standing where he had left her, and Mistyfoot and Crowfeather peered anxiously around her flank.

"Is Squirrelflight hurt?" Mistyfoot called.

"No, I think she's fine," Brambleclaw replied. "She wants me to go down there. Will you keep watch?"

Mistyfoot nodded, and Brambleclaw turned back to the cliff. When he looked at it closely, he saw that it wasn't as sheer as the gorge. It was steep, but there were plenty of pawholds on jutting stones and tussocks of grass. Half slipping, half scrambling, he made his way down until he reached Squirrelflight, who was standing among the brambles looking rather disheveled.

"There!" She spun around, impatiently twitching her tail. "See?"

Brambleclaw followed her gaze more slowly. They were standing on the edge of a bramble thicket; a wide, grassy space stretched in front of them, surrounded by walls of stone. Where he and Squirrelflight had come down, the walls were fairly low, but on the opposite side of the clearing they stretched above their heads for many fox-lengths.

"It's a good thing you didn't fall down on that side," he meowed.

"Yes, I know, but don't you see, Brambleclaw?" Squirrelflight demanded. "This is ThunderClan's new camp!"

"What?"

"*Look* at it," she insisted. "It's perfect."

Brambleclaw unhooked a bramble from his fur and padded into the center of the clearing. The stone walls rose all around him except for a gap not far away, which was choked with dead ferns and grass with whiskery, seedy stems. There were more bramble thickets all around him, and he could see one or two cracks that might lead to caves in the highest part of the wall. He could see what Squirrelflight meant. The place could make a good camp, but something about it spooked him all the same.

"I don't know . . ." he began, not wanting to crush Squirrelflight's excitement but unable to ignore the disquiet that made his paws itch. "Look at the surface of the stone, how smoothly it's been cut. Only Twolegs could have done that, and we can't camp anywhere near Twolegs."

"But that must have been ages ago," Squirrelflight argued, coming to join him in the center of the clearing. "Look at the grass and bushes growing up the walls. They didn't spring up overnight, did they? And there's no scent of Twolegs."

Brambleclaw tasted the air. Squirrelflight was right. No Twolegs had been there for a long time. She was right about the bushes, too. Twolegs must have cut out the stone—maybe to build their nests—and then gone away and left the hollow in the middle of the forest. In a way, it reminded him of the ravine that had sheltered the old ThunderClan camp. Perhaps that would make it feel like home to the Clan.

He forced himself to be calm. His Clanmates needed him to be strong, and not see danger in every shadow and stirring leaf. "It might do, I suppose."

Squirrelflight flicked her ears. "Don't get too enthusiastic, will you?" she mewed.

"I'm just wondering what it would be like to defend. That part over there would be fine"—he gestured with his tail to the highest, steepest wall—"but it's pretty low where we came in. And what about that gap?"

"Well, it's an easier way in and out than the one we took just now! We can fill it in with thorns or something to keep out uninvited visitors."

She bounded over and prowled through the long grass, sniffing here and there. Watching her, Brambleclaw felt a wave of homesickness sweep over him, and he closed his eyes. The feeling seemed to pick him up and swamp him like the waves at sun-drown-place, and for a few heartbeats he thought he would drown in it. He wanted the old ThunderClan camp with its strong thorn walls and the gorse tunnel that was so easy to defend. He wanted to lie down in the warriors' den under the thornbush, or visit Cinderpelt in her den among the soft green ferns. He wanted to eat fresh-kill by the nettle patch while the apprentices scuffled by their favorite tree stump, their fighting moves carefully imitated by the kits outside the nursery.

The pain of knowing he could never go back was almost too much for Brambleclaw to bear. The Twoleg monsters would have torn up every part of the camp by now, all the places that were so deep in his heart. It wasn't fair! Why had StarClan let this happen?

The wind picked up, rattling the branches of the trees that surrounded the hollow and jolting Brambleclaw back to his surroundings. Taking a deep breath, he padded over to Squirrelflight, who was still nosing about in the gap between the walls.

"Are you okay?" she asked. "You're limping."

"Oh—there's a thorn in my pad." Brambleclaw had almost forgotten about it.

"Lie down and let me look."

When Brambleclaw obeyed, she licked experimentally at his pad and managed to get the end of the thorn between her teeth. With a sharp tug it came away.

"There," Squirrelflight meowed. "Now give it a good lick."

"Thanks. You're nearly good enough to be a medicine cat!"

Squirrelflight gave a little *mrrow* of amusement. Then the laughter died from her eyes and she looked closely at him. "You don't like it here, do you?"

"It's not that." Brambleclaw paused in rasping his tongue over his injured pad. "It's just . . . well, I suppose I wanted to find a camp exactly like the one we left behind, in a ravine with gorse to keep out invaders. . . ."

He trailed off, afraid Squirrelflight would think he was being ridiculous; instead she pressed her muzzle affectionately against his. "There isn't a cat among ThunderClan who doesn't want our old home back. But it's gone now. StarClan has brought us to a new place, and we've got to find out how to live here. Don't you think this hollow would make a good camp? Twolegs don't come here, and there's no sign of Thunderpaths."

Gazing into her shining eyes, Brambleclaw knew that he had brought with him from the forest everything that was truly important. "You're right," he murmured, leaning into the warmth of her fur. "I couldn't do this without you. You know that, don't you?"

Squirrelflight's tongue rasped gently over his ear. "Stupid furball."

Brambleclaw returned the affectionate lick, then froze as he heard the sound of something approaching through the gap.

"Hi, there." It was Crowfeather's voice, muffled by a mouthful of vole. He shouldered the long grass aside as he came up to them and dropped the fresh-kill at their paws. "You've been so long, we started to think a fox might have gotten you."

"No, we're fine," replied Brambleclaw.

"If a fox had gotten *me*," Squirrelflight added, "you would have heard about it, don't worry."

"I daresay we would," Crowfeather meowed, pushing the vole toward them. "This is for you," he went on. "We've all had ours. We hunted while we were waiting for you to come back."

"Thanks, Crowfeather," mewed Brambleclaw.

The WindClan warrior acknowledged his thanks with a wave of his tail.

"Well, what do you think of the new ThunderClan camp?" Squirrelflight demanded.

"Here?" Crowfeather blinked, and turned slowly around while the ThunderClan warriors shared the vole in swift, hungry bites. "I suppose it's okay," he meowed at last, "if you want to be closed in like this. It would be easy to defend, but it wouldn't do for WindClan."

"We're not offering it to WindClan," Squirrelflight pointed out.

Crowfeather flicked his ears, and Brambleclaw wondered if he was worried about finding somewhere suitable for his Clan. Surely he'd wait until they explored the ridge of hills before seriously looking for a camp? Now that they'd found this hollow, amid the right sort of woods for voles and squirrels and birds, Brambleclaw was starting to believe there might actually be territories for every Clan around the lake.

Tawnypelt and Mistyfoot padded into the hollow, tasting the air as they gazed around at the sheer walls of rock.

"No foxes or badgers," Mistyfoot remarked. "Pretty sheltered, too."

"All the same, you'll need to be careful," Tawnypelt urged Brambleclaw. "If Twolegs made this place, how do you know they won't come back?"

"Twolegs haven't been here for seasons," Squirrelflight replied calmly. "There's no scent of them, and there wouldn't be so much undergrowth if they were still cutting out the rock."

But Tawnypelt's words made Brambleclaw unsheathe his claws and sink them into the rain-damp ground. The memory of Twoleg monsters ripping through their old home was too recent; it was all too easy for him to imagine them coming here to cut more stone out of the hollow. And yet ThunderClan would be mousebrained not to use a place that seemed to have nearly everything they would need for a safe and sheltered camp. In the end it was Firestar who would have to make the decision.

"Are you ready?" Mistyfoot interrupted his thoughts. "It's way past sunhigh."

Brambleclaw nodded. He looked around, trying to get his bearings. He wasn't sure what direction they should take to return to the lake, when his nose was filled with unfamiliar smells. Not far away from the entrance to the hollow, he noticed that the ground sloped upward.

"Let's go that way," he suggested. If they gained some height, they might be able to see the lake.

The rest of the patrol murmured agreement, and the cats padded side by side out of the hollow. As they pushed through the undergrowth, leaving the sheltering stone walls behind them, Squirrelflight paused and looked over her shoulder. "We'll come back, won't we?"

She spoke so quietly that Brambleclaw wasn't sure if she was talking to him, but he replied anyway. "Yes," he said, stretching forward to touch his muzzle to the tip of her ear. "I think we will."

"Come on," called Crowfeather. "We want to be back before it gets dark." He didn't add that they still had to find somewhere for WindClan to live, but Brambleclaw knew that must be in his thoughts.

He trotted up the slope with Squirrelflight beside him, leaving the hollow to be swallowed up once more among the close-growing trees. Wet grass brushed at his fur, chilling him through, but above his head the clouds had cleared away to reveal the pale blue sky of leaf-bare. The sun shone, though there was little warmth in it.

Brambleclaw stopped and looked down at the sweep of leafless branches below. The stone hollow was totally hidden, safe and secret in the surrounding forest. Could it really become ThunderClan's new camp? He had expected to feel more certain when he discovered somewhere his Clanmates might be able to live; he had thought it would feel like *home*. Instead there was something oppressive about this place, as if the rocks themselves did not want to welcome the newcomers.

As they climbed, the trees began to thin out, and the dense undergrowth gave way to stretches of crisp fallen leaves. After a while Brambleclaw saw glimpses of open moorland between the trunks, and soon they reached the edge of the forest, with the ridge of hills rolling away in front of them. The lake was a gleam of silver in the valley below. Straight ahead lay a gray-green swell of moorland grass, rippled by the wind. Gorse thickets were dotted over it, and Brambleclaw could hear the sound of running water. There could be no doubt that they had found a home for WindClan.

"Hey, Crowfeather!" he called. "What do you think?"

The WindClan warrior's eyes gleamed, but he did not reply until he had opened his jaws and carefully tasted the air. "Rabbits!"

"Right, that's WindClan sorted out," Squirrelflight meowed. "Let's get back to the others."

Crowfeather shot her a look from narrowed eyes.

"Only joking," Squirrelflight mewed quickly. "Come on; let's find somewhere for your camp."

Brambleclaw knew they needed to look for a camping place for WindClan, but already the sun was slipping down the sky, casting long shadows over the grass.

"Actually, we should get back to the others," he began awkwardly. "I'm sorry, Crowfeather. I don't think we've time to explore these hills properly. Tallstar can send another patrol tomorrow to check out a site for your camp. I think we should head straight across the ridge to the end of the lake now."

Crowfeather's tail-tip twitched. For a few heartbeats he stood motionless, studying the sweep of hillside before lowering his head to sniff the grass. Brambleclaw was worried that he was about to insist they explored further, but in the end he just meowed, "It's okay. You're right; we should be heading back."

There was a guarded look in his eyes as he spoke, and Brambleclaw guessed he wasn't sorry that cats from other Clans weren't getting a chance to explore WindClan's new territory. Pain stabbed at the young tabby's heart. Crowfeather was ferociously loyal to his Clanmates; it wasn't surprising that he would be the first to start setting up the old barriers again.

They started to follow the slope up to the top of the ridge, with the lake stretching out below them like a shining sheet of sky. Brambleclaw padded beside Squirrelflight, gazing from side to side over this new stretch of territory. They climbed a shoulder of the hill to a stream that foamed over rocks and vanished into the trees they had left behind. They followed it uphill for a few fox-lengths until they came to stepping-stones where they could cross. A smaller stream joined it here, gurgling down a steep, grassy slope.

Before they reached the top of the hill they came to a spot where the ground fell away, as if some enormous monster had taken a bite out of the hillside. But not a Twoleg monster, Brambleclaw realized; this hollow had been formed by time and weather alone. Boulders were scattered over the ground in the middle, while gorse and other shrubs grew thickly around the edges. Inside, it would be sheltered from the wind, but not as closed-in as the walls of stone that encircled the possible ThunderClan camp.

Brambleclaw narrowed his eyes. "What about that for your camp, Crowfeather?" he asked.

Crowfeather kneaded the ground in excitement as he looked down the slope. "It looks good," he agreed. "I'll check it out. You go on, and I'll catch up."

"Are you sure?" Brambleclaw meowed. "I don't think we should leave you on your own."

"I'll be fine," Crowfeather promised, flexing his hindlegs, ready to dash off. "There's no scent of Twolegs or foxes. And I can find my own way back to the camp by the horseplace. I can smell those creatures from here!"

Before any of the others could argue, he streaked off down the hill. Brambleclaw watched him pause on the edge of the dip before plunging into the gorse cover, the trembling branches the only sign of where he had been a moment before.

"I hope he's right about the Twolegs and foxes," murmured Mistyfoot, coming over to stand beside Brambleclaw.

Too late, he wondered if he should have consulted Mistyfoot before letting Crowfeather go off on his own. He opened his mouth to defend the WindClan warrior, but she stopped him, speaking gently to take any sting out of her words. "It's all right, Brambleclaw. I can see how much respect these cats have for you. That's something to be proud of, not to apologize for. Few cats are born leaders, but I think you are."

He blinked at her, partly grateful and partly surprised. It seemed strange having a RiverClan cat make a judgment like that about him. He wondered what Mistyfoot thought of his half brother, Hawkfrost, who was a RiverClan warrior. Was Tigerstar's other son a born leader, too?

Suddenly a gust of wind buffeted them so hard that Brambleclaw's eyes watered, and for a couple of heartbeats he thought it would sweep him off his paws. It brought a strong scent of horse with it. Shaking his head to clear away the tears, Brambleclaw spotted the horseplace at the far end of the ridge, and beyond it the small copse where the four Clans waited for the patrol to return.

"We're almost there!" Squirrelflight exclaimed. She bounded forward, and the other cats followed, their paws flying over the smooth ground. It was much faster to travel out here than in the forest, and for a moment Brambleclaw understood why WindClan cats ran more swiftly than any other, and seemed restless when they were closed in by ferns and tree trunks.

The sun was setting behind the pine trees, turning the

surface of the lake to fire, as they trekked down the hill. They had just reached the bottom when Crowfeather caught up, panting.

"Well?" Squirrelflight demanded.

Crowfeather swiped his tongue around his jaws as if he had just swallowed a juicy piece of fresh-kill. His eyes gleamed with enthusiasm. "It's great!" he mewed. "There's a tunnel under one of the gorse bushes that looks as if it might lead to an old badger set, but the badgers are long gone. There's not even any scent left."

"You could use the set as a den," Tawnypelt suggested.

Crowfeather sniffed. "WindClan cats sleep outside. Only badgers and rabbits live in burrows," he reminded her.

In twilight they slipped along the edge of the lake, past the fence of the horseplace. All Brambleclaw's senses were alert for dogs and Twolegs, but they saw nothing except for one huge horse looking over the fence. Squirrelflight jumped as it blew out a noisy breath, then hissed to hide how startled she had been.

Moments later they heard a loud meow coming out of the darkness. "Who's there?"

"It's okay, Hawkfrost, it's only us," Mistyfoot called.

The RiverClan warrior emerged from the shadows, his powerful shoulders flexing smoothly under his tabby pelt. "Leopardstar and the other leaders sent me to look out for you," he meowed. "They're all expecting you. Follow me."

Brambleclaw blinked. It was strange to think that he and Hawkfrost were kin, both sons of Tigerstar. They were alike in so many ways, yet Brambleclaw struggled to feel any kin-ship or loyalty to the RiverClan warrior. He was too quick to order other cats around, too openly hungry for power in his Clan, and he made Brambleclaw ask himself questions about their shared inheritance that he would have preferred to ignore. Such as, where did Hawkfrost's ambition come from? Did he share Tigerstar's hunger for power at any cost? And if he had inherited this from their father, what did that mean for Brambleclaw?

Hawkfrost led them to the trees near the horseplace where the Clans had stopped to rest the day before. Firestar and Blackstar were talking together beside the tree stump, but otherwise the clearing looked deserted.

As soon as the patrol appeared, Blackstar leaped up on the stump and let out a yowl. "Cats of all Clans! Gather around!"

At once the shadowy shapes of cats began to appear out of hollows and clumps of long grass. One or two jumped down from low-hanging branches. Mudclaw pushed his way through his Clanmates and joined Blackstar on the stump, forcing Leopardstar to sit on the ground again.

Firestar padded over to stand in front of Brambleclaw. "Welcome back," he meowed. "No trouble, I hope?"

"Nothing we couldn't handle," Brambleclaw replied. He glanced guiltily at Squirrelflight as he remembered the fight they had nearly lost against the kittypets.

"One of you had better come up on the stump so we can all hear you," Firestar decided. "Mistyfoot, would you like to join us?"

Mistyfoot dipped her head. "Actually, Firestar, I think Brambleclaw should speak on behalf of the patrol. He has more experience with describing unknown places."

Brambleclaw looked quickly at her, but there was no edge to the RiverClan deputy's words. Instead she stepped back to let him reach the tree stump. "Thanks," he murmured as he went past. Mistyfoot just blinked.

Brambleclaw bunched his hindlegs underneath him and sprang onto the stump. It was a tight squeeze, and his flank brushed against Blackstar's as he shuffled around to face the cats below. The ShadowClan leader drew away with the faintest hiss, but Brambleclaw tried not to let Blackstar's hostility ruffle his fur. His heart pounded at the thought of describing the long journey around the lake to all four Clans. The cats gazed up at him, and Brambleclaw could feel their hunger for his news pulsing through the air. Briefly he wondered if this was what it was like to be a Clan leader, with every cat hanging on his words.

Then he heard Dustpelt's voice raised impatiently above the rustle of the branches overhead. "Get on with it, Brambleclaw! Tell us what you found."

Brambleclaw swallowed uncomfortably, wondering where to start. He couldn't say that choosing a new home was not all he had hoped for. In spite of Midnight's directions, the dying warrior, the starlight reflected in the lake, he didn't feel as if the Clans truly belonged in this territory. It was too easy to imagine Twoleg monsters tearing through the woods, turning the ground to mud and shattering the walls of the stone hollow until the newly built ThunderClan dens were exposed to the sky, and every cat was as helpless as a newborn kit. . . .

But that wasn't what the Clans wanted to hear, and none of the other cats on the patrol had seemed to doubt that this was where they belonged now. They could be right, Brambleclaw told himself firmly. They had proved that the Clans could live here; what more could he expect?

"It's good news," he began, taking a deep breath. "We have found territories that are suitable for all the Clans—reeds and water for RiverClan, pine forest for ShadowClan, leafy woods for ThunderClan, and moorland for WindClan."

As murmurs of excitement broke out, Leopardstar called. "What about prey?"

"There seems to be plenty," Brambleclaw replied, "given that it's leaf-bare. We didn't go hungry, that's for sure."

"And Twolegs?" queried another cat—Brambleclaw thought it was a ShadowClan warrior, but he couldn't be sure.

"We saw some evidence that they visit places around the lake, but there are none there now," he meowed. "Mistyfoot thinks there'll be more of them around in greenleaf. That's when they used to bring their kits to swim in the river, back in the forest."

He noticed several of the cats glance anxiously at each other, and felt the familiar tremor of fear at the thought of what Twolegs had brought to the forest, apart from their kits. He was relieved when Mistyfoot added, "We'll be able to keep out of their way. They won't be a big problem."

"Well . . . that's all." Brambleclaw wasn't sure what else to say. "Maybe each of us should tell our own Clans what we saw in more detail."

"We need to decide where the boundaries will be," Blackstar growled.

"Right," meowed Firestar from where he was sitting at the base of the stump, next to Leopardstar. "We can do that when we have a clearer idea of each territory. Thanks, Brambleclaw."

Brambleclaw dipped his head gratefully at his leader; he may have led his friends to sun-drown-place and back again, and explored the territory around the lake, but he felt as helpless as a kit among the other Clan leaders. His fur prickled, and he noticed Hawkfrost staring at him from the edge of the cats seated around the stump. Twitching his ears uncomfortably, Brambleclaw jumped down. He winced as Hawkfrost came over to meet him and braced himself for a hostile comment, perhaps a challenge about where the new boundaries should be.

To his surprise, there was a friendly gleam in the RiverClan warrior's blue eyes.

"Thanks for finding the new territories, Brambleclaw," he meowed. "I'm almost sorry that we'll be going our separate ways now. I'd have liked to hunt with you."

Brambleclaw blinked. Warriors of different Clans could not hunt together—but that wasn't the real reason Hawkfrost's suggestion startled him. Did the RiverClan warrior feel something like kinship with him? If he and Hawkfrost had been members of the same Clan, might they have been friends like Firestar and Graystripe, who had risked their lives for each other countless times?

"Well, we'll meet at Gatherings," he began.

"Brambleclaw, what are you doing?" Squirrelflight padded up with a glare at Hawkfrost. "Firestar is waiting for us."

"Of course. And Leopardstar will be waiting for me." Hawkfrost dipped his head in farewell and padded away.

"Why are you talking to *him*?" Squirrelflight demanded crossly when Hawkfrost was out of earshot. "You know he can't be trusted."

"I don't know anything of the kind," Brambleclaw retorted.

Squirrelflight snorted. "Yeah, right. That cat has too much ambition for his own good."

Brambleclaw felt his neck fur start to rise. "Really?"

"He wishes Mistyfoot had never come back, so that he could still be deputy. I've heard him arguing with her more than once."

"He wants the best for his Clan, that's all," Brambleclaw meowed. There was something in him that understood exactly how Hawkfrost must have felt when Mistyfoot had escaped from the Twolegs, and claimed back her place as RiverClan deputy.

"That's not all." Squirrelflight paused, flicking her tail-tip back and forth. "I can tell Leafpaw doesn't trust Hawkfrost, and she knows him better than we do. She was in the forest while he was RiverClan deputy."

"Have you asked her why she feels that way?"

Squirrelflight shook her head. "I don't need to ask her. I just know how she feels."

Brambleclaw narrowed his eyes. "So you don't have anything against Hawkfrost except for what Leafpaw feels about him? Because she's your sister, right? Well, Hawkfrost is *my* brother."

"Are you telling me you feel loyal to him because of that?" Squirrelflight exclaimed. "But you hardly know him!"

"Neither do you. But you think you know him well enough to say he can't be trusted." Brambleclaw unsheathed his claws and let them sink into the fallen leaves. "Or are you accusing him because of who his father was?"

Squirrelflight's green eyes stretched wide. "If that's what you think, then you don't know me at all!" she hissed. She whirled around and stalked away with her tail in the air.

Brambleclaw stared after her in dismay. He and Squirrelflight had quarreled ever since she became an apprentice. But he had never expected to hear such cold dislike in her voice.

Icy claws pricked down Brambleclaw's spine. If Squirrelflight distrusted Hawkfrost because of who his father was, did that mean she didn't trust *him?*

CHAPTER 5

❧

When Brambleclaw had finished speaking and leaped down from the tree stump, Leafpaw looked around for Squirrelflight. She was dying to hear about their new territory, and to know if her sister had found any useful herbs.

She spotted Sorreltail and bounded over. "Have you seen Squirrelflight?"

The tortoiseshell warrior shook her head.

Leafpaw was about to keep looking when a sharp pang sliced through her like a claw. She caught her breath, tucking her nose against her chest to take away the pain. Something was wrong with Squirrelflight, something was troubling her, but Leafpaw had no idea what it might be. The patrol had come safely home, and it sounded as if there were territories for all the Clans around the lake, so why should Squirrelflight feel such a jolting mixture of shock and anger?

"Are you okay?" Sorreltail asked.

"What? Oh, yes, fine. I just need to ask Squirrelflight something." Leafpaw tried to speak calmly, but her voice shook. Luckily there was so much noise around them that Sorreltail didn't seem to notice.

"I'll help you look," she offered. "I can't wait to hear about our new home!"

Leafpaw nodded, and began to weave her way through the other cats, searching for the familiar dark ginger pelt. She felt a rush of relief when she spotted her sister with some other ThunderClan cats, her tail waving animatedly as she explained something to them. There certainly didn't seem to be anything wrong now—but Leafpaw knew she hadn't mistaken the lightning strike of anger and dismay that had jolted through her.

She padded over with Sorreltail beside her.

"It's a stone hollow, with walls all around," Squirrelflight was mewing. "There's plenty of space inside for dens, the nursery, even a training area."

She was doing a great job of sounding normal, but as she drew closer, Leafpaw could feel waves of unhappiness coming from her. Squirrelflight's eyes were too wide, too bright, and she kept looking around as if trying to spot a cat who wasn't there. After a moment Leafpaw realized that the missing cat must be Brambleclaw. She guessed he was talking to other members of the Clan.

"Is this hollow empty?" Dustpelt asked. He was sitting in front of Squirrelflight with Ferncloud at his side; their one surviving kit, Birchkit, was rolling around in the grass with Tallpoppy's three kits, all far too excited to sleep. "It would be just like you, Squirrelflight, to expect us to camp in a badger's set."

Squirrelflight's tail curled up indignantly. "Dustpelt, I

promise I'll eat any badgers you find in there. Foxes, too. We didn't scent anything like that."

Dustpelt grunted.

"I think it sounds great." Brightheart stepped up to Squirrelflight and pressed her muzzle against the younger warrior's side. "How did you find it?"

"I . . . well, I fell into it," Squirrelflight admitted.

Cloudtail let out a snort of laughter. "Why doesn't that surprise me?"

"Now look—" Squirrelflight spun around to face the white warrior, but before she could say any more a yowl rose into the air.

"Cats of all Clans!"

Leafpaw turned to see that Cinderpelt had climbed onto the stump, the moonlight turning her gray fur to silver. She signaled with her tail for silence, and the excited mewing gradually died away.

"Before we separate and go into our own territories," the ThunderClan medicine cat meowed, "we must decide where we're going to hold the next Gathering. StarClan will expect us to meet together when full moon comes."

"But where?" asked Russetfur, the ShadowClan deputy. "Did the patrols find anywhere like Fourtrees?"

Mistyfoot, who was sitting near the base of the stump, rose to her paws. "No," she replied, raising her voice so all the Clans could hear her. "Nowhere like that. But we didn't have time to explore everywhere properly."

"StarClan will show us a place." Littlecloud spoke up from

where he was sitting beside Russetfur and Blackstar.

"They might have shown us already." Mothwing sprang to her paws, her blue eyes shining. She began to describe the island close to the shore of the lake. "It's safe, sheltered, and not too far away. Perfect for Gatherings," she finished.

"But we'd have to swim to get there!" The protest came from Mousefur, a ThunderClan warrior. "I'm not swimming in that lake every full moon, not if StarClan themselves come down and beg me."

"And what about the elders?" croaked Runningnose, the former ShadowClan medicine cat.

A chorus of agreement rose up. Leafpaw glanced worriedly from one face to another. Even though she had her own doubts about gathering on the island, she couldn't think of a better option. But she didn't see a single cat who showed any enthusiasm for Mothwing's suggestion.

Hawkfrost padded over to stand next to Mothwing. Dipping his head politely to Cinderpelt, he meowed, "May I suggest that I take a patrol of RiverClan cats to explore the island more fully? If the Clans can't use it for Gatherings, it sounds like the ideal place for the RiverClan camp."

Almost before he had finished speaking, Mistyfoot took a pace toward him. "I already told you where RiverClan are going to camp," she mewed quietly, the fur on her neck bristling. "There's a place where two streams meet, not far from the lake, with trees for shelter, and no sign that Twolegs come near, even in greenleaf."

"But think how safe the island would be," Hawkfrost

pointed out. "We'd have a lake full of fish right outside our dens. Have you thought that your choice of camp might be too open? And that Thunderpath you mentioned can't be far away."

Mistyfoot bristled. "Are you questioning my judgment? I know what my Clan needs."

Hawkfrost curled his lip, and Leafpaw tensed, half expecting the two RiverClan warriors to leap at each other.

"Enough!" The word, spat out, came from behind Leafpaw. She turned to see Leopardstar stalking up to her quarreling warriors. "Do you want to shame RiverClan?"

Hawkfrost stepped back, and the fur on Mistyfoot's shoulders lay flat, though Leafpaw could tell it took some effort.

"Hawkfrost, you can take a patrol to the island if you wish," Leopardstar went on. "We'll make a decision about where to site the camp when you come back."

"Of course, Leopardstar," Hawkfrost meowed, dipping his head. "I'll pick some other cats and leave as soon as it gets light." He stepped back, and was instantly surrounded by his Clanmates, all clamoring to come with him to the island.

Leafpaw shivered. It had been strange to see such an open challenge to Mistyfoot's authority. Hawkfrost must feel very confident of his place within the Clan if he dared to pick a fight with his deputy in front of his leader as well as the other Clans.

Leafpaw thought she could see the same concern in her mentor's blue eyes as Cinderpelt called for silence again. "So," she meowed, "where shall we meet for the next Gathering?"

"We'll have to come back here," Firestar decided. "Unless StarClan shows us a different place before the next full moon."

Mudclaw turned to face Firestar. "I don't think that's a good idea. We're much too close to that Twoleg nest on the other side of the horseplace."

"That can't be helped," Blackstar replied, and Firestar nodded.

"We've been here for two days and nights now, and we haven't had so much as a sniff of a Twoleg. But if you have a better idea, let's hear it."

Mudclaw lashed his tail. "Suit yourself," he snarled. "The great Firestar's word is law, as always."

The cats began to slip away from the tree stump, back into the shadows. Ferncloud signaled with her tail for Birchkit to come to her. "It's time you got some sleep, little one. We have a long journey ahead of us tomorrow."

Birchkit abandoned his play fight with Tallpoppy's kits and bounced over. "Can Toadkit and Applekit and Marshkit come too?" he asked.

"No, we belong to ShadowClan," Tallpoppy explained gently. "We'll have our own territory now."

"But that's not *fair!*" Birchkit wailed, and all four kits clustered together, gazing at the two queens with huge, pleading eyes. "If they can't come, I don't want to go."

Leafpaw flinched. They were so innocent! They had no idea how different their lives had been from the lives of their older Clanmates. Their earliest memories would be the horror of starving in the forest, every cat fearing for its life, until they found new friends when the Clans came together for the exhausting trek through the mountains. They had no sense of Clan rivalry, or the importance of being a warrior in the service of one Clan alone. They probably hardly knew there were four Clans at all.

"Don't be so silly." Ferncloud padded over to her kit and gave his ears a sympathetic lick. "That's the warrior code. When you're apprentices you'll meet again at Gatherings."

"It won't be the same," Toadkit muttered, with a mutinous look at his mother.

"And there are no other ThunderClan kits for me to play with," Birchkit added sadly.

Ferncloud and Tallpoppy looked at each other, and Leafpaw saw genuine regret in their eyes—it wasn't just their kits who had made strong friendships across Clan boundaries.

Finally Tallpoppy dipped her head and gathered her three kits around her with a sweep of her tail. "Say good-bye now," she mewed briskly.

"Good-bye," Toadkit and Marshkit chorused, while Applekit darted up to Birchkit and touched her nose to his.

"Good-bye." Birchkit stared after his friends as they padded away, and then turned to follow his mother, his tail drooping.

Leafpaw felt her heart ache for the lonely kit, and for all the cats who would miss friends they had made in other Clans. A couple of tail-lengths away she spotted Thornclaw saying good-bye to Ashfoot and Onewhisker from WindClan; he jumped guiltily when he saw Leafpaw watching, as if he felt he had been disloyal to his Clan by becoming friends with them.

"It's okay," Leafpaw meowed, padding over to touch noses with the ThunderClan warrior. "It's hard to give up new friends like this." *I'm one of the lucky ones*, she thought gratefully. *I can still be friends with Mothwing.* Clan divisions weren't so important to medicine cats, especially where the other medicine cats were concerned.

She decided to go and ask Cinderpelt if there was anything she could do to help the cats prepare for tomorrow. As she wove her way through the other cats, she came across Crowfeather standing over a WindClan elder, a skinny tom with creamy brown fur, who was comfortably curled up in a nest of dry leaves underneath a tree.

"Look, Rushtail," Crowfeather was meowing frustratedly, "WindClan is gathering farther down the hill. If you stay here, you'll get mixed up with ThunderClan."

"So? ThunderClan never did me any harm," rasped the elder. "I'm not moving a pawstep from here, young fellow, until I've had something to eat."

Crowfeather rolled his eyes. "Great StarClan!"

"Can I help?" Leafpaw offered, wondering if Rushtail was being stubborn, or if he really felt too weak to move. She might be able to find some herbs that would help restore his strength, like the traveling herbs they used to eat before journeying to the Moonstone.

But when Crowfeather turned around to face her, his eyes were cold. "I don't need help from ThunderClan, thanks," he mewed curtly.

"I'm sorry." Leafpaw took a step back, struggling not to show how cross she was that he was refusing her help for no good reason. "I only thought—"

"Take it easy, Crowfeather." Leafpaw felt a light touch on her shoulder and glanced around to see Squirrelflight. "There's no need to be so prickly," her sister added to the WindClan warrior.

Crowfeather dug his claws agitatedly into the ground. "Our journey's *over*, Squirrelflight," he meowed. "We have to remember we belong to different Clans now."

Squirrelflight snorted. "You always were a difficult furball, Crowfeather. But I won't stop you if you're determined to make everything harder than it needs to be. Just watch it when you talk to my sister, that's all."

Crowfeather looked back at Leafpaw and muttered something that might have been an apology. "But I can manage Rushtail on my own, thanks," he added.

Just before she left, Leafpaw saw him bend over the elder again. "Rushtail, if I fetch you some fresh-kill, will you move then?"

"I might." The old tom settled himself more comfortably and closed his eyes. "As long as it's good and plump."

"Leafpaw, are you coming?" Squirrelflight called.

Leafpaw turned to see Sorreltail bounding over to her. "Was that Crowfeather?" she asked. "His tongue's as sharp as a fox's teeth. Is he giving you trouble? I'll sort him out for you." Her amber eyes gleamed with anticipation.

"No, he's fine." Leafpaw touched her friend's shoulder with the tip of her tail.

Glancing back to where Crowfeather had disappeared in search of fresh-kill, she knew that was not entirely true. But she could not think of any herb that would heal his broken heart.

CHAPTER 6

Brambleclaw shifted uneasily among the dead leaves. A branch was digging into his flank, but that wasn't what had woken him. He couldn't get used to sleeping alone, without the warmth of Squirrelflight's body beside him. He thought she had gone to sleep next to Ashfur, but he wasn't sure. She certainly wasn't anywhere near him.

There was another prod in his side. Brambleclaw looked up blearily to see that it wasn't a branch after all, but a paw. Barkface was standing over him.

"Where's Firestar?" the WindClan medicine cat demanded.

Brambleclaw scrambled up, yawning. Above his head the sky was just beginning to grow light. "Most of ThunderClan are over there, under the trees."

"Find him for me, will you?" Barkface's voice sounded close to breaking. "Tallstar is asking for him."

Brambleclaw knew the WindClan leader must be close to losing his last life. "I'll fetch him," he promised.

"Thanks. We're under that gorse bush over there." Barkface pointed with his tail. "I've got to find Onewhisker." He dashed off.

Brambleclaw bounded toward the nearest ThunderClan warriors. Tallstar was the eldest of the leaders, and his death would be a great loss to all four Clans, not just WindClan. For a few heartbeats he despaired of finding Firestar in the dim predawn light, but then he spotted him sharing tongues with Sandstorm near the tree stump.

"Firestar, Barkface says Tallstar wants to see you," Brambleclaw meowed as he raced up to them.

Firestar stiffened, and exchanged a glance with Sandstorm. "I'll come at once," he replied.

"Does Barkface need any help?" Sandstorm asked. "Cinderpelt was here a moment ago. Tell Barkface to send a cat with a message if he wants her."

Brambleclaw nodded, and followed Firestar across the open ground to the gorse bush where Tallstar lay dying. Its outer branches swept the ground, and there was no sign of any cats at first, but as Brambleclaw approached he heard the sound of harsh, uneven breathing. Ducking down, he peered through a gap to see Tallstar stretched out on his side in a nest of dead leaves.

"Firestar's here," he meowed, stepping back to let his leader enter the makeshift den. "I'll wait outside," he added to Firestar.

"Is that Brambleclaw?" Tallstar's voice came weakly from beneath the bush. "Don't go. You should hear what I have to say, too."

Brambleclaw glanced hesitantly at Firestar, and when his leader nodded he flattened himself against the ground to creep under the low branches beside him.

Tallstar was alone; Barkface hadn't come back yet with Onewhisker. The WindClan leader's chest heaved as he fought for breath, and Brambleclaw winced at the effort it cost him to raise his head.

But in the faint moonlight that filtered through the branches, Tallstar's eyes shone with the light of StarClan. "Firestar, I must thank you," he rasped. "You have saved my Clan."

Firestar gave a murmur of protest.

"And Brambleclaw . . ." Tallstar went on. "You journeyed a long way to find this place for us, facing dangers no cat has seen before. Even Graystripe, may he walk with StarClan, would agree you will make a worthy deputy for ThunderClan."

Brambleclaw gasped. He didn't dare look at his leader, who stiffened beside him. He knew that Firestar had never stopped grieving for Graystripe, and clung to the belief that his friend was still alive. He had refused to name another deputy so far, even though it seemed extremely unlikely that Graystripe would escape from the Twolegs who had taken him away from the forest.

Ambition gripped Brambleclaw like an eagle's talons. Hard as it was to admit it, he knew that he wanted to be deputy, and then leader, of his Clan. Was this what Tigerstar had felt? he wondered. His father's hunger for power had been so strong that he was prepared to lie and murder and betray to achieve it. *I could never do that,* Brambleclaw thought.

If he became deputy it would be through loyalty to his Clan, hard work, and respect for the warrior code.

But Tigerstar's dark heritage would always be with him, overshadowing all he tried to do. *They look at me and see Tigerstar.*

He recovered himself in time to dip his head to Tallstar and murmur, "It wasn't just me. It was all of us together."

"You're tiring yourself, Tallstar." Firestar's voice was gentle. "You need to rest."

"Rest will do me no good now," the WindClan leader meowed.

Firestar did not try to pretend that there was any hope he would get better. "You will be a noble addition to the ranks of StarClan," he told him. He crouched down so he could press his muzzle to Tallstar's.

"Before then . . . before then I must say . . ." Tallstar started to choke, and his paws scrabbled in the dried leaves.

"Brambleclaw, find Barkface," Firestar ordered.

"No." Tallstar managed to catch his breath again, and signaled with his tail for Brambleclaw to stay. "Nothing . . . any medicine cat can do for me now." His eyes half closed and he took several gasping breaths before continuing. "There's something important I have to say. Where's Onewhisker?"

Firestar glanced at Brambleclaw, who shook his head.

"Barkface went to get him," he meowed. "I'll go and look too."

"Quickly . . ." Tallstar rasped as Brambleclaw backed out. "Tell them . . . that it is time. . . ."

When Brambleclaw straightened up and looked around,

the dawn light was strengthening, but he still couldn't see any more than dark shapes and the occasional blur of a pale-colored pelt. Most cats were still sleeping in hastily flattened dens among the long grass, roughly divided among the four Clans. He was trying to work out which of the shadowy groups was WindClan when he spotted a solitary cat racing up from the direction of the lake. To his relief he recognized Onewhisker.

"Barkface said Tallstar's dying." The WindClan warrior gasped as he halted beside the bush, dropping his mouthful of dripping moss. "I only went to the lake to get him a drink."

"He wants to see you," Brambleclaw meowed.

Onewhisker slid under the branches into Tallstar's den, and Brambleclaw followed him in time to see the warrior place the moss beside Tallstar's head. The dying leader feebly licked up a few drops, then raised his head again.

"Before I go to StarClan, there is something I must do." His voice was stronger now. "Firestar, Onewhisker, listen. Mudclaw is a brave warrior, but he is not the right cat to lead WindClan. In these last moons we have learned that the future of our Clans lies in friendship. I want no rivalry between WindClan and ThunderClan after I am gone. We must have no enemies. But this will not happen if Mudclaw rules the Clan."

Brambleclaw saw Firestar exchange a glance with Onewhisker; both cats seemed uncomfortably aware that Tallstar's ideal of lasting friendship wouldn't happen, who-ever was in charge of the Clan. It was natural for Clans to be rivals—that was part of the warrior code.

"I can still choose the cat who will lead WindClan after me," Tallstar rasped. "From this moment Mudclaw is no longer deputy of WindClan."

Three pairs of eyes stared at him in astonishment.

"I say these words . . . before StarClan," Tallstar gasped out. "WindClan must have . . . a new deputy. Onewhisker, you must lead the Clan when I am gone."

Brambleclaw and Firestar exchanged a swift, startled glance. These were not the right words to choose a deputy, even though it was clearly what Tallstar intended. Brambleclaw felt an icy tingle in his fur. Would StarClan accept Onewhisker as the leader of WindClan if he had not been appointed as deputy in the way demanded by the warrior code? He opened his mouth to say something, but closed it again when he caught sight of the expression on his leader's face. Firestar seemed even more shocked than Brambleclaw, his neck fur bristling and his claws digging into the ground, but he said nothing.

"Tallstar, *no*." Onewhisker sounded horrified, but Tallstar took no notice. His glittering, star-filled gaze traveled from his new deputy to Firestar and then to Brambleclaw.

"I am grateful to have brought the Clan this far," he murmured. "Onewhisker, treat our friends well when you lead our Clan. Remember everything ThunderClan has done for us."

"Tallstar, I'll do my best, but . . ." Onewhisker stretched out a paw to touch his leader's shoulder, but Tallstar's head had slipped down into the leaves. His eyes closed, and his breathing became quick and shallow.

Brambleclaw felt a faint breeze touch his fur and heard the murmur of pawsteps. Something brushed his pelt, and he thought he saw starlight reflected for a moment in Firestar's eyes. It suddenly felt as if the tiny den was packed full, with sleek-furred flanks sweeping against him on every side.

Brambleclaw jumped at a scuffling sound behind him, and in a heartbeat the den was empty once more. He turned to see Barkface squeezing under the branches.

Dropping a packet of leaf-wrapped herbs beside Tallstar, he meowed, "Cinderpelt gave me these."

He broke off, staring at his leader.

"It is too late for herbs," Firestar mewed quietly.

Onewhisker crouched down and pushed his nose into Tallstar's fur. The WindClan leader's black-and-white flank had stopped rising and falling now, stilled forever with the departure of Tallstar's spirit.

"He walks with StarClan now," Barkface murmured.

Brambleclaw felt his throat swell with grief. Tallstar had not been his leader, but he had been a noble cat, and nothing would be the same now that he was dead.

After a few moments Firestar curled his tail to touch Onewhisker on the shoulder. "Onewhisker, you need to tell your Clan. Remember what Tallstar said: he . . . he appointed you deputy, and he wants you to be leader now."

Onewhisker raised his head, his eyes filled with a chaos of

grief and confusion. "Firestar, I can't do this," he pleaded. "I *can't* take over as leader!" More hesitantly, he asked, "Do we have to tell them what he said? I . . . I know that wasn't the right way to choose a new deputy. Tallstar was dying, he couldn't think clearly. . . ."

"Tallstar knew exactly what he wanted, whether he used the right words or not," Firestar told him firmly, though his eyes were sympathetic. "He wanted you to be deputy instead of Mudclaw, and he wanted you to succeed him as Clan leader. Would you betray his trust, and the honor he has given you?"

Brambleclaw saw Barkface's eyes stretch wide, and he remembered that the medicine cat had not arrived until after Tallstar had finished speaking.

"He said *what?*" Barkface demanded. When Firestar explained, the medicine cat looked troubled. "I can understand what he said was a shock," he mewed to Onewhisker, "but you can't do anything about it. If that's what Tallstar wanted, it means that you're Clan leader in the sight of StarClan. Do you think they would give nine lives to Mudclaw now, knowing that Tallstar changed his mind?"

"Mudclaw!" Onewhisker stared at the other cats in dismay. "What am I going to say to him?"

Firestar pressed reassuringly against his side. "If you like, I'll make the announcement to the Clans while you figure out what to say to individual cats."

Onewhisker's eyes flooded with relief. "Would you, Firestar? Thanks."

Firestar nodded, but Brambleclaw felt a flicker of unease. He knew that the two cats had been friends long before Firestar became Clan leader, but surely this was a time when Onewhisker should be acting on his own, however hard it was. There was going to be enough shock from WindClan without suggesting that Firestar, a cat from a completely different Clan, had been involved.

The ThunderClan leader pushed his way out through the branches. Brambleclaw and the others followed as Firestar padded across and leaped up on the stump at the edge of the deserted clearing.

Onewhisker was about to sit among the roots when Firestar gestured with his tail to a spot beside him. "You should be up here," he meowed. "What is your Clan going to think if you sit down there like an ordinary warrior?"

Brambleclaw could see exactly what Firestar meant, and he fought down a prickle of impatience. It was time Onewhisker got over his shock and started behaving like a leader. "Go on," he urged.

Onewhisker gave him a doubtful look, then jumped up to stand beside Firestar.

The ThunderClan leader let out a yowl. "Cats of all Clans! Gather to hear the news I have to tell you."

All around the clearing, Brambleclaw watched the cats stir in their makeshift nests, like a ripple in long grass when wind passed over it. From close by he heard some cat mutter crossly, "What does he want now?"

Firestar repeated his yowl until one by one the cats slipped

out of their makeshift dens and crept forward until they surrounded the stump.

Squirrelflight padded sleepily over to Brambleclaw, her
jaws gaping in a huge yawn. "What's happening? What does
Firestar want?"

"It's best you hear it from Firestar," Brambleclaw meowed.
He couldn't begin to put into words what had happened
before Tallstar lost his ninth life.

Too late, he remembered his quarrel with Squirrelflight;
she obviously hadn't forgotten, however, and interpreted his
guarded response as reluctance to speak to her at all.

"Fine," she mewed. She glanced coolly at him, then padded
a couple of tail-lengths away before sitting down.

"Cats of all Clans, I have some very sad news," Firestar
began. "Tallstar has gone to hunt with StarClan."

"Tallstar dead!" exclaimed Tornear. "He became leader
before I was born. What will happen to WindClan without
him?"

Beside him, his apprentice, Owlpaw, bowed his head, too
overcome to speak. Mosspelt, a RiverClan queen, touched
the young cat on his shoulder with the tip of her tail. "He was
a noble cat," she murmured. "He will be welcomed by
StarClan, and walk with the best of them."

From somewhere near the back a single voice rose up in a
wail of grief. Brambleclaw echoed it in his heart.

"I was there when he died," Firestar went on, with a glance
at Brambleclaw, "and he said—"

He broke off as a mottled brown warrior thrust his way

forward and halted at the foot of the stump. "What's that?" he demanded, his eyes flashing anger. "Tallstar is dead? Why did no cat tell me?"

It was Mudclaw.

CHAPTER 7

❧

Firestar looked calmly down at the WindClan warrior. "Tallstar died just a few moments ago," he meowed. "There's been no chance to tell any cat."

"Mudclaw, you're our leader now," meowed Webfoot. "We will all grieve for Tallstar, but we need you to help us settle in our new home."

A murmur of agreement came from his Clanmates. Mudclaw dipped his head in acknowledgment, but when he turned back to Firestar his eyes still gleamed with fury. "You should have come to find me before calling this meeting. Why should a ThunderClan cat announce WindClan's news?"

Firestar's tail-tip twitched. "Tallstar wanted it to be this way. Listen to what I'm trying to tell you, please." Addressing all the cats, not just Mudclaw, he went on: "Just before he died, Tallstar made Onewhisker his deputy." His gaze swept over Brambleclaw, but he didn't meet the warrior's eye. Brambleclaw's fur prickled; was Firestar really willing to ignore the fact that Tallstar hadn't used the right ceremony to appoint his new deputy?

"*What?*" Mudclaw screeched in disbelief.

"You mean Mudclaw *isn't* our leader?" Webfoot queried. He unsheathed his claws in confusion and sank them into the ground.

"Mouse dung to that!" A black WindClan she-cat drew her lips back in a snarl. "There's no cat better able to lead the Clan."

Brambleclaw listened uncomfortably. If it were up to him, he thought Onewhisker would make a better leader than Mudclaw, but he didn't have the right to judge. And he could imagine exactly how Mudclaw must be feeling, to have the leadership he had been waiting for snatched out of his paws in a heartbeat.

Onewhisker looked down at Mudclaw. "This is as much of a shock to me as it is to you," he meowed. "And I would like you to carry on being WindClan's deputy. I'll need your support and experience every pawstep of the way."

Mudclaw's neck fur bristled. "You don't think I *believe* this load of fox dung, do you?" he spat. "Every cat knows that Tallstar practically handed our Clan over to Firestar before he left the forest. He's always felt more loyalty to ThunderClan than they ever deserved. And now Firestar tells us that *his friend* Onewhisker is to be leader! Did any other cat witness this convenient change of mind?"

His paws heavy as stone, Brambleclaw padded forward until he stood beside Mudclaw. "I did." The words stuck in his throat like a tough bit of fresh-kill. "I was there. I heard Tallstar make Onewhisker his deputy."

He almost added, *but he didn't use the right words*, then stopped himself. Firestar had said nothing about that.

The clearing and the tree stump faded away, and Brambleclaw was back in the ravine, an apprentice of less than seven moons, grudgingly searching the elders' pelts for ticks. All the apprentices hated this duty, but sometimes it was made bearable by the chance to listen to stories about the old days in ThunderClan, before the apprentices were even born. As Brambleclaw fixed his teeth gingerly around a tick at the base of One-eye's tail, he could hear the old cat talking to Dappletail about when Bluestar appointed Firestar—then called Fireheart—to be her deputy. The former deputy, Tigerclaw, had been revealed as a traitor who was plotting to kill his Clan leader—and Brambleclaw's fur had crawled even then to hear his father spoken of in dark, grim tones. Tigerclaw had been chased out of the camp, and Bluestar had appointed Fireheart in his place. But she had been so distressed by Tigerclaw's treachery that she had delayed the ceremony until long after moonhigh, which was the time limit set down by the warrior code. Several cats in the Clan, even those who liked and respected the flame-colored warrior, had grave doubts about his right to be called deputy, and it had been many moons before Fireheart had proved himself worthy of taking Tigerclaw's place.

Brambleclaw shook his head, jolting himself back to the copse on the lakeshore. His blood thickened icily in his veins. There had been something wrong with Firestar's deputy ceremony, just like Onewhisker's! No wonder the ThunderClan leader wanted to defend Onewhisker when doubts were cast on his right to lead the Clan. If Firestar had ever had any doubts about his own position as deputy, he had kept them to himself; he obviously believed Onewhisker should do the same.

Mudclaw narrowed his eyes at Brambleclaw. "You were there too, were you? *Another* ThunderClan cat, what a surprise! What did Firestar offer you if you backed him up? Did he promise to make you deputy of ThunderClan?"

Any temptation to blurt out the truth vanished in an instant, as Brambleclaw struggled with the urge to leap on the WindClan warrior's back and claw his fur off. Just managing to stay where he was, he glanced up at Firestar and saw cold fury in his leader's green eyes.

"How dare you doubt my word, or my warrior's?" Firestar hissed at Mudclaw. "Tallstar's decision was made in the sight of StarClan."

"How do you know?" Mudclaw challenged. "Are you a medicine cat all of a sudden?"

"His decision was clear enough." Firestar spat back.

Mudclaw spun around to face his Clanmates. "Are you going to sit here and accept this?" he demanded. "Do we let ThunderClan choose our leader for us?" Whipping around to glare at Onewhisker again, he added, "How many of our warriors do you think will follow you, you sniveling, crow-food-eating traitor?"

Before Onewhisker had time to reply, Crowfeather padded forward and stood at the edge of the tree stump. His fur was ruffled and his eyes stunned with grief, but when he spoke his voice was calm.

"I will follow Onewhisker. I made the journey to the sun-drown-place with Brambleclaw, and I know he does not lie. If he says that Tallstar made Onewhisker deputy before he went to hunt with StarClan, then I believe him." Raising his head to meet Onewhisker's gaze, he meowed, "Onestar, I greet you as the leader of my Clan."

More voices came from WindClan. "Yes! Onestar! Onestar!" But others sounded uncertain, or openly defiant, and Brambleclaw could see it wasn't going to be easy for Onewhisker to believe in his right to lead his Clan. He spotted Blackstar and Leopardstar at the edge of the crowd, exchanging a glance of amused satisfaction. They weren't disappointed to see quarrels in WindClan, that was for sure.

Onewhisker dipped his head toward Crowfeather. "Thank you," he mewed. "But don't call me Onestar yet," he begged. "I haven't received my name or my nine lives from StarClan." His ears flattened with embarrassment, and Brambleclaw guessed he was afraid he would never be approved by StarClan because of the way in which he had become WindClan's deputy.

"And you never will!" Mudclaw snarled, as if he could read Onewhisker's most hidden thoughts. "You are not our leader! Come down here and fight me if you dare. Then we'll see who'll make the better leader for WindClan."

Onewhisker gathered his haunches under him, ready to leap down and meet Mudclaw's challenge, but Firestar raised his tail to stop him. Brambleclaw braced himself to intercept Mudclaw if he launched himself onto the tree stump.

"Stop!" An outraged cry came from Barkface. "Sheathe your claws, Mudclaw," he told the WindClan deputy. "Clan leaders have never been chosen by fighting. And do you want to start a fight with Tallstar's spirit still watching over us? We should be sitting in vigil for him, not bickering over who will take his place. You betray him by behaving like this. He always expected the best from his senior warriors." He paused, with a long glance at Firestar, and then added, "I believe what the ThunderClan cats tell us. This was Tallstar's choice, and you must accept it."

With a visible effort, Mudclaw flattened his neck fur and sheathed his claws. "Very well," he growled. He looked up at Onewhisker, and the hatred in his eyes was like poison. "You're brave enough standing there with your ThunderClan friends to back you up. But if you think I'll serve as your deputy, you're wrong."

Onewhisker dipped his head. "Very well," he meowed. "I'm sorry if that's your decision."

Mudclaw's only reply was to spit. Then he turned away to follow Barkface and some of the other WindClan warriors as they went to bring out Tallstar's body for the vigil.

"Onewhisker," Firestar mewed quietly, "you have to appoint another deputy. *Now.* You can't lead this Clan alone, and you will need all the support you can get if Mudclaw decides to make things difficult."

For a moment Brambleclaw wondered if he would choose

Crowfeather, who was watching the leaders closely. But Crowfeather had been made a warrior too recently, and besides, he carried the taint of being friendly with ThunderClan, thanks to the journey he had made with Brambleclaw and Squirrelflight. Onewhisker needed an experienced warrior who was trusted by WindClan but not too popular with cats in other Clans; a choice that every cat would approve, perhaps even Mudclaw.

Onewhisker closed his eyes to think. Then he opened them again and looked down at his Clanmates. "I say these words before the spirit of Tallstar, and the spirits of all StarClan, that they may hear and approve my choice." Brambleclaw found himself letting out a sigh of relief that the correct words were being used this time.

"Ashfoot will be the new deputy of WindClan."

Brambleclaw wasn't even sure that he knew who Ashfoot was. Then he saw a gray she-cat standing with a look of utter shock on her broad face. Crowfeather bounded over to her and pressed his muzzle to hers, while the other WindClan cats called out, "Ashfoot! Ashfoot!"

Brambleclaw suddenly remembered that she was Crowfeather's mother; he had seen her once or twice before at Gatherings, though he hadn't spoken to her. She was obviously a popular choice among her Clanmates. Brambleclaw narrowed his eyes. Onewhisker had made a wise decision, just as he hoped.

Onewhisker leaped down from the stump, and Firestar followed. Ashfoot came forward to touch noses with her leader. "Thank you, Onewhisker," she meowed. "I'll do my best. I never imagined—"

"I know," Onewhisker interrupted, giving her ear a quick lick. "That's one reason why I chose you. I don't want a cat who thinks she deserves power. I want a cat who will help me make our Clan strong again when we reach our new home."

Ashfoot let out a purr. "Then that is what I will do."

Turning to Firestar, Onewhisker meowed, "Thanks, Firestar. I'm sorry that was so difficult. I never thought Mudclaw would accuse you of lying."

Firestar shrugged. "I wasn't surprised. Mudclaw had taken on many leadership duties long before Tallstar died. It must have been a shock for him to learn he wasn't going to be leader after all. But at least you seem to have most of the Clan behind you now."

Onewhisker nodded, but a flicker of anxiety crept into his expression. "How will I get my name and my nine lives from StarClan, Firestar? There's no Moonstone here. Do you think I should take some of my warriors and go back through the mountains to Highstones?"

Firestar twitched his tail. "I think that's the most mouse-brained thing you could do. The journey there and back would take nearly a moon. And Mudclaw wouldn't be sitting on his paws doing nothing while you were away; that's for sure."

He flicked his ears toward the cats who had brought Tallstar's body into the clearing. Mudclaw was sitting a little way apart from them, staring at Onewhisker with an ominous look in his eyes. Brambleclaw felt his belly twist. The new WindClan leader must be more than mousebrained if he thought the problems with Mudclaw were over.

"You're right." Onewhisker sighed. "This isn't the time to leave the Clan. But we'll have to find some way of sharing tongues with StarClan, won't we?"

"There must be another Moonstone close by," Ashfoot meowed with sturdy common sense. "StarClan wouldn't have brought us here otherwise. We'll find it as quickly as we can— and until we do, your Clan's loyalty will have to be enough to keep you as our leader."

Onewhisker still looked troubled, and Brambleclaw could understand why. It wasn't just Mudclaw. Webfoot and Nightcloud clearly weren't happy with the change of leader either, and there might be others. Onewhisker's leadership wouldn't be completely safe until he had his nine lives and his new name. And would StarClan grant them to him, when Tallstar had not followed the age-old ceremony in appointing him deputy?

"We can't do any more now," the WindClan cat mewed wearily. "Though dawn is already here, we must sit vigil for Tallstar."

He led the way across the clearing and crouched beside the unmoving black-and-white shape, pushing his nose into Tallstar's cold fur. Ashfoot and Crowfeather settled down on each side of him, as if they wanted to shelter him while he grieved for his dead leader. Their grief must be even greater, Brambleclaw knew, because they could not sit vigil for a whole night; soon the Clans would move off to their new homes. His mind whirled, and for a moment he felt as if the entire warrior code were tumbling around him, shattering under the pressure of moving to their new home.

"Onewhisker chose wisely in making Ashfoot his deputy," Firestar remarked, jolting Brambleclaw back from his troubled thoughts.

Brambleclaw knew he was right, but it felt as if he had a prey bone stuck in his throat, and he couldn't say anything in reply. What was there to say, when Firestar had refused to make a similar choice for ThunderClan? He swallowed hard, searching for words that would express his respect for Firestar's friendship with Graystripe, while making it clear that he didn't believe ThunderClan could survive without a deputy forever.

Firestar turned his green gaze on him and seemed to guess what he was thinking. "We have no proof that Graystripe is dead. And if he isn't, then one day he'll return to ThunderClan. How can I appoint another cat in his place?"

"RiverClan appointed Hawkfrost as deputy when Mistyfoot went missing," Brambleclaw ventured.

Firestar's eyes narrowed. "That was different. When Mistyfoot disappeared, no cat knew what had happened to her. It seemed impossible that she could still be alive. But now we know that Twolegs trapped the cats that went missing. If they wanted them dead, they would have killed them right away, but they didn't. Graystripe is being held prisoner somewhere, and sooner or later he'll escape and come back to us." His claws scraped against the ground, leaving deep scratches in the dirt. "I won't give up hope until I've seen his body with my own eyes."

Is it me you're trying to convince, Brambleclaw wondered bleakly, *or yourself?*

Without another word, Firestar turned and headed toward the cats who had gathered around Tallstar's body. Brambleclaw watched him with guilt and frustration churning in his belly. He wanted to be deputy—and what was so dreadful about that?

Remember Tigerstar, a small voice whispered in his ear, and every hair on Brambleclaw's pelt pricked with horror.

I'm nothing like Tigerstar! I'm a loyal warrior. I've worked hard and risked my life for my Clan. No cat could say I didn't deserve to be deputy.

He saw Squirrelflight slip silently out of the shadows and touch noses with her father. They settled down side by side just outside the circle of grieving WindClan cats, their flame-colored pelts mingling together.

A pang of envy shook Brambleclaw, sharp as a winter wind. He had quarreled with Squirrelflight over Hawkfrost, and his sister, Tawnypelt, belonged to another Clan. He didn't have any cat to share that uncomplicated affection that Squirrelflight had with Firestar.

How many times do I have to prove myself? he wondered desperately. Hawkfrost didn't seem to have the same trouble in RiverClan, even though Tigerstar was his father too. Brambleclaw felt a sudden desire to seek him out and talk to him, but with the Clans on the brink of going their separate ways, he knew that the moment was past.

Brambleclaw wanted to be deputy so much that it *hurt*. Why couldn't Firestar and Squirrelflight trust him? He shut his eyes, his claws sinking into the ground as a wave of hunger swept blackly over him, turning his blood to ice.

CHAPTER 8

❧

Leafpaw crouched not far from Tallstar's body, watching the cats who came to keep vigil for the dead leader. Daylight spread steadily from beyond the ridge of hills, revealing a gray sky with clouds hanging low over the trees. A damp, chilly wind blew from the lake and made the branches rattle together like mouse bones.

The dead leader's body looked grim and stark. Leafpaw shivered. It felt very strange to be sitting in vigil in the cold light of morning. Usually the ceremony was carried out at night, when the unmoving shape would be muffled by shadows as comforting as soft, black fur.

Glancing away from Tallstar's body, Leafpaw let her thoughts wander. Anxiety gnawed at her, sharp as a fox's fangs. Onewhisker couldn't go all the way back to the Moonstone to receive his name and his nine lives from StarClan; he was too tired to make the long journey twice over again, and it was obvious Mudclaw would seize upon his absence to make trouble. But what would happen to the Clans if their leaders didn't share tongues with StarClan? The warrior code would fade away like mist in sunshine, and they would be nothing more than rogues.

"StarClan *must* guide us!" she mewed out loud.

Cinderpelt glanced around from where she was talking to Barkface. "Leafpaw? What's the matter?" She padded over, looking concerned.

Leafpaw shook her head. "Sorry I disturbed you, Cinderpelt. I was just thinking about Onewhisker. What's he going to do if he can't go to Highstones?"

Cinderpelt stretched out her tail and touched Leafpaw gently on the head. "Don't worry," she reassured her. "Star-Clan will show us a new place to share tongues with them."

"But *when?*" Leafpaw gazed into her mentor's blue eyes. "Onewhisker needs his name and his nine lives *now.*"

"Leafpaw, be patient. StarClan can't be hurried. There'll be an answer, you'll see. And meanwhile," she added more briskly, "you could be doing something useful instead of worrying. Look, Mothwing has the right idea. She's fetching water for all the kits and elders."

On the other side of the clearing, the RiverClan medicine cat was padding toward a group of WindClan cats, her mouth filled with dripping moss. Leafpaw realized with a guilty pang that she had done nothing except fret over things she could not help.

"Sorry, Cinderpelt," she meowed, getting to her paws. "I'll go and fetch some moss too."

Cinderpelt nodded. "You'll feel better if you're busy."

Leafpaw headed for the lake, but she had barely left the copse of trees when she spotted several cats bounding up the slope. Their pelts were slick with lake water, and Leafpaw recognized Hawkfrost in the lead. It was the RiverClan patrol that had gone to explore the island as soon as the first streaks of dawn appeared.

Curious, she turned back and followed them into the center of the clearing.

Hawkfrost leaped onto the tree stump and let out a yowl to summon all the cats to listen to him. Leafpaw wondered if he should have done that.

"What's he playing at? The stump's for the leaders, just like the Great Rock at Fourtrees." Sorreltail echoed Leafpaw's thoughts as she trotted over to join her friend. "Hawkfrost isn't even a deputy anymore."

But no cat challenged the RiverClan warrior. Instead the Clans gathered quickly to hear Hawkfrost's news.

"Well?" Leopardstar prompted. "Did you make it to the island? What did you find?"

"Everything we could have hoped for," Hawkfrost declared. "I can't imagine a better place for a camp. StarClan must have had it in mind when they brought us here. There's the lake to fish in, trees for shelter, and it's safe from predators—or anything else that might attack us," he added, his eyes flashing toward the rival Clans.

Several mews of agreement came from the RiverClan warriors, and Blackclaw called out, "Well done, Hawkfrost!"

The tabby warrior dipped his head. "I'm only trying to do what's best for the Clan," he replied.

Leafpaw was surprised to hear a loud "Huh!" coming from

just behind her. She glanced over her shoulder to see Squirrel-flight glaring at Hawkfrost with unmistakable hostility.

Quietly Leafpaw wriggled backward until she reached her sister. "What's the matter?"

"I don't trust him," Squirrelflight muttered, not taking her eyes from the RiverClan warrior.

"Me neither," Leafpaw meowed. She thought back to the day in the forest when Sorreltail had accidentally crossed the RiverClan border while chasing a squirrel. Hawkfrost had caught her, and only Mothwing's warning about making trouble between the Clans had made him let her go. He had made his ambitions perfectly clear then, even hinting that RiverClan might move into ThunderClan territory while they were weak from lack of prey.

Leafpaw and Sorreltail had decided not to say anything about the incident to Firestar or their Clanmates. Sorreltail didn't want to confess that she had crossed the border, and she pointed out that any ambitious young warrior might have dreams of taking over another Clan's hunting ground. Leafpaw had wished she could dismiss Hawkfrost's greed for territory and power quite so lightly.

"I knew you didn't trust him," Squirrelflight mewed quietly. "I could tell all along. I'm glad some cat agrees with me."

Mistyfoot padded to the foot of the tree stump, her tail-tip twitching. "Hawkfrost, I've already told you what a mouse-brained idea it is to camp on the island. Warriors can swim over there, yes, but what about kits and elders? And what if something happens to the fish in the lake? We'd never be able to carry fresh-kill across from the shore."

Hawkfrost looked straight past her and meowed, "Leopardstar, what do you think?"

The RiverClan leader hesitated before replying. "What you say is true, Hawkfrost," she meowed at last. "The island would be easier to defend than any camp on land. But Mistyfoot's right, as well. We can't make our home some-where that kits and elders would struggle to reach, and our isolation would make us vulnerable as well as safe. We will camp in the place she found."

Leafpaw braced herself for an explosion of anger from Hawkfrost, but it never came. Instead he dipped his head to Leopardstar and leaped down from the stump.

"Good." Squirrelflight sounded satisfied.

"Be fair," Leafpaw warned. "You can't blame him for want-ing to find a safe home for his Clan."

Squirrelflight let out a snort of disgust. "That's the last thing he was trying to do. He just wanted to challenge Mistyfoot. If I were her, I'd watch my tail. And don't tell me that you don't agree," she added, "because I won't believe you."

"I know," Leafpaw admitted. "All the same, he hasn't *done* anything yet."

Squirrelflight narrowed her eyes. "Just give him time," she meowed darkly.

Worn out by the day's early start, Leafpaw dozed, stirring only when she felt a tail-tip brush against her ear. Blinking, she looked up to see Cinderpelt.

"I'm going to help take Tallstar's body away for burial," her mentor meowed. "Firestar's getting ready to leave now."

Leafpaw scrambled up, shaking scraps of dead leaf from her pelt. "Sorry, Cinderpelt!" she stammered. "Why didn't you wake me sooner?"

"You needed the sleep," Cinderpelt murmured.

By now the clouds had thinned to reveal a pale yellow sun. Cats were gathering around Firestar near the tree stump; Brackenfur was leading Longtail with his tail draped over the blind cat's shoulders, while Ferncloud gently scolded Birchkit, who was bouncing around and getting under every cat's paws.

Excitement surged through Leafpaw, and she was instantly wide awake. They were about to see their new home! "Is there anything I can do to help?" she asked.

"Yes, please. I'd like you to make a quick trip to the marshy place to collect some more horsetail. We might not get another chance for a while."

Leafpaw nodded. "Sure. But may I find Mothwing first? I want to say good-bye."

"You'll see her again at Gatherings," Cinderpelt pointed out, then added gently, "Okay, but don't be long."

Leafpaw darted away. To her relief she spotted Mothwing almost at once, padding through the trees with another mouthful of soaked moss. She must have watered every kit and elder in all four Clans by now, Leafpaw realized guiltily.

"Hey, Mothwing!" she mewed. She stopped, wrinkling her nose at the pungent smell that came from her friend's fur.

Amusement lit Mothwing's blue eyes. "Mouse bile," she mewed ruefully. "Heavystep insisted I sorted out his ticks before I did anything else this morning. Since then I've been so busy fetching water that I haven't had time to wash it off. To be honest, I've gotten used to the smell by now."

"I'm sorry." Leafpaw felt worse than ever. "I should have come to help you."

Mothwing shrugged. "It doesn't matter. I've nearly finished. Do you want some water for your elders?" She pushed the soaked moss across the ground toward Leafpaw.

"Thanks," she meowed, wondering if she had time to take some to Longtail before she fetched the horsetail.

She bent down to pick up the moss, but sprang back when a strong scent filled her mouth and nose—an odd, sour odor that reminded her of crow-food. She straightened up and swiped her tongue over her lips.

"What's the matter?" Mothwing asked.

"I'm not sure. It smells a bit strange, that's all. Where did you get it from?"

"There's a pool over there. . . ." Mothwing gestured with her tail. "I was lucky to find water that close, so I haven't had to trek all the way down to the lake."

"Show me," meowed Leafpaw.

Mothwing led her out of the clearing until they came to the edge of the marsh. She padded confidently across the boggy ground, leaping between tussocks of scratchy grass when the bits in between got too muddy even for a RiverClan cat's paws. They were traveling level with the lakeshore, but farther from the water.

Eventually Mothwing stopped beside a small, stagnant pool fed by a stream that trickled through the long marsh grass toward the lake. Even before she reached the water, Leafpaw recognized the same sour taste in the air. She crept forward cautiously to look down into the pool. The water was black and still, but Leafpaw leaned over until her reflection blocked the light and she could see all the way to the bottom. Narrowing her eyes, she spotted a mass of sodden dark fur lying on the peaty soil. It looked as if a rabbit had fallen into the pool and drowned.

Letting out a hiss of disgust, she pulled back. "Look," she meowed to Mothwing, moving so that the RiverClan cat could crouch next to her.

Mothwing's eyes widened. "The pool was reflecting the sky when I came here before," she murmured. "I never saw the dead rabbit. And I can't smell anything but that wretched mouse bile. Do you think the elders will be okay?" she asked worriedly.

Leafpaw opened her mouth to tell her the water might give them bellyache, but when she met her friend's anxious gaze she couldn't do it. "I'm sure they'll be fine," she mewed awkwardly. After all, if the water was tainted there was nothing Mothwing could do about it now. "Best not give them any more of it, though."

"No, I won't." Mothwing's tail lashed in annoyance. "Now I've got to go all the way to the lake! I'll see you at the next Gathering, Leafpaw."

"I hope so," Leafpaw called as her friend bounded down the slope. "Wash your paws!" she added, though she was not sure Mothwing heard her.

She stepped away from the water and rubbed her paws carefully on the grass in case any of the poison had soaked into the ground around the pool. A little way off, far enough that its roots would be safe from the tainted water, she spotted a thick clump of horsetail.

She would be able to pick some for Cinderpelt, and then they could leave. *Everything will be fine once we're in our new territory,* she told herself. She glanced after Mothwing, and a tremor of anxiety rippled through her fur.

The RiverClan medicine cat had meant well when she fetched water from the pool for the kits and elders. But what would the tainted water do to the cats who had drunk it?

CHAPTER 9

Brambleclaw slipped through the trees, jaws parted to distinguish
ThunderClan scent from among the mingled Clan scents
that hovered in the air. It wasn't easy; they had traveled
together for so long that the Clans no longer kept their separate, distinctive scents. Cats were darting everywhere, trying
to say good-bye to friends in other Clans. There was so much
activity, so much tension crackling between different cats
that Brambleclaw could almost imagine he was in the thick of
a battle—except in this battle there were no enemies.

Already it was sunhigh, and Firestar was eager to set out
for the new territory. He had sent Brambleclaw to make sure
no cat was left behind when they set out for their new home.

Brambleclaw spotted Mousefur saying good-bye to
Heavystep from RiverClan. The ThunderClan warrior
looked thin and tired. Perhaps when they reached their new
camp it would be time for her to join the elders.

"Hi, Mousefur," he meowed. "Firestar would like us all to
gather near the stump now." He carefully avoided giving her
a direct order; Mousefur had a short temper, and he didn't
want his tail snapped off.

"Okay, I'm coming." Mousefur gave Heavystep's ear a quick lick. "Go safely," she told him. "I'll see you at the Gathering."

"Good-bye, Mousefur." Heavystep watched her go before nodding to Brambleclaw and slipping into the trees where RiverClan was gathering.

Brambleclaw almost ran into Squirrelflight, who skidded around the trunk of a tree right under his paws.

"Hi, I was looking for you," she panted. "Come with me."

She doubled back and led him down into a small hollow where Tawnypelt and Crowfeather were waiting. "We have to say good-bye properly," she meowed. "This is the end of *our* journey, now the Clans are separating."

A thorn of sorrow pierced Brambleclaw's heart. Squirrelflight was right. Their quest was at an end. They had faced danger side by side, and somewhere amid the fear, the darkness, and the desperate race to save their Clanmates, they had found true friendship. But their first loyalty had to be to their Clans. It seemed like nine lifetimes ago that they had first left the forest, and sometimes it was even hard to remember how strong their friendship had been on their long journey to sun-drown-place. Brambleclaw looked at Squirrelflight and wondered if she would still trust him with her life.

He padded over to Crowfeather and Tawnypelt and touched noses with them. Gazing into their eyes, he saw memories swimming there like fish.

"We'll never forget what we did," Tawnypelt murmured. "We'll be stronger all our lives for it."

All four cats stood in silence until Crowfeather mewed somberly, "We should be six."

Brambleclaw flinched as he thought of the two cats who would never return to their Clan: Feathertail, who had selflessly given her life, and Stormfur, left behind with the Tribe of Rushing Water.

"We *are* six," Squirrelflight mewed softly. "They'll always be with us as long as we remember them."

Crowfeather's gaze was fixed on the far distance. In a voice almost too low to hear, he murmured, "Sometimes remembering is not enough."

Tawnypelt gave herself a shake. "Well, this won't catch any prey," she meowed. "I'd best be off. I'll see you all at the Gathering."

She turned and bounded away, the others calling goodbyes after her.

Crowfeather dipped his head. "May you travel safely," he mewed, beginning to back away.

"We'll be traveling together for a while," Brambleclaw pointed out. "We have to cross your territory to reach ours."

"But we must keep with our own Clans now." Crowfeather turned and disappeared over the top of the hollow.

Brambleclaw stared after him, wishing there were something he could do about Crowfeather's stubborn belief that he had to do everything alone. His grief for Feathertail seemed to have convinced him that friendship brought nothing but pain.

Squirrelflight brushed his ear with her tail-tip. "Come on.

Firestar will be looking for us."

On their way back to the clearing they caught up with Mousefur's apprentice, Spiderpaw, who was saying good-bye to a couple of RiverClan apprentices. Squirrelflight gave him a friendly cuff around the ear and told him to come with them before he got left behind.

When they reached the stump they found the rest of ThunderClan sitting in small groups, waiting to leave.

Dustpelt was trying to check that every cat was there. "Brambleclaw and Squirrelflight are missing," he meowed irritably to Firestar as Brambleclaw came within earshot. "And Spiderpaw—oh, there you are," he added as he spotted them. "Right, Firestar, that's every cat."

"Good," meowed Firestar.

He leaped onto the tree stump, where Blackstar was already waiting. Leopardstar joined them a moment later, and Onewhisker raced across from WindClan and sat below them, among the roots. There was only room for three cats to stand on the stump—but Brambleclaw noticed Mudclaw give a tiny satisfied nod, as if he was pleased Onewhisker hadn't been able to stand with the other leaders. A chill ran through his fur. This was not the start WindClan needed for their new life beside the lake.

The rest of the cats stirred restlessly, and one or two stood up and clawed the ground. They were too excited at the prospect of finding their new homes to sit quietly and listen to their leaders.

"The four of us have been discussing possible boundaries,"

Blackstar began, "and we need to tell you what we have decided."

Brambleclaw's ears pricked. Wasn't it rather early to settle this? After all, his patrol hadn't had a chance to explore every pawstep of the new territories. But maybe it was better to prepare the cats for the extent of each territory, to avoid one Clan claiming more than their share.

"Tawnypelt reported a small Thunderpath running alongside the pine woods," Blackstar went on. "ShadowClan will take that for its boundary with RiverClan. Farther around the lake, the clearing where the stream runs through the middle can be the boundary with ThunderClan."

"We don't know how far upstream the clearing goes," Tawnypelt reminded him from where she sat among her Clanmates. "We'll need to mark the boundary through the trees as well."

Blackstar nodded. "We'll check that out as soon as we arrive."

"Then ThunderClan's territory will begin at the clearing," Firestar meowed. "And Brambleclaw says there's a stream on the other side of the woods, at the foot of the ridge of hills, that might make a good boundary with WindClan."

"RiverClan's territory will begin here at the horseplace." Leopardstar spoke up. "And stretch as far as the Thunderpath at the edge of the pinewoods."

"Then WindClan territory will be from the horseplace to the stream that Firestar mentioned," Onewhisker meowed.

Brambleclaw caught Tawnypelt's eye across the clearing

and nodded. That sounded fair. Each Clan would have a good stretch of territory with access to the lake and plenty of space for hunting the prey they were most used to.

"This is only a rough idea," Firestar warned. "We need to get to know the territory better before we put down our scent markers. We'll announce the exact boundaries at the next Gathering."

"And let's try to do it without fighting," Barkface called out. "Before you claw some warrior's ear off, kindly remember that we medicine cats haven't had time to build up our stores of herbs yet."

A ripple of amusement passed through the cats, and Brambleclaw spotted more than one warrior nodding in agreement. But it wasn't the threat of a low supply of herbs that made fighting seem wrong. Much more than that, it would feel strange to fight cats who had struggled side by side to survive the destruction of the forest and the long journey through the mountains.

"Let's get going," Firestar urged. "And may StarClan be with us all." He jumped down and padded over to the ThunderClan cats, his tail sticking straight up in the air with barely restrained excitement. "Brambleclaw, Squirrelflight, you'd better lead, as you know the way."

Brambleclaw dipped his head and went to the front of the Clan. This felt right—after all, he had brought them this far. His Clanmates should know how much he had done for them, to find their new home. And maybe, just maybe, Firestar would realize that he deserved to be made deputy.

As they began to make their way through the trees, Onewhisker hailed them, bounding over with his Clan behind him. "I thought we'd travel together for a while," he meowed to Firestar. "We're going in the same direction."

Firestar nodded. "Good idea."

As they continued, Brambleclaw noticed that Crowfeather was among the cats at the front of his Clan, but the young warrior didn't even glance sideways at Brambleclaw. Instead, he kept his gaze fixed straight ahead, padding determinedly down toward the shore of the lake where they would pick up a trail that led to the ridge of hills. Just behind him, Brambleclaw saw Mudclaw scowling at Onewhisker, but it was impossible to tell whether his hostility came from simple envy, or because he didn't want to travel with ThunderClan.

A little way off, RiverClan and ShadowClan were heading slantwise across the slope in the opposite direction. Narrowing his eyes, Brambleclaw recognized Hawkfrost at the edge of his Clanmates. At exactly the same instant, he turned and met Brambleclaw's gaze. Murmuring something to the warrior beside him, he bounded away from his Clan and came over.

"Brambleclaw." Hawkfrost dipped his head in the formal greeting, but his ice-blue eyes were friendly. "Good luck in your new territory. May StarClan be with you."

"And with you," Brambleclaw responded.

"I'm looking forward to meeting you again at Gatherings," Hawkfrost added. His eyes searched Brambleclaw's as if there were more that he wanted to say, but a yowl from one of his Clanmates made him jerk his head around. The two Clans had almost reached the shore of the lake, and if he wasn't careful he would have a long run to catch up. "I have to go," he meowed to Brambleclaw. "Until the Gathering, then." He blinked, then whipped around and raced back to his Clan.

"Until the Gathering!" Brambleclaw called after him, and his heart twisted with regret that the opportunity to know his half brother better was gone.

"Do you think we can get a move on?" Squirrelflight complained. "Or are you planning to stand gossiping all day?"

"He was only trying to be friendly!" Brambleclaw retorted angrily.

"Friendly?" Squirrelflight hissed, her eyes stretched wide with disbelief. "We can do without *his* friendship. Look at the way he tried to grab the island for RiverClan's camp."

"He wasn't trying to *grab* the island. No other Clan can use it. He was only trying to do his best for RiverClan."

"If you believe that, you'll believe anything." Squirrelflight whisked around with her tail in the air and stalked on.

As Brambleclaw followed her, he could see tension prickling in every hair on her pelt. His belly clenched with pain. Of all the friendships he had made on the long journey, surely this one should have survived the separation of the Clans? Instead, it had vanished as quickly as dew in morning sunlight, because Squirrelflight couldn't bear to see him with his half brother. And if she thought he would rather be friends with Hawkfrost than with her, she was wrong. It was

Squirrelflight that Brambleclaw wanted, and he missed her so much it took his breath away.

ThunderClan and WindClan followed the edge of the lake, slipping quietly past the fence of the horseplace and then climbing the hill a little way so they could look down on the shining expanse of water. On the shore near the island Brambleclaw could just make out two groups of tiny dots, moving slowly: ShadowClan and RiverClan, heading for their own new territories. At that distance he could not distinguish individual cats, but he knew that his sister, his half brother, and his half sister Mothwing would be among them, and whatever trouble Hawkfrost had caused between him and Squirrelflight, he wished them well.

The cats padded across the hillside together until they reached a narrow fold in the hill with rocks jutting out of the tough grass and a trickle of water along the bottom.

Onewhisker stopped and gathered his Clan around him with a wave of his tail. "We'll leave you here," he meowed to Firestar. "This should lead up to the ridge where Crowfeather found our camp." Dipping his head, he added, "Our thanks go with you to your new home. Without you, WindClan would never have seen these hills."

Brambleclaw heard a suppressed hiss from among the WindClan warriors. He couldn't see which cat it came from, but he didn't need to. Mudclaw would be the first to resent any suggestion that WindClan owed thanks to ThunderClan.

Firestar swept his tail lightly across Onewhisker's shoulder. "Go well. StarClan has found a good home for all of us." Lowering his voice, he added, "If there's any trouble, let me know. ThunderClan will be glad to help."

Brambleclaw wasn't sure he had been meant to hear that, and he drew away in case Firestar realized he was aware of the ThunderClan leader's promise. Brambleclaw's fur pricked. Surely it was a bad idea for Onewhisker to rely on the leader of another Clan for support? And not just that—Onewhisker knew that Firestar and Brambleclaw were the only other cats who knew what Tallstar had said, and not said, when appointing his new deputy. He was relying on them to keep his secret, to be loyal to him beyond the demands of the warrior code, and support his leadership even though it might not be approved by StarClan.

The two leaders made their farewells, echoed by other cats in both Clans as WindClan began the steep climb up the ravine. The ThunderClan cats stood watching them for a while; Brambleclaw noticed Leafpaw, a bunch of herbs in her jaws, looking after the departing Clan with her head tipped questioningly to one side. He wondered if something was worrying her—perhaps StarClan had warned her of trouble on the way for WindClan—but before he could ask, Firestar called his Clan together.

Somehow, now that ThunderClan was on their own, the lake and the land around it seemed to stretch away farther than before, even more unknown and more threatening. Brambleclaw was acutely aware of every rock or bush that might hide an enemy. His pelt bristled. It was strange that he hadn't felt the same sense of danger on the patrol. But apart from Mistyfoot, he had faced many dangers with those cats beside him, and he could trust them to look out for themselves as well as one another. Now he had to worry about the safety of his whole Clan, who were less practiced at traveling through unfamiliar territory.

Firestar obviously shared his misgivings. "Every cat stay alert," he called, and added more quietly, "Brackenfur, Dustpelt, keep guard on the side nearest the lake. Cloudtail and Brightheart, you take the other side. Sandstorm and Sorreltail, stay at the back and make sure no cat falls behind."

The warriors took up their positions and the Clan moved on. The cheerful meows and joking died away, and the cats padded on in silence, their eyes wide and watchful.

The cold gray light was beginning to fade when they came to a stream at the foot of a gentle slope. On the other side was the wood where Squirrelflight had discovered the stone hollow. Brambleclaw's ears twitched uncomfortably as he wondered what his Clanmates would think of their new home.

"We crossed this stream before," Squirrelflight muttered as they paused on the bank. "Once we're on the other side, we're really in ThunderClan territory!"

"If we decide to make this our boundary," Brambleclaw reminded her. "It's not decided yet."

The stream was too wide to leap, and the cats hesitated on the bank, looking for stepping-stones or tree branches that might help them cross. As the last of the light died, turning the woods ahead to a rustling mass of shadows, Brambleclaw sensed his Clanmates' anxiety rising. Ferncloud curled her tail around Birchkit's shoulders to keep him away from the water, and even the apprentices looked scared.

"What about Longtail?" Mousefur called out. "How do you expect him to get across here?"

"Mouse dung!" Squirrelflight muttered crossly. "We'd better climb the hill to the place we crossed before. It was easier farther up."

"No, hang on," Brambleclaw meowed. They didn't have time for that, not if they wanted to reach the stone hollow before dark. "The water doesn't look deep. Let's see if we can wade across."

He dipped one paw in the water, shivering at its icy touch, then stepped out into the current. The pebbly bottom shelved gently, and he found that even at the deepest place the water didn't lap much higher than his belly fur.

"Come on!" he called as he leaped out on the opposite bank, shaking each leg in turn to get rid of the water. "It's easy!"

A couple of yowls of protest rose from the other bank. "If you think I'm getting wet, you've got bees in your brain!" Mousefur called across to him.

Brambleclaw sighed. It would take far longer to climb the hill to the stepping-stones, and if the Clan had to blunder about in the dark looking for their new camp, then the chances were that some cats would discover it the same way

Squirrelflight had—by falling over the edge of the cliff. To his relief, he saw Firestar beckoning to his Clan with his tail.

"Come on!" he meowed impatiently. "We've come all this way. We're not going to let a stream stop us now, are we?"

One by one, the Clan began to cross. Cloudtail and Sandstorm went first, wading slowly through the water with their tails washed sideways by the current. Dustpelt carried Birchkit across next, his head tipped back to save the kit from getting too wet, and behind him Brackenfur and Sorreltail guided Longtail. Squirrelflight finally persuaded Mousefur into the water by promising she'd soon be in a warm den, on a bed of dry moss; the older warrior grumbled every pawstep of the way until she pulled herself out on the other side and glared at Brambleclaw as she shook herself dry. Behind her, Squirrelflight rolled her eyes, as if she wasn't looking forward to collecting all the moss she'd promised on the other side of the stream.

Firestar crossed last. "Right," he meowed as he joined Brambleclaw on the bank. "Where's this camp?"

Brambleclaw exchanged a glance with Squirrelflight. They hadn't approached the hollow from this direction, and in the gathering darkness everything looked different. Squirrelflight was obviously no more certain than he was. She looked blankly back at him and gave the tiniest shake of her head.

Brambleclaw tasted the air, trying to judge their position from the stream and the slope of the hill. "It's this way," he meowed at last, hoping he sounded more confident than he felt.

The Clan followed him into the trees. Brambleclaw veered in front of his Clanmates to walk beside Squirrelflight. "What if we can't find it?" he mewed quietly.

Squirrelflight's green eyes glinted in the darkness as she turned to look at him. "Then we'll have a lot of furious cats on our tails. Stop worrying," she added. "It's around here somewhere. We found it even though we weren't looking for it before, remember?"

Brambleclaw didn't tell her that was precisely what he was afraid of—that they'd find the hollow only when a cat fell into it. He suddenly felt very small and vulnerable as he padded through the dead leaves, with smooth gray trunks rising up on every side. *Even if we find the hollow, will the others think it's any good?* he wondered desperately.

He was just beginning to hear uneasy muttering from the other cats, who must have realized they weren't following a direct route, when he saw Squirrelflight's ears prick up.

"Look!" she meowed. "That gap between the trees over there, with the clump of dead bracken . . . I've seen that before."

"Are you sure?" Brambleclaw asked, but Squirrelflight was already racing ahead. He followed her into a small clearing and skidded to a halt in front of the tangle of thorns where Squirrelflight had disappeared when she first found the stone hollow.

She was standing in the middle of the clearing, her eyes shining. "This is it!" she yowled triumphantly. Spinning around, she called to the rest of the Clan, "Come on, we're here!"

Spiderpaw let out a screech of excitement. He broke away from the rest of the Clan and dashed forward, straight into the brambles. Brambleclaw stared in horror. They had found the hollow again, but that wasn't the way in!

"Come back!" Mousefur called after her apprentice.

There was no reply. Brambleclaw caught a glimpse of his long black tail waving among the thorns and sprang forward, but Squirrelflight was faster.

Yowling, "No!" she burrowed among the thorns after Spiderpaw. Brambleclaw slid underneath the branches and found them on the very edge of the cliff. Squirrelflight had pinned Spiderpaw down with a paw on his neck, her flanks heaving with effort. Beneath her, the apprentice peered over the sheer rock wall, his eyes bulging.

"Stupid furball!" Squirrelflight exclaimed. "Do you want a broken neck?"

"Sorry," Spiderpaw mumbled. "You said we were here, so I thought—"

Squirrelflight batted him across the ear with one paw, her claws sheathed. "Get back to the others," she rasped. "And maybe you should try thinking less and listening more next time!"

Brambleclaw almost snorted out loud, hearing Squirrel-flight give the same advice she'd heard so many times. He waited until they had crawled away from the cliff before following them out of the brambles.

"What's going on?" Ferncloud, Spiderpaw's mother, demanded as they came into the clearing. "Is there something dangerous in those bushes? Why didn't you warn us before?"

Unease, sharp as a claw, raked down Brambleclaw's spine. "Er . . . we've found the camp," he meowed. "It's in a hollow on the other side of those brambles." Hastily he added, "It's not dangerous once you know where the edge is. Come and see. Not that way!" he growled as Whitepaw bounded curiously over to the thorns.

He and Squirrelflight led the other cats down the slope, weaving between brambles and hazel trees until they reached the gap in the circle of stone. Brambleclaw nervously watched his Clanmates as they filed in and stood looking around at the towering walls. The sky was almost completely dark now, with clouds covering the half-moon, and Brambleclaw had to admit the hollow looked dark and uninviting. There seemed to be more brambles and thornbushes than he remembered, making it feel cramped and overgrown. Some of the undergrowth would be useful for shelter, but the rest would have to be cleared.

Mousefur was the first to speak. "This isn't a camp! Where are the dens? There's not enough space for a snake to sun itself here."

"Hey!" Squirrelflight protested. "You didn't think StarClan would have it all ready for us, did you? I know there's a lot of work to do, but think how easy it will be to defend, surrounded by these cliffs."

"I think it looks great," Thornclaw meowed. "We'll soon sort out proper dens, and somewhere for the nursery."

"I want to explore!" Whitepaw exclaimed, bouncing on

her paws. "Can we, Brackenfur? Please!"

Her mentor gave her a gentle nudge. "Wait until tomorrow, when it's light."

Goldenflower was standing beside Longtail, her tail curled across his shoulders. "It's a huge clearing with stone walls," she mewed softly. "It's quite dark, but I think the walls are covered with ferns and moss. Can you hear that trickle of water? It sounds more like rain draining off the rock than a proper stream. The hollow is full of brambles and thorn thickets, but there's plenty of space for the Clan."

"Then StarClan have brought us to an excellent place," Longtail meowed. "I can easily imagine us building our camp here."

Their optimism cheered Brambleclaw up, even though not all the cats shared it. Ferncloud was looking around doubtfully, and Sootfur was sniffing the air with an irritable look, as if he expected prey to leap into his paws.

Mousefur snorted. "Those bushes will be cold and wet and full of ticks, I shouldn't wonder."

Squirrelflight's eyes narrowed, but before she could make a stinging retort Sandstorm flicked her warningly on the ears with her tail.

"Come on, it's got a lot going for it," she mewed bracingly. "Those walls will shelter us from bad weather. And like you said, Squirrelflight, it should be easy to defend."

"We'll have to do something about that, though." Dustpelt nodded his head toward the entrance. "The whole of Shadow-Clan could be through there in a couple of heartbeats."

Even though Brambleclaw had thought exactly the same thing when he first saw the hollow, he couldn't help feeling annoyed. Did his Clanmates expect the camp to be perfect from the first moment they set paw inside it?

"It's too late to do anything tonight," Firestar meowed. "And far too dark. But you're right, it looks a likely place for a camp," he added to Brambleclaw. "We can make up our minds for sure when we see it in daylight. Dustpelt, Thornclaw, could you check that we're not sharing the place with any foxes or badgers? The rest of us can start finding places to sleep."

The two warriors peeled off from the group and began to circle the hollow in opposite directions, scenting the air every few pawsteps and peering into clefts in the rock and underneath bushes. Feeling as if he couldn't walk another step, Brambleclaw watched until they were swallowed by the shadows at the foot of the cliff.

"What about fresh-kill?" Rainwhisker asked. "Do we have to go to sleep hungry?"

One or two voices were raised in agreement, and Brambleclaw felt his neck fur begin to rise.

"It's not long ago we went to sleep hungry every night," Squirrelflight muttered into his ear. She sounded as disappointed as he was with their Clanmates' reaction to the hollow. "Why are they complaining so much?"

"We've been very well fed since we reached the lake," Brambleclaw reminded her. "Our bellies are used to being full again. But it won't do any cat harm to wait until morning to eat."

"We'll send out patrols at dawn," Firestar promised his Clan.

There was some muttering at that, but gradually it died away, and the group began to split up as cats looked for sleeping places.

"Brambleclaw, do you know if there's a sheltered place for Birchkit?" Ferncloud asked anxiously. "I'm afraid he'll come down with whitecough if he doesn't have somewhere warm to sleep."

"I don't know," Brambleclaw admitted, "but I'll help you look. There are brambles near the wall just a bit farther up."

"And what about some moss for bedding?" Mousefur broke in. "Are we expected to sleep on bare earth? Squirrelflight said there would be a warm den waiting for me once I crossed that wretched stream."

"I can't do everything!" Brambleclaw snapped, his patience giving way. "You'll have to do the best you can for tonight."

Mousefur curled her lip and turned away with her shoulders hunched. Brambleclaw felt his fur prickle, and looked up to see Firestar watching him. The Clan leader's eyes were expressionless, but Brambleclaw knew that if he wanted to be Clan deputy, losing his temper with one of the older warriors wasn't the best way of going about it.

"Sorry," he mumbled, padding after Mousefur. "I'll come and help when I've settled Ferncloud, okay?"

"No, I'll do it." Brackenfur came over and pressed his muzzle against Mousefur's shoulder. "Don't take it out on Brambleclaw," he told her. "He's doing his best."

Mousefur sniffed. "His best is pretty poor, then."

"You'll feel better when you've had a good sleep," Brackenfur promised. "Come on, let's take a look among the ferns over there."

With a sympathetic glance at Brambleclaw, he headed for the rock wall. Mousefur followed him, her tail trailing over the damp grass. Brambleclaw felt a stab of pity for her. The elderly warrior wasn't usually this difficult; she must be exhausted from the journey, and as scared as any of them about finding a new home.

As he helped Ferncloud look for a nest for her kit, he thought about the way Brackenfur had dealt with Mousefur. The ginger warrior had been good-humored and calm in spite of her ill temper, showing his moons of experience in caring for his Clanmates. Didn't that mean he deserved to be deputy more than Brambleclaw? Brambleclaw curled his tail in discomfort. Not just Brackenfur—several other cats had been warriors for longer than him, like Dustpelt and Cloudtail.

But that wasn't the only reason Brambleclaw might never become deputy. He carried a burden that no other ThunderClan warrior shared: Tigerstar. When they were leaving the forest, Firestar had declared that all Tigerstar's children had earned their places within their Clans; he had been trying to persuade Hawkfrost and Mothwing to stay in RiverClan rather than leave with Sasha, their rogue mother, but Brambleclaw knew he had been thinking of Brambleclaw and Tawnypelt, too. Even so, no cat could forget the degree of hostility between Firestar and Tigerstar that had almost destroyed every Clan in the forest with the heat of its flame, and Brambleclaw doubted that his leader would ever be able to look at him and not see the ghost of his old enemy padding at his shoulder.

By the time he had found a place for Ferncloud and Birchkit among the brambles and scraped up some dead bracken to make a nest, most of the other cats had found sleeping places. Instinctively he looked around for Squirrelflight, spotting her among a patch of ferns with some of the younger warriors.

Brambleclaw called her name, but if she heard him she didn't reply. Instead she curled up beside Ashfur, her dark ginger fur mingling with his gray pelt. Brambleclaw took a step toward her, then turned away. If she was waiting for him to apologize for speaking to Hawkfrost, she would have to wait a very long time.

Looking for a sheltered spot of his own, he passed his mother, Goldenflower, who had just settled Longtail into a nest of dried bracken. It looked as if the tabby warrior was asleep already, his sightless eyes tightly shut and his tail curled over his nose.

"Cheer up," Goldenflower meowed. "Everything's going to be fine; I know it is."

Brambleclaw slumped down beside her. He was too tired to pretend this was how he had wanted the Clan to arrive in their new home. "It wouldn't hurt for every cat to be a bit more enthusiastic," he complained.

Goldenflower pressed her muzzle against his flank and let out an affectionate purr. "We're exhausted. What do you expect? Every cat knows how much we owe to you. If we'd stayed in the forest, we would be dead by now. Instead, you brought us here. We're *safe*."

"I know, but—"

"So the journey's end isn't quite what you hoped for. Right now I can't see that that matters." She drew her tongue over his ears in a brisk lick; for a moment Brambleclaw felt like a kit again, and wished himself back in the nursery with Tawnypelt beside him, and nothing more urgent to worry about than their next feed, or whether it was warm enough to play outside.

"Get some sleep," his mother told him, moving away and breaking the illusion. "Everything will look better in the morning."

CHAPTER 10

❧

Leafpaw and Cinderpelt had found a rocky overhang at the back of the stone hollow.

"This won't do permanently," Cinderpelt warned. "We need a proper cave with walls to store our supplies, like the one we had in the forest. But it'll be okay for tonight."

Leafpaw crept in after her mentor and found a dry place at the back for the horsetail stems she had carried from the marsh.

"Get a good night's rest," Cinderpelt advised her, settling down and tucking her nose under her tail. "There'll be plenty to do in the morning."

Leafpaw knew she wouldn't be able to close her eyes until she had asked the question that ran icy claws along her spine. "Cinderpelt? D-do you think this is the right place for us?" she mewed bravely. "Is this really where StarClan meant us to be?"

Cinderpelt yawned. "We'll know that when StarClan's ready to tell us. Now stop worrying and go to sleep." She pushed her nose further into her tail, and her breathing became slow and even as she drifted off.

Leafpaw did not find sleep so easy to come by. She sat

beneath the overhang with her paws tucked under her, gazing into the shadow-filled hollow. *StarClan, where are you?* she begged silently. But only one or two lonely stars glimmered from the cloudy sky, and Leafpaw felt as if her warrior ancestors were too far away to watch over her Clan tonight.

She must have dozed at last, because she opened her eyes to find she was dreaming. She was standing on a dark sweep of hillside, looking down at the glitter of Silverpelt reflected in the shiny black lake. The island should have been a thicker patch of shadow against the water, but instead it shone with moonlight, each tree picked out in a shaft of silver. Leafpaw felt as if the place were calling to her, as if there were more she needed to learn about it. *But we can't go there,* she reminded herself. *Not every cat can swim like RiverClan.*

A breeze picked up, whispering over the star-filled lake and ruffling Leafpaw's fur. She felt a surge of hope run through her, even though the voices of her warrior ancestors remained silent. But Leafpaw was not afraid. They had been silent before on the long journey through the mountains, and she had learned that sometimes the only thing a cat could rely on was the strength that lay within. Everything would be all right if she and the others made it so. They would make their camp here; they would explore every part of the woods until they knew the good places for prey, for water and bedding, the spots where each healing herb grew, and the places where they could play and relax in the sun. It seemed strange and daunting now, but eventually it would be their home. Pawstep by pawstep, they would make it happen.

As she stood gazing down at the lake, Leafpaw realized that the surface of the water was changing. The glitter of starlight faded and the water turned steadily redder, until waves of scarlet lapped against the shore. Leafpaw looked up in surprise, but the sky was as dark as before, so this couldn't be a reflection of sunrise. The water seemed thick and slow-moving, surging lazily over the pebbles—and in that instant, Leafpaw knew that it wasn't water at all. The lake was filled with blood, fed by streams that ran like gaping wounds. Another gust of wind buffeted Leafpaw's fur, hot and dusty this time, bringing with it the stench of crow-food.

Shaking with terror, she heard a voice speak clearly in her mind:

Before there is peace, blood will spill blood, and the lake will run red.

"Cinderpelt! Cinderpelt!"

Leafpaw woke with a jump. It was still dark. Sorreltail was peering under the rocky overhang, anxiously calling Cinderpelt's name. Somewhere in the hollow, the eerie yowl of a cat in pain tore the quiet of the night.

"What is it? What's happening?" Leafpaw asked, scrambling up and prodding Cinderpelt in the flank.

"It's Mousefur," mewed Sorreltail. "She says she has a pain in her belly."

"I'll come," Cinderpelt meowed, getting to her paws.

"If Mousefur has bellyache, we need water mint or juniper berries," Leafpaw told her. "There were masses of them at the other end of the lake. Do you want me to fetch some?"

Her mentor looked serious. "It would be better to find a supply nearby, but if we need them before daylight, then you'll have to go back."

They followed Sorreltail across the hollow to the clump of ferns where Mousefur had made her nest, stumbling over stones in the darkness. Leafpaw tasted the air in an attempt to discover if any of the herbs they needed were growing nearby, but it was impossible to make out the special scents among so many, and against the overwhelming scent of cats.

When she and Cinderpelt reached Mousefur, the brown warrior was lying on her side, her body twisted with pain, her jaws gaping as she let out another anguished yowl.

"Mousefur, listen to me." Cinderpelt crouched down beside her. "Do you know what caused this? Have you eaten any crow-food?"

Mousefur blinked eyes glazed with pain. "Crow-food? No," she rasped. "Do you think I'm mousebrained? My belly . . ." Her words trailed off into another yowl.

A horrible suspicion forced itself into Leafpaw's mind. Beckoning Cinderpelt aside, she murmured, "Mousefur must have drunk some of the water Mothwing found. I think it might have been tainted. It smelled bad, and when she showed me the pool she got it from, there was a dead rabbit in there."

Cinderpelt let out an exasperated sigh. "And she didn't think to . . . Well, no point in going into that."

"What are we going to do?" Leafpaw asked anxiously.

Cinderpelt turned to Sorreltail. "Do you know if any other cat drank the water?"

Sorreltail shook her head.

"Goldenflower and Longtail might have," Cinderpelt went on. "Check it out, would you, Sorreltail?"

The tortoiseshell warrior nodded and vanished into the darkness.

"Try to lie still, Mousefur," Cinderpelt urged. "Let me feel your belly." She patted gently with her paw. To Leafpaw, the brown warrior's stomach looked unnaturally distended.

"Haven't you got some herbs I could take?" Mousefur fretted.

Cinderpelt shook her head. "We haven't had time to look for any yet."

Mousefur opened her mouth to say something else, then retched and began to vomit.

"That could be a good sign," Cinderpelt meowed to Leafpaw. "At least she's getting rid of the poison."

Leafpaw nodded, feeling utterly helpless. Mousefur was suffering because the medicine cats could do nothing without their stock of herbs. "We'll have to find more supplies as soon as it's light," she mewed. "Especially water mint and juniper berries. I'll take some to the other Clans, in case they drank the water too."

Cinderpelt's blue eyes widened in surprise, and Leafpaw winced. She had become too used to thinking of all four Clans as one, with shared problems and shared solutions. It seemed natural to help them if she thought their elders might be suffering the same thing as Mousefur. But now that the boundaries between them were being reestablished, was she being disloyal to her own Clan?

"We should check on WindClan at least," she added persuasively. "Their cats are the weakest, so they'll be in the most danger."

Cinderpelt nodded. "You can go in the morning, but you'd better take a warrior with you. We'll speak to Firestar as soon as we can. Well?" she prompted, as Sorreltail reappeared.

"Goldenflower says she had a bellyache, but she's been sick, and it isn't too bad now," the tortoiseshell warrior reported. "Longtail is asleep, and he looks okay, so I didn't wake him."

"Thanks," meowed Cinderpelt. "Longtail's younger, of course, so he should be stronger. I'll have a word with him when he wakes."

"Mothwing meant to be kind," Leafpaw murmured. She didn't want her friend to get into trouble for not noticing the rabbit at the bottom of the pool.

To Leafpaw's relief, Cinderpelt didn't seem to blame Mothwing too much. "I know. Any cat can make a mistake." Then the medicine cat's eyes darkened and she went on: "But Mothwing would be the first to admit she has much less experience than the other medicine cats, and no mentor to guide her now that Mudfur is dead. I hope for RiverClan's sake that she doesn't make this sort of mistake too often. She'll need all the help StarClan can give her, that's for sure."

Weak after her vomiting, but more comfortable, Mousefur managed to sleep. Sorreltail stayed to keep an eye on her, with instructions from Cinderpelt to fetch her if the pain returned. The sky was already turning gray behind the trees at the top of the cliff, and though Leafpaw felt exhausted there was no point in going back to the makeshift den. As soon as the light grew stronger, she and Cinderpelt went to look for Firestar.

A wind had sprung up, rattling the leafless branches and tearing the clouds into ragged strips, but the undergrowth sheltered by the ring of stone hardly stirred. A gleam of pale sunlight slanted into the hollow, leaving the foot of the cliff in shadow but striking a gentle warmth into the ferns by the entrance. The cats that hadn't been disturbed by Mousefur's illness awoke to a far different place from the dark and unwelcoming hollow of the night before. Leafpaw heard them call cheerfully to one another, and spotted Birchkit emerging from a bramble thicket to pounce on a dead leaf. The sight of the kit playing just as he had done back in the forest, before the prey vanished and they were dulled by starvation, made Leafpaw's heart lift, and she offered silent thanks to StarClan. She forced the terrifying bloodstained prophecy from her dream to the back of her mind, and told herself that this must be the right place for ThunderClan to settle.

They found Firestar in an open space near the center of the hollow; he had already gathered some of his warriors around him.

"We need to get out there right away and mark our boundaries," Leafpaw heard Dustpelt meow as they approached. "If we don't, WindClan and ShadowClan will claim all the woodland—and the prey—before you can say mouse."

"We need to explore the territory as well," Sandstorm pointed out. "For all we know, these woods could be crawling with foxes and badgers."

"Not to mention hawks," Thornclaw added.

Sandstorm murmured agreement. "I'll see to the hunting patrols, if you like," she meowed to Firestar.

The Clan leader gave her a grateful nod. "Thanks, that would be great." Leafpaw felt a little stab of pride to think that her mother was one of the best hunters in the Clan.

Dustpelt flicked his ears. "I'll take charge of guarding the camp—I don't like the look of that entrance gap. I'll get the apprentices and see what we can do with some thorns."

"And I'll take care of the boundary patrols," Brambleclaw offered.

"That's a huge job," Firestar warned, "especially as we don't even know where the boundaries are going to be yet. Brackenfur, will you and Brambleclaw do that together?"

The two warriors nodded.

"Cloudtail, I want you to take a patrol and work outward from the camp," the Clan leader ordered. "Report back on anything you think I should know about. It's not just the boundaries we need to think about—I want to know what's inside them, too." Cloudtail agreed with a wave of his tail.

"What about me?" Thornclaw asked.

Cinderpelt limped forward. "Excuse me, Thornclaw. Firestar, we have a problem." She quickly told him about

Mousefur's bellyache. "I want to go out and find the right herbs," she explained, "and then take some to WindClan. All the Clans could have drunk the water, but WindClan is weakest, so they're most at risk."

Firestar thought for a moment before he replied. His expression was hard to read, and Leafpaw wondered if he was reluctant to spend time and energy helping another Clan now that they were establishing their new territories.

"We can't leave WindClan to suffer if there's something we can do," Cinderpelt urged.

"All the medicine cats know how to treat bellyache," Firestar reminded her. "But you're right, Cinderpelt: WindClan have been through enough, and it's the kits and elders who'll suffer. Thornclaw can go with you."

"Thanks. I'll just check on Mousefur and the others, and then we'll go."

Leafpaw followed Cinderpelt back to Mousefur's nest. The brown warrior was asleep, with Sorreltail dozing beside her. Longtail and Goldenflower had joined them; Goldenflower was asleep too, but Longtail raised his head as they approached and pricked his ears toward them as if he could see as clearly as ever.

"Hi, Cinderpelt, Leafpaw," he greeted them; Leafpaw knew he had recognized them by their scent, but it didn't stop a thorn-sharp claw of sympathy raking through her.

Sorreltail blinked her eyes open and scrambled to her paws. "I think everything's fine," she meowed. "Mousefur's been asleep ever since you left."

"Her scent is almost back to normal," Longtail added. "Goldenflower's, too, but I think she drank less of the water to start with."

Cinderpelt bent her head over Mousefur and then Goldenflower, sniffed them, and listened to their breathing. "They'll be okay now," she meowed, straightening. "You might as well go, Sorreltail. You'll be needed on one of the patrols. Thanks for staying with Mousefur."

The young warrior raced off, waving her tail at Leafpaw as she passed.

"What about you, Longtail?" Cinderpelt prompted. "Did you have a bellyache as well?"

"A bit," mewed the blind warrior. "Sorreltail said it was the water Mothwing gave us. I thought it smelled a bit odd, but when a medicine cat gives it to you—"

"Mistakes happen," Cinderpelt meowed. "Leafpaw and I are going to look for herbs to restock our supplies in case any other cats show the same symptoms."

"Good luck," Longtail meowed. There was a wistful note in his voice, as if he would have liked to come with them to explore the new territory.

The medicine cats went back to the center of the camp, where the warriors were dividing up their patrols. Leafpaw spotted Brambleclaw heading purposefully toward Squirrelflight, but before he reached her, Ashfur bounded over.

"Hey, Squirrelflight!" he meowed. "Sandstorm says she wants you for the hunting patrol."

"Sure," Squirrelflight replied.

There was a look of mingled frustration and disappointment in Brambleclaw's eyes as he watched her pad away, but he didn't try to stop her. Leafpaw sighed. There was definitely something wrong between the tabby warrior and her sister, though she had no idea what it was.

"Wake up." Cinderpelt prodded her in the side. "Thornclaw's ready. Let's go."

Leafpaw's paws tingled with excitement as they headed for the gap in the rock wall. Dustpelt was giving orders to Spiderpaw and Whitepaw about clearing unwanted thorns from the camp to build a barrier. "I don't want so much as a mouse to get in and out," he meowed.

"What, not even cats?" Spiderpaw asked cheekily, waving his tail.

Dustpelt sighed. "We'll leave a tunnel, mousebrain."

Leafpaw pushed her way into a patch of ferns, which looked less prickly than the bramble bushes next to it, and paused in the middle, breathing in the strong green scent around her. On the other side, beyond the gap that led into the stone hollow, the unknown forest lay waiting.

No—ThunderClan's new territory lay waiting.

CHAPTER 11

"Are you stuck?" Thornclaw asked, nearly bumping into Leafpaw as he pushed through the ferns.

Leafpaw sprang forward, out of the sharp-smelling stems. "Sorry," she puffed.

Thornclaw followed more slowly and looked at her. "It's all a bit strange, isn't it?" he mewed. "But this is as strange as it will ever feel, remember that. We only have to explore once for it to seem more like home."

Feeling comforted, Leafpaw padded beside him, away from the hollow. When she glanced back a few moments later, the stone cliffs had vanished among the trees, and all she could see were smooth gray trunks and branches that trembled in the wind. She was pleased to think her Clan-mates were sheltered by the towering walls, invisible and safe in the middle of the wood.

Voices sounded up ahead, and they rounded a sturdy oak tree to find Cloudtail, Brightheart, and Sorreltail sniffing suspiciously at a gap between the roots. This was the patrol that Firestar had sent out to explore the territory that lay closest to the hollow.

"Fox," Leafpaw heard Cloudtail meow.

Brightheart lifted her head and carefully tasted the air. "It's very stale," she decided. "I don't think the fox can have been there for moons."

"Shall I go in to look?" Sorreltail offered.

Brightheart shook her head. "Didn't your mentor ever warn you about going into strange holes? We can smell there's nothing there. Let's keep going."

Sorreltail called out a greeting to Leafpaw, then followed the warriors as they headed deeper into the woods.

Leafpaw stopped to let Cinderpelt catch up, and gazed around her. Trees stretched away on all sides, their branches interwoven so tightly that only tiny splinters of sky showed through. The trees weren't as tall as the ones in the forest they had left, but Leafpaw guessed that in greenleaf their leaves would form a thick, cooling canopy. Most of the ground was covered by short grass with spikes of snowdrops thrusting upward, and the occasional clump of thornbushes and bramble thickets. It was more exposed than Leafpaw was used to, and she hoped that ferns and other plants would grow in newleaf to provide homes for prey, and to make the cats feel safer as they patrolled their territory.

Cinderpelt reached her and limped steadily on, following the sound of running water. "We're not likely to find juniper here," she commented as the three cats padded side by side. "Leafpaw, what else might we use for bellyache?"

"Water mint?" she suggested. "Or chervil root?"

"They would both be fine," Cinderpelt agreed. "Water

mint should be easier to find than chervil root."

They reached the stream, which flowed in a deep cleft between the tangled roots of overhanging trees. Leafpaw stood on the bank and looked for signs of the leafy green plant, but all she could see was water sliding over gray stone about a tail-length below her, with bright green ferns trailing over the edge of the bank.

"Let's try on the other side," Thornclaw suggested when they came to a place where the banks sloped down and they could splash across.

Cinderpelt agreed, but it was much the same: open woodland with little in the way of undergrowth. Then Leafpaw smelled damp soil, a bit like the marsh at the far end of the lake. Water mint didn't have to grow in a stream—sometimes wet earth was enough. She raced ahead, pushing her way through some spiky tussocks of grass, and spotted the tall, leafy stems half-hidden in a clump of bracken.

"Good work!" Cinderpelt praised her, coming to join her. "There's enough here to supply us regularly."

Tipping their heads to one side, they bit through several stalks. Leafpaw's eyes watered as sap clung to her fur, filling her mouth with the pungent scent.

"I'd better get back to camp," Cinderpelt meowed when they had finished picking the water mint. "Thornclaw, will you take Leafpaw to WindClan now?"

"We'll see you home first," meowed Thornclaw. "I don't think any cat should be alone in these woods until we know a bit more about them."

He led them back by a different route, calculating from the way the ground sloped that it should lead more quickly to the stone hollow. They passed beneath some beech trees, and Leafpaw's belly rumbled as the scent of squirrel flooded over her.

Thornclaw tasted the air with a gleam in his eyes, and Leafpaw guessed he was ravenous too. "Do we have time to hunt?" he asked Cinderpelt.

The medicine cat set down her stems of water mint. "If we don't take too long."

"This won't take long at all," Thornclaw promised. He flicked his ears toward the nearest tree, and Leafpaw spotted a squirrel among the roots, nibbling a beechnut.

Thornclaw paused for a moment to judge the direction of the breeze, then began stealthily working his way around so that he approached the squirrel from downwind. Bunching his hindquarters under him, he pounced; the squirrel gave one spasmodic kick, and was still.

"Come on," he called. "There's enough for all of us."

The fresh-kill was delicious, and Leafpaw offered a quick prayer of thanks to StarClan for bringing them to a place where the prey was plump—and slow. Her mouth was filled with the scent of the squirrel, so she had no warning when three cats suddenly appeared around the trunk of a tree a little way off. They paused for a heartbeat when they spotted the ThunderClan cats, and then loped toward them. As they drew closer, Leafpaw realized it was a WindClan patrol made up of Tornear, his apprentice, Owlpaw, and Whitetail.

Swallowing his last bite of fresh-kill, Thornclaw rose to his paws, but Tornear spoke first.

"What are you doing here?" he demanded. "This is WindClan territory."

"What do you mean, WindClan territory?" Thornclaw stared at him in surprise. "The boundaries haven't been marked yet."

"We're marking them now," Whitetail explained, sounding faintly embarrassed. "Firestar said the stream that runs along the foot of the hill would be the boundary, and this is on WindClan's side."

"Firestar also said that was only a suggestion," Thornclaw reminded the WindClan warriors. He waved his tail around. "Look. Trees. This is the sort of place where ThunderClan are best at hunting. You need moorland and rabbits, right?"

"There's not as much moorland here as there was in the old place," Tornear explained. "We need to extend the territory into these woods, or we won't be able to support our Clan."

"Well, you're not extending it here," Thornclaw meowed firmly, but the fur along his spine bristled, and Leafpaw guessed he felt very uncomfortable. It was impossible for any cat to forget how close the Clans had been on their journey. Back in the forest, claws would have been unsheathed by now, but here, there was no instinct to fight over territory they hadn't finished exploring.

"Do you think StarClan will send a sign to show us where the boundaries should be?" she asked Cinderpelt.

The medicine cat shook her head. "StarClan would never favor one Clan above another, or get involved in disputes. This is something the Clans have to sort out for themselves."

The warriors stood around awkwardly for a few more moments. Whitetail spotted the pile of water mint stems. "Are those for bellyache?" she asked.

"Yes," Leafpaw replied. "Are some of your cats ill too?"

Whitetail cast a swift glance at Tornear before she replied. "Yes," she answered. "Morningflower and Darkfoot."

"Morningflower?" That was worrying. Leafpaw knew the WindClan queen had always been a friend to ThunderClan. "What is Barkface doing for her?"

"There's not much he can do without herbs," Tornear meowed. "The last I heard, he'd gone looking for juniper. I just hope he doesn't take too long. Morningflower looked pretty sick to me."

Leafpaw spun around to face her mentor. "I can take some water mint to WindClan right now," she mewed. "These cats can show me the way, and Thornclaw can go back to the hollow with you."

"Of course," Cinderpelt meowed. "Be as quick as you can."

All the warriors looked relieved to have something more urgent to think about than the issue of boundaries. Thornclaw and Cinderpelt set off toward the stone hollow, while Leafpaw went in the other direction with the WindClan cats. They led her to the edge of the trees—just as they had said, the stream curved into the woods here, away from the foot of the hills—and across open moorland. Then they climbed more steeply beside another stream that fell in a series of tiny, bubbling waterfalls. A few stunted thorns grew along the banks, with traces of rabbit scent clinging here and there. So there was prey for WindClan here, Leafpaw thought. Had Tornear been telling the truth when he said it might not be enough?

At last they came to the top of a rise, fringed by bushes, and Leafpaw found herself looking down into the WindClan camp. The sides weren't as steep as the cliffs around ThunderClan's hollow, but the smooth, bare slopes gave no cover for attackers.

Leafpaw spotted Onewhisker and Ashfoot talking with a couple of the warriors near a scatter of boulders in the center of the dip.

"I'll take you straight to Morningflower," Whitetail meowed.

"And I'll let Onewhisker know you're here," Tornear added, heading down the slope with Owlpaw.

Whitetail led Leafpaw to a knot of gorse bushes at the far side of the hollow. Leafpaw's pelt pricked under the stares of WindClan warriors as she padded past, but they were curious rather than hostile.

Morningflower lay on a bed of ferns in the shelter of the bushes. Darkfoot was curled up a tail-length away, but Leafpaw couldn't take her horrified gaze from the old she-cat. Morningflower lay limply stretched out, her breathing harsh and shallow. Her belly was distended, and a sour smell of vomit came from her. Her eyes were closed, and she was still except for the occasional twitch of her flank. To Leafpaw, she looked as if she were barely a pawstep away from joining StarClan.

Setting down the water mint stems, Leafpaw bent her head closer to Morningflower, but before she could do more than set one paw gently on her belly, she was interrupted by a furious snarl.

"What do you think *you're* doing?"

CHAPTER 12

Fox!

Brambleclaw lifted his head to taste the air more carefully. The scent clung to the bramble thicket beside him, strongest around a rough-edged tunnel that looked as if it had been made by slender bodies pushing regularly through it.

"It was here not long ago," he warned Brackenfur. "There might be an earth nearby."

They were leading a patrol to find landmarks for the boundaries of the new territory, and to put down the first scent markers. Rainwhisker was with them, and Dustpelt had come too, leaving Whitepaw and Spiderpaw dragging thorns into place to block the camp entrance.

"We'll report it to Firestar," Brackenfur decided. "We need to be careful until we find out whether it lives here or was just passing through."

Brambleclaw nodded. His fur tingled with excitement, all his doubts about the hollow forgotten now that it was daylight and the cats could see what a good place it made for a camp. He had been glad when Firestar chose him to patrol the new boundaries; every pawstep made the woods feel more like ThunderClan territory, and he deliberately brushed against brambles and tree trunks as he walked along, to leave a scent trail that was unmistakably theirs.

He let Brackenfur take the lead as they padded on. As they skirted a clump of hazel, Dustpelt stopped to sniff a low-hanging branch. He looked up, and his eyes were so full of concern that the other three went over to examine the scent as well. They looked apprehensively at each other as they scented Twolegs.

"At least it's stale," Brackenfur pointed out. "Days old, I'd say."

"But they come here." Dustpelt curled his lip. "If I never see another Twoleg, it'll be too soon."

Brambleclaw took a deep breath to stop his heart pounding. He felt exactly the same way, but it would be a sign of weakness to show his fear in front of these warriors. This was their home now, and they couldn't live every day expecting to have it snatched away from them. He let his tail-tip rest briefly on the older warrior's shoulder. "This is the first scent we've picked up since leaving the hollow," he pointed out. "And we're a long way away from a Thunderpath. There won't be any monsters."

Dustpelt flicked his ears and padded on without speaking. The others followed, Brambleclaw keeping to the back, half-afraid the others would see the terror in his eyes as he tried to push away images of the forest crashing down around them.

"Let's hunt!" Brackenfur suggested.

"Good idea," Rainwhisker agreed. No cat mentioned that

it would be a welcome diversion from thoughts of Twolegs and monsters, but they all concentrated on tracking prey as if they had been starving for a moon.

Brambleclaw slowed down to drink in the mingled scent of squirrel and rabbit and birds. He jumped when he heard an alarm call, and saw that Rainwhisker had brought down a starling. Nodding appreciatively, he headed past the young warrior, farther into the forest, until he spotted a thrush pecking among the gnarled roots of a dead tree. Crouching low enough for his belly fur to brush the fallen leaves, he crept forward until he could pounce on it and dispatch it with a swift blow to the neck.

As he lowered his head to take a bite, a weight landed on his back and he felt claws digging into him. Instinctively he flung himself sideways and rolled over to dislodge his attacker. Scrambling away from slashing claws, he caught a glimpse of ginger fur and at first thought it was Brackenfur. Had his Clanmate gone mad? But when he scrabbled for a foothold and managed to spin around, he saw that he was facing a snarling ShadowClan warrior.

"Rowanclaw! What are you doing?"

"What do you think?" growled the ginger tom. "Defending the ShadowClan boundary, of course."

"What?" Brambleclaw looked around and realized that the beeches and oak trees that grew around the ThunderClan camp were mixed with pine here.

"Don't pretend you didn't know! You crossed our scent markers."

"I didn't notice any scent marks at all!" Brambleclaw protested. "They must be too faint." He shied away from the other possibility—that the Clans' scents had become so mixed while they were traveling together that no cat could tell one from the other now. If that were true, it would be impossible to set any boundaries at all.

"Too faint!" Rowanclaw sneered. "Mouse dung! Admit it, you were trying to steal our territory."

"*You're* trying to steal *ours*," Brambleclaw retorted furiously. "Back at the horseplace, we said we'd use the clearing on either side of the stream as the boundary. You must have crossed it, because I certainly haven't."

"There *isn't* a clearing here, mouse brain," Rowanclaw snarled. "The stream veers deeper into our territory and the trees grow right up to both banks. We have set the boundary in a straight line, carrying on from where the stream runs through the clearing. Try looking out for the scent marks next time, and you'll know exactly where ShadowClan begins."

He unsheathed his claws, bunching his hindquarters under him, and Brambleclaw braced himself for a fight. But before Rowanclaw could pounce, a tortoiseshell streak burst out of the bushes and bowled him over. It was Tawnypelt.

"What are you doing?" she spat. "It's much too soon to start fighting over territory."

Rowanclaw glared at his Clanmate. "What a surprise, it's the half-Clan warrior!" he hissed. "We all know you'd rather defend your brother than your Clan."

"That's not true!" Tawnypelt protested.

"No, it's not." Brambleclaw padded forward to stand next to his sister. "I know Tawnypelt is loyal to ShadowClan."

Rowanclaw's disbelieving gaze raked him like a claw. "If you ask me," he growled, "all the cats who went to see that badger have forgotten which Clan they belong to."

With a furious yowl, Brambleclaw was about to spring at him when three more ShadowClan cats appeared: Cedarheart, Oakfur, and Talonpaw. Brambleclaw's belly clenched. He could hardly take on an entire ShadowClan patrol, and what would Tawnypelt do if her Clanmates forced her to join in the fight against her brother?

To his relief he heard Brackenfur's voice behind him. "Brambleclaw! What's going on?"

Glancing back, he saw his three Clanmates racing through the trees. The ShadowClan warriors crouched down, unsheathing their claws, but before the warriors could leap on one another a new voice rang out.

"Stop!"

Firestar padded out from a patch of thorns behind Brambleclaw, his eyes narrowed in fury. "I can't believe how stupid you are being, all of you. If we can't establish our boundaries peacefully, we'll end up shedding the blood of every cat in the forest."

Stung, Brambleclaw took a step back, and saw his Clanmates flatten their neck fur as well. The ShadowClan warriors did the same, though their tails twitched angrily.

"They crossed our scent markers," Rowanclaw muttered.

"No, we didn't," Brambleclaw insisted. He had expected support from his Clan leader; instead, Firestar was behaving as if he didn't even want him to defend their territory. "We might need to fight," he argued. "This is our home now, and we have to be ready—"

"That's enough." Firestar's eyes were cold. "If ShadowClan has set scent markers already, then this is their territory."

"*If* they did," Dustpelt put in. "I didn't smell any."

"We will not accuse another Clan's cats of lying," Firestar hissed. "Rowanclaw, where is the stream and the clearing that we said we'd use as a boundary?"

The ShadowClan warrior jerked his head toward his own territory. "The stream's back there, and there isn't a clearing this far away from the lake." Twitching his tail contemptuously toward Brambleclaw, he added, "I already told *him* that."

"Then ShadowClan has the right to be here," Firestar decided. "ThunderClan will find other places to hunt. Come on, we're going back to camp."

Brambleclaw couldn't believe what he was hearing. He clamped his teeth together to stop himself from challenging his leader in front of warriors from another Clan. The most he could do was glare at the ShadowClan patrol as he swung around and followed Firestar back through the trees.

As he approached the dead tree where he had killed the thrush he noticed a faint scent hanging in the air; it was the ShadowClan marker, but it was so weak that he hardly recognized it, and it definitely held traces of ThunderClan, Wind-Clan, and RiverClan scents as well. Brambleclaw didn't feel any less furious now that he knew ShadowClan hadn't been lying. It wasn't ShadowClan he was angry with; it was Firestar.

Why had his leader assumed that Brambleclaw and the other ThunderClan cats were in the wrong? Why hadn't he stopped to listen to their explanation for crossing the boundary? Brambleclaw curled his lip. If he carried on like this, Firestar would end up handing the entire forest over to the other Clans.

On their journey to sun-drown-place, he and the other five cats had discussed everything, and even when Brambleclaw emerged as the natural leader, they had still made all the important decisions together. Why couldn't Firestar be more like that? Every cat in the Clan had an opinion about their new home, and blindly following orders wasn't always the best solution.

Before they reached the hollow, Firestar stopped. "Brackenfur, I want you to go that way." He pointed with his tail to an area no cat had explored yet, where the trees grew more thickly. "See what you can find, and whether there are any good landmarks for the boundary. But I need one of you to come back with me—Brambleclaw, you'll do."

Brambleclaw watched the other three cats vanish into the bracken before turning to follow Firestar. "What do you want me to do?"

"We need a lot of moss and bedding for the new nests," Firestar replied. "I want you to collect as much as you can before it gets dark."

"What?" Brambleclaw stopped dead, his anger surging up again. "That's a job for an apprentice!"

"Usually, yes, but the apprentices are busy building a barrier at the camp entrance. Just do it, Brambleclaw. You know every cat has to pitch in until our new home is fully established."

"Okay," Brambleclaw muttered.

He let Firestar go on, and stopped at the foot of a tree to claw at the moss between the roots, taking out his anger on the close-packed stems. Whatever Firestar said about every cat pitching in, this was a punishment for his scrap with the ShadowClan patrol. Brambleclaw had only been trying to defend his Clan's territory. He wanted to be trusted, to be given responsibility, and here he was collecting moss.

Padding back with a ball of moss clenched between his teeth, he met Squirrelflight and the rest of the hunting patrol, laden with fresh-kill.

"Hi, Brambleclaw!" Squirrelflight called to him, setting down the squirrel she was carrying. "This place is great for prey!"

Brambleclaw couldn't share her excitement. The only thing he'd been allowed to hunt for his Clan was a heap of bedding. Not bothering to put the moss down so he could answer, he brushed past his Clanmate and stalked into the camp.

CHAPTER 13

❧

"I said, what are you doing here?"

Leafpaw felt her pelt bristle as she met Crowfeather's furious glare. "I've come to help!" she hissed. "Morningflower and Darkfoot are ill. I've brought herbs for them."

"How do you know what's wrong?" Crowfeather asked suspiciously.

"Because we've got the same problem in ThunderClan," Leafpaw retorted. There was no need to tell him about Mothwing and the tainted water. She didn't want to give the prickly WindClan warrior the smallest chance to accuse Mothwing of deliberately poisoning the elders.

"Back off, Crowfeather," Whitetail mewed. "I asked Leafpaw to come."

The dark gray warrior let out a snort of disgust; he didn't say anything else, but he watched Leafpaw closely as she began to examine Morningflower. She found his presence thoroughly off-putting, but she couldn't tell him to go away, not in his own camp.

Once she was sure that Morningflower was suffering from the same illness as Mousefur and the others, Leafpaw chewed a few mint leaves into a pulp and used her claws to part Morningflower's jaws. Pushing the pulp into her mouth, she stroked her throat to make her swallow.

Whitetail crouched close by. "Will she die?"

"I don't know," Leafpaw admitted. Silently she added a prayer to StarClan: *Please let her get well.*

As she waited for the healing herbs to work, she heard Darkfoot stirring; the old tomcat raised his head and looked around with bleary eyes. "Great StarClan, my belly aches," he complained. "Where's Barkface with that juniper?"

"He's not back yet," Whitetail meowed. "But Leafpaw's here with some water mint."

"Leafpaw?" Darkfoot blinked. "She's a ThunderClan cat." Before Leafpaw could explain, he added, "ThunderClan, WindClan, who cares, so long as she knows what she's doing." He chewed the mint leaves Leafpaw set in front of him, and rested his head on his paws again.

A choking sound from Morningflower drew Leafpaw's attention back to her; the old she-cat was retching feebly, her legs jerking.

"What have you done to her?" Crowfeather snarled. "She's getting worse!"

He tried to nudge Leafpaw away. She leaped backward, and he bared his teeth at her when she tried to dodge around him and get back to her patient.

"Stop!" Spinning around, Leafpaw saw Onewhisker padding into the bushes, with Tornear just behind him.

"Crowfeather, what do you think you're doing? Leafpaw has come to help."

"She shouldn't be here," Crowfeather growled.

"Are you saying she shouldn't do us a favor? She shouldn't try to save the life of one of our cats?" Onewhisker's voice was level, but tense with anger. When Crowfeather didn't reply, he added, "Since you're taking such an interest, you can stay and keep an eye on her. If she needs you to do anything, you do it. Leafpaw, don't be afraid to ask."

Leafpaw dipped her head. "Thanks, Onewhisker. I think Whitetail and I can manage."

"I want Whitetail for a hunting patrol," Onewhisker told her. "But Crowfeather hasn't got anything else to do." He beckoned to Whitetail and padded away.

Crowfeather glared at Leafpaw. "Treat me like an apprentice and you're crow-food," he hissed.

Much as he had ruffled her fur, Leafpaw couldn't help feeling that Onewhisker had been a bit tough on Crowfeather. "Let's just concentrate on helping Morningflower," she mewed. "We need to get some more water mint down her."

She chewed up more of the leaves, and asked Crowfeather to hold Morningflower's jaws open while she pushed the pulp into her mouth, praying that the old cat wouldn't vomit it up again. She flinched as Crowfeather's flank brushed hers, making her fur tingle like the air before a storm. He leaped back too, then stepped forward again without meeting her eyes, as if he were embarrassed.

Morningflower had gone limp again, as if she were exhausted. Leafpaw sat beside her, stroking her belly gently with her tail. She was acutely conscious of Crowfeather watching her, and wished he would go away.

After a while she thought that the old she-cat's breathing was growing stronger. Darkfoot was dozing again, occasionally letting out a rusty purr.

"Are they getting better?" Crowfeather whispered.

"I think so," Leafpaw replied. "I'm sure Darkfoot will be fine. It's Morningflower I'm worried about."

"Leafpaw." A shadow fell across Morningflower's body, and Leafpaw looked up to see Barkface. "It's good to see you." He spoke around a leaf-wrapped bundle; when he set it down the leaves fell back to show a few shriveled juniper berries.

"Barkface, I hope you don't mind," Leafpaw began nervously. "I met some of your Clan in the woods, and they said Morningflower was very ill. We've had the same trouble, so—"

Barkface interrupted her with a wave of the tail. "You're very welcome. I've no idea yet where the best herbs grow—I found only one juniper bush, and birds must have taken most of the berries." Sniffing carefully at Morningflower, he added, "She's better than when I left. What are you giving her—water mint? Good thinking, though I'd use juniper myself, if I could find enough."

"Can I go, then?" Crowfeather asked loudly.

"Oh, yes, yes." Barkface waved him away. "I can take over now."

Leafpaw watched him go, wondering why she was feeling

disappointed. She hated the idea of falling out with any cat, but it hurt even more when Crowfeather was a friend of Squirrelflight's—though what her sister saw in him, she couldn't begin to guess.

"You'd better go too, Leafpaw," Barkface meowed. "You've done good work here, and your own Clan will be needing you."

Leaving what was left of the water mint, Leafpaw rose to her paws. "Let me know how Morningflower gets on."

"I will. I'll get a message to you somehow," Barkface promised.

Leafpaw pushed her way out of the bush. Onewhisker was in the center of the camp with some of his warriors around him, and she decided to tell him she was leaving. Her steps faltered when she saw that one of the cats talking to the Clan leader was Mudclaw.

Onewhisker spotted her. "How's Morningflower?" he asked.

"I think she'll be fine. Barkface is with her now."

"We can't thank you enough for what you've done," the WindClan leader meowed, his eyes warm. "Tornear told me that when he met you, he and Thornclaw were having a dispute over the boundary in the woods. I've decided that we'll leave that area to ThunderClan from now on. We'll put our scent markers at the edge of the trees, close to the foot of the hill."

"That's very generous of you!" Leafpaw began, but she was interrupted by a growl from Mudclaw.

"Are you completely mousebrained?" rasped the former deputy. "You're giving away WindClan territory for a pawful of healing herbs? Barkface was perfectly capable of treating the sick cats without this apprentice sticking her nose in."

Onewhisker spun to face him. "Mudclaw, you are a fool if you think this is about nothing more than herbs. Think of everything ThunderClan has done for us. How many lifetimes would it take to repay them? Without their friendship, every cat in WindClan would be crow-food by now."

Mudclaw snarled, curling his lip to reveal sharp yellow teeth, and Leafpaw had to sink her claws into the ground to stop herself from shrinking away. One or two of the other warriors were looking uneasy, too, including Crowfeather. She waited for him to back Mudclaw up, and say that she shouldn't have come, but the lean gray warrior said nothing.

"I don't want to hear of any fighting over the border with ThunderClan," Onewhisker growled. "That stretch of woodland isn't much use to us. Since when has WindClan hunted among trees?"

"There's more than prey among trees." Webfoot stepped forward to stand beside Mudclaw. "Herbs, for one thing. I know Barkface needs plants that we'd never find on open moorland."

"That's enough!" Onewhisker snapped. "There's plenty of territory left, and Barkface never had trouble finding supplies before."

His warriors dipped their heads, but none of them looked

happy about their leader's orders. Mudclaw turned away, muttering, "Traitor!" in a voice just loud enough to be overheard.

Leafpaw's belly clenched with anxiety. She guessed several of the WindClan warriors would agree with Mudclaw, that Onewhisker was not putting the good of his own Clan first by harking back to their old alliance with ThunderClan. She wondered what would happen if Mudclaw were to challenge him for the leadership. How many cats would support him with tooth and claw?

"You'll want to be getting back," Onewhisker meowed. "Crowfeather, please go with Leafpaw as far as her camp and tell Firestar my decision."

Crowfeather looked up, his eyes wide. "Me?"

Oh, no, Leafpaw thought. Aloud she hissed, "You don't have to. I'm perfectly capable of looking after myself. Just because I'm a medicine cat doesn't mean I don't know how to use my claws."

Onewhisker flicked his ears at her. "Crowfeather, that was an order."

Crowfeather still looked appalled, but he heaved an exaggerated sigh. "Come on. I'll only get into trouble if I don't go with you."

Leafpaw could see she would have to give in. As Crowfeather whisked around and headed up the slope to the edge of the camp, she nodded a hasty farewell to Onewhisker and bounded after the dark gray warrior. He set a fast pace, not asking Leafpaw if she could keep up. He was so rude, she couldn't be bothered trying to make conversation, but even in the silence the air between them crackled like greenleaf lightning. He obviously hated the idea that a ThunderClan cat had done his Clan a favor.

As a medicine cat, Leafpaw lived outside the Clan-based rivalries held by other cats. If this was what it felt like, she was glad she didn't have to treat cats like enemies just because they came from different Clans. Although Crowfeather had been one of the journeying cats, he had fallen back quicker than any cat into the old ways. With his bristling fur and awkward sidelong glances, he seemed only too ready to rekindle the old rivalries.

Leafpaw heaved a sigh of relief when they came to the stream. They were higher up than the place where ThunderClan had crossed the night before, and Crowfeather led her nimbly across some stepping-stones back into ThunderClan territory. Not long after she recognized the bushes that surrounded the top of the stone hollow. Leafpaw took the lead and followed the slope of the land down to the gap in the cliffs. When they reached the entrance she saw that a thorn barrier was partly in place, and inside, a fresh-kill pile had appeared on a cleared space among the brambles.

Firestar was standing by the thicket where Ferncloud and Birchkit had spent the night. Squirrelflight was helping Ferncloud drag out long tendrils of bramble.

"We could make a good nursery in here," Ferncloud panted, reaching up with her hindpaw to unhook a thorn from her flank. "It's right up against the rock wall, so it'll be sheltered in bad weather. We need to make more space inside, though."

"That won't take long," Squirrelflight assured her, energetically dragging away a bramble twice as long as she was, while Birchkit pounced playfully on the other end.

Brambleclaw appeared with a ball of moss and carried it through the entrance of the new nursery. Leafpaw was impressed that a warrior was prepared to help with apprentice tasks; Brambleclaw was obviously determined to settle his Clanmates into the home he had found for them. Ferncloud followed him inside to help him arrange it. Birchkit gave up hunting the end of Squirrelflight's bramble, and bundled after his mother.

"Firestar, Crowfeather's here." Leafpaw dipped her head to her Clan leader. "He came back with me from WindClan."

"Thanks." Firestar padded over to the young WindClan warrior. "Is everything okay?"

"Leafpaw helped Morningflower." Crowfeather sounded distinctly ungrateful. "And Onewhisker asked me to tell you that ThunderClan can be the first to set scent markers in the woodland across the stream. He's happy for WindClan's boundary to be set at the edge of the trees."

Firestar's eyes stretched wide in surprise; he clearly hadn't expected to win that territory so easily. "That's very good of Onewhisker," he replied. "Thank him for me."

"And thanks for bringing me back," Leafpaw added. Just because Crowfeather had behaved like a fox with a thorn in its paw didn't mean she had to be rude too.

Crowfeather gave her a long look, hostility and something else in his eyes. He seemed about to say something, then just nodded and headed out of the camp.

"Hey!" Squirrelflight called after him. "Ignore your old friends, why don't you?"

The WindClan warrior didn't look back, and vanished among the ferns.

Firestar stared at the quivering green fronds that had swallowed Crowfeather up. "Onewhisker's being very generous," he remarked, though he didn't sound quite as pleased as Leafpaw would have expected. "Quite different from ShadowClan," he added.

"ShadowClan?" Leafpaw echoed, wondering what had made her father think of them.

"There was nearly a fight!" Squirrelflight told her excitedly. "Brambleclaw crossed ShadowClan scent markers, and a ShadowClan patrol tried to chase him off."

"We could have dealt with them," Brambleclaw mewed, reappearing from the nursery without his burden of moss. "I suppose they were only putting their Clan's interests first. I wonder if Onewhisker could say the same. I mean, he's just given away a fair chunk of good hunting territory."

He sounded curious rather than hostile, but Squirrelflight rounded on him with her tail fluffed up.

"At least he's loyal to his old friends!" she flashed. "Something you seem to have forgotten about."

Anger flared in Brambleclaw's eyes. Instead of speaking, he clamped his jaws shut and stalked off. Firestar shook his head worriedly, followed him for a few paces, then veered off and went to talk to Thornclaw by the fresh-kill pile.

"What was all that about?" Leafpaw asked her sister in dismay. "Why has everything gone wrong between you and Brambleclaw?"

Squirrelflight shrugged. "Don't ask me. He's been in a foul mood ever since we came here." She gave up trying to pretend she didn't care, and gazed at Leafpaw with eyes that were green pools of hurt and bewilderment. "I don't think he likes me anymore."

Leafpaw couldn't think of anything to say to comfort her. She could heal wounds and knew the right herbs for belly-ache, but the breach between her sister and Brambleclaw was totally beyond her. That was a part of life that a medicine cat would never know. She thought she should probably feel relieved that she would never have to suffer such pain. Then she saw the hunger in Squirrelflight's gaze as it followed Brambleclaw out of the camp, and remembered how deeply the two cats cared for each other. A tiny empty space appeared inside her when she realized no cat would ever feel that way about her.

Dustpelt emerged from the bramble thicket with another long tendril dragging behind him, and almost tripped over Birchkit as the kit hurled himself at the trailing end. "Birchkit! You're more trouble than a fox in a fit."

"Don't scold him," Ferncloud murmured, following her mate into the open. "It's great that he feels happy enough to play."

Dustpelt purred agreement, his eyes shining as the two cats watched their kit growl fiercely at the bramble, gripping it between his teeth and shaking his head from side to side.

As Leafpaw looked on, the hollow place inside her got bigger. She would never feel for another cat what Squirrelflight felt for Brambleclaw, or enjoy the closeness of a mate and kits. She had never doubted her decision to give her life to StarClan and tread a medicine cat's solitary path—but suddenly she couldn't help wondering if she was missing something.

CHAPTER 14

Cool grass swept against Brambleclaw's pelt as he prowled through the undergrowth. He could hear the scuttering of tiny creatures underneath the bushes, and his senses were flooded with the scent of prey.

Before he could make a catch, he emerged into an open space. An almost-full moon hung in the clear sky, outlining every grass stem and leaf with pale silver rays. Just in front of him the ground fell away into a cleft, with rocks jutting from its steep sides.

Brambleclaw stared in astonishment. This was the ravine leading down to the old ThunderClan camp. He lifted his head and sniffed cautiously. There was no harsh tang of Twoleg monsters in the air, no noise louder than the gentle rustle of the wind in the trees. Their home was safe! The destruction of the forest, the fear and hunger, the long journey through the mountains, had been nothing more than a dream.

Brambleclaw pelted down the ravine to the gorse tunnel at the bottom, his heart nearly bursting with happiness. In a few heartbeats he would see all his Clanmates again: Graystripe would never have been captured by Twolegs; all Ferncloud's kits would still be alive; the elders would be in their den, querulously ordering the apprentices to get rid of their ticks.

Trembling with excitement, Brambleclaw pushed his way through the gorse tunnel into the camp, his jaws parted to let out a yowl of greeting. Then he stopped dead. The clearing was completely empty, except for one cat sitting alone in the middle of the open space.

The cat raised his head and gazed at Brambleclaw with scorching amber eyes.

It was Tigerstar.

Brambleclaw almost choked with shock and disbelief. Graystripe's capture, the death of Ferncloud's kits, the endless journey—all those things were real. *This* was the dream, and it had suddenly become a nightmare.

Tigerstar kinked his tail and beckoned Brambleclaw to come closer. Brambleclaw stiffened, then padded slowly forward. As he drew closer he saw his father more clearly, his muscular shoulders and broad head, his burning amber eyes.

"Welcome," Tigerstar rumbled. "I have waited for many moons to speak with you."

Brambleclaw stopped a couple of tail-lengths away. He had no idea what to say. All he could think was that he was the image of his father—the breadth of his shoulders, the shape of his head, the exact shade of his eyes. He could have been staring at his reflection in a pool.

"I have seen your courage and strength," Tigerstar went

on. "I am proud to call you kin."

"Th-thank you." Brambleclaw kneaded his forepaws on the ground. "Why have you come here? Did StarClan send you?"

"I do not hunt with StarClan," spat Tigerstar. "There is more sky than Silverpelt, and there are hunting grounds that not even StarClan knows of."

His gaze slid past Brambleclaw. "Welcome," he meowed. "I hoped you would come. I've looked forward to meeting you."

Brambleclaw spun around to see Hawkfrost emerging from the gorse tunnel. He watched in stunned silence as the RiverClan warrior padded across the clearing and sat beside him. The moonlight cast a pair of identical shadows on the hard-baked ground in front of them, and Brambleclaw realized that a half-blind kit would know at once that all three were kin.

He told himself that he ought to feel something stronger than bewilderment and curiosity to find out more about his father and half brother. They came from three different Clans; beyond that, Tigerstar had murdered many cats and betrayed his own Clanmates to satisfy his hunger for power. Yet Brambleclaw could not shake off the feeling that he had waited a long time for this moment. For all the differences between them, the same blood ran in their veins.

"Are you Tigerstar?" Hawkfrost asked, reminding Brambleclaw that Hawkfrost had arrived in the forest after his father was killed. "Are you my father?"

Tigerstar nodded. "I am. So, how are your new territories?"

"It's hard being somewhere so different," Hawkfrost admitted.

"We all miss the forest," Brambleclaw added.

"Soon the land by the lake will seem like home to you," Tigerstar promised. "Establish your boundaries and guard them with tooth and claw, because territory is what binds a Clan together."

"Yes!" Hawkfrost's eyes gleamed. "RiverClan has set its scent markers already. Yesterday Blackclaw and I drove out a badger that was living in our territory."

"Good, good." Tigerstar's ears pricked, and he raised his head as if he heard a voice calling him. Above the trees, the sky was growing pale with the first light of dawn. "I must go now," the dark tabby meowed. "Good-bye, Brambleclaw, Hawkfrost. We will meet again as we walk the path of dreams; of that I'm sure."

He rose to his paws. At that moment a cloud drifted over the face of the moon, plunging the clearing into darkness for a single heartbeat. When it cleared, Tigerstar was gone.

"I must go too." Hawkfrost touched noses with Brambleclaw and began padding back to the camp entrance.

"No—wait. Don't go!" Brambleclaw called.

"I *have* to go; I'm on the dawn patrol. What are you talking about, Brambleclaw?"

Brambleclaw blinked and sat up. Cloudtail was looking at him with a puzzled expression as he groomed scraps of moss out of his pelt. "Is there something wrong?" he asked. "Do you want me to tell Brackenfur I can't go on the patrol?"

Brambleclaw shook his head, dazed. "No, no, I'm fine." He lay down again and closed his eyes tightly, as if he could force out the thorn-sharp grief that tore at his belly.

The dream had faded, and he was in the stone hollow again. Tigerstar, Hawkfrost, and the old ThunderClan camp were gone.

Brambleclaw slept dreamlessly for a while, and awoke feeling less confused and wretched. He padded out of the ferns and arched his back in a stretch. The sky was brighter now, outlining the bare branches at the top of the rock wall. A pulse of excitement ran through him as he remembered that tonight the moon would be full, and the Clans would meet for a Gathering.

He glanced around the camp. The clearing looked very different from the first time he had seen it. Many of the brambles had been uprooted to form a barrier blocking the camp entrance. The biggest thicket had been turned into the nursery. The apprentices were using a shallow cave in the rock wall as their den, while the warriors slept under the spreading branches of a thornbush almost as big as the one in the old camp. The elders still hadn't found a den they could agree on; every night they would try a different spot, and wake up complaining that it was too damp or too drafty. Brambleclaw suspected Goldenflower and Longtail were rather enjoying the search for the perfect place, because it meant they got to inspect every corner of the hollow, and had even started advising the other cats on the best places to bask in the sun or eat fresh-kill out of the rain.

Gradually, the stone hollow was becoming more like home, but Brambleclaw couldn't shake off the memory of his dream, when he had gone back to the camp in the ravine. It wasn't just a longing to be back in the forest that tugged at his paws and made him restless; he kept thinking of his father and half brother, too. What had Tigerstar meant about hunting in different skies? Was he keeping watch over Firestar and the whole of ThunderClan from wherever he hunted now?

Brambleclaw shook his head violently, as if the dream were a cobweb clinging to his pelt. Their old home had gone, and there was nothing to be gained by fretting over memories. Focusing on practical duties, he saw that the fresh-kill pile near the entrance to the camp was getting low. At the same moment, Dustpelt emerged from the nursery and padded across to meet him.

"Hi," Brambleclaw meowed. "Want to go hunting?"

"Great!" Dustpelt's eyes gleamed. "Who should we take with us?"

Brambleclaw wondered if he should go and look for Squirrelflight, but then he heard a cat call out Dustpelt's name, and glanced around to see Brackenfur racing toward them.

"Dustpelt," he panted as he skidded to a halt, "you had Whitepaw fetching fresh bedding all day yesterday. Can I have her for warrior training today? It's time we got the apprentices back into a proper routine."

"Sure," Dustpelt replied. "Do you want to come hunting with us?"

"Bring Spiderpaw too," Brambleclaw suggested. "Mousefur isn't well enough for patrols yet."

"Good thinking." The voice came from behind Brambleclaw; he spun around to see Firestar coming over.

"I've just had a word with Mousefur," Firestar went on. "Yesterday Spiderpaw chased away a young fox that was sniffing around the entrance to the camp. We both think he's ready to be a warrior, so we're going to hold his ceremony at sunhigh. You can tell him this will be his last hunt as an apprentice."

Brambleclaw's tail curled up with satisfaction. Making a new warrior was one of the most important things a Clan could do, and Spiderpaw's ceremony would be one more thing to make the stone hollow feel like home. It would be something to report at the Gathering, too.

Firestar wished them luck in their hunt and padded off, while Brackenfur went to fetch the two apprentices. Soon the five cats were climbing the slope around the edge of the hollow before striking off into the trees above the camp. They had almost reached the highest point of the cliff when they heard a plaintive mew behind them.

"Wait for me!"

Brambleclaw looked back to see Birchkit struggling after them, stumbling over tussocks of grass in his efforts to keep up.

"Birchkit!" Dustpelt exclaimed. "What do you think you're doing?"

The kit looked up at his father with pleading eyes. "I want to go hunting too. *Please,* can I?"

Brackenfur rolled his eyes at Brambleclaw. "Kits!"

Dustpelt didn't share their amusement. "No, of course not," he meowed sharply. "You can't go hunting until you're an apprentice."

"But I'm good at hunting!" Birchkit boasted. "Look, I'll show you. I'll catch that bird."

He nodded at a robin that was perched on one of the thornbushes at the very edge of the hollow. Before any cat could stop him, he wriggled his haunches under him and launched himself at it.

"No!" Dustpelt and Brambleclaw yowled, springing after him.

Brambleclaw reached him first and fastened his teeth in his scruff, just as the thornbush gave way under Birchkit's weight and he began to slide down into the hollow. Another heartbeat and he would have tumbled over just like Squirrelflight, except at this point the cliff was twice as high, and no cat who fell that far could expect to survive.

Scrambling backward, Brambleclaw dropped Birchkit on solid ground, well away from the edge. The kit crouched there shivering; Dustpelt stood over him, bristling with fury.

"Are you completely mousebrained?" he hissed. "Don't you think there's a reason kits stay in the nursery with their mother until they're apprenticed?"

Birchkit nodded, his eyes huge and scared. "I'm sorry," he whimpered.

"Don't be too hard on him," Brackenfur urged. "He didn't mean any harm."

Dustpelt whirled around to glare at him. "What difference does that make? He would be dead if it hadn't been for Brambleclaw." He prodded Birchkit with his tail. "I haven't heard you thank him yet."

Birchkit flattened his ears and ducked his head. "Th-thank you, Brambleclaw. I'm really sorry."

"That's okay," Brambleclaw meowed. He felt very sorry for the frightened kit—the scare had been enough to keep him in the camp for several moons, judging by Birchkit's terrified face.

"Come on, stand up; you're not hurt." Dustpelt bent over his kit and gave him a few fierce licks. Brambleclaw knew that he had been so angry only because he had nearly lost the last kit of his litter. "Go home to Ferncloud, and let's have no more of this nonsense."

Birchkit nodded, and Dustpelt pressed his muzzle comfortingly against his side before the tiny cat set off back toward the camp entrance. His father watched him until he was out of sight.

"We'll have to make a rule," he decided. "No kits anywhere near the edge of the cliff. That goes for apprentices too," he added, flicking his ears at Whitepaw and Spiderpaw, who had watched the near-miss in wide-eyed silence.

Whitepaw nodded; Spiderpaw's tail curled up as if he were reminding himself that the rule wouldn't apply to him after sunhigh. He seemed to have forgotten that he had nearly fallen over himself when the Clan first approached the camp.

"We could put scent marks along the edge," Brambleclaw suggested. "That way every cat would be reminded."

"Good idea," mewed Dustpelt. "Have a word with Firestar when we get back. Come on; let's hunt before Spiderpaw misses his warrior ceremony."

As Brambleclaw padded after the others, his paws still tingled with the sense of danger. He glanced back at the thornbushes and pictured Birchkit's tiny body, battered and broken in the clearing below. *Have I really brought the Clan somewhere safe?* he wondered.

Since they had arrived nearly half a moon ago, there had been no sign from StarClan to suggest they were still being watched by their warrior ancestors. Was this really the place where they were meant to be?

Brambleclaw led the patrol across the stream into the stretch of woodland that Onewhisker had given to ThunderClan. It was not long before he spotted a squirrel scuffling at the foot of a tree. Brambleclaw crept forward and brought it down with a skilful blow that snapped its neck.

"Well done!" Dustpelt called.

Brambleclaw began scratching earth over the squirrel, pausing as Whitepaw padded up to him.

"Do you think we should really take that?" she asked nervously. "Territory on this side of the stream was supposed to be WindClan's."

"But Onewhisker gave it to us." Brambleclaw went on

covering the fresh-kill. "This is our prey." His fur prickled with irritation that an apprentice was suggesting he would steal food from another Clan. It wasn't his problem if WindClan wanted to give away their hunting grounds.

Whitepaw didn't protest again when he led his patrol farther into the trees.

By sunhigh the whole Clan had eaten well, and there was a good pile of fresh-kill left over. When they had finished their meal, they stayed in the center of the hollow, where bushes had been cleared away to make a space for the Clan to gather. It was time for Spiderpaw's warrior ceremony.

There was no Highrock like the one in the old camp. Instead, Firestar had found a ledge a few tail-lengths above the heads of the other cats, which he reached by leaping up a tumble of broken rock that made rough stepping-stones up the cliff. Just below the ledge—already cats were beginning to call it the Highledge—there was a narrow cleft that opened into a cave where Firestar had decided to make his den. Of all the dens in the new camp, this was most like the one in the ravine, enclosed by lichen-covered walls and with a dry, sandy floor.

Firestar raised his voice in a yowl, his pelt a splash of orange flame against the blue-gray rock. "Let all those cats old enough to catch their own prey join here beneath the ledge for a Clan meeting."

Brambleclaw's pelt tingled to hear the familiar words ring around the hollow. He watched the leggy black figure of

Spiderpaw, his pelt groomed until it was as glossy as a raven's wing, cross the clearing to stand beside his mentor, Mousefur. She looked thin and shaky, as if she were still not quite recovered from her bellyache, but her eyes shone with pride as her apprentice joined her.

Brambleclaw wriggled forward, hoping to sit beside Squirrelflight, but he stopped when he saw that she was sitting with Ashfur, Sootfur, and Rainwhisker. Their heads were close together and their shoulders shook gently as if they were sharing a joke. Brambleclaw curled his lip, suddenly feeling hollow and cold. He sat gloomily beside the nearest cat, who happened to be Cloudtail, and tried to concentrate.

"Trouble?" murmured the white warrior. He glanced past Brambleclaw and flicked his ears toward Squirrelflight. "What have you done to ruffle her fur?"

"Nothing," Brambleclaw replied stubbornly. The reasons for their quarrel were too complicated and private to share with any cat.

"Hey, don't worry." Cloudtail gave him a sympathetic flick with his tail. "It'll blow over."

"Maybe." Brambleclaw sighed; he really didn't want to discuss it.

"We have a ceremony to perform," Firestar meowed as soon as all the cats were settled. "Mousefur, are you satisfied that Spiderpaw is ready to become a warrior?"

The brown warrior dipped her head. "I am."

Firestar ran lightly down the broken rocks until he reached the floor of the hollow, and beckoned Spiderpaw closer to him with his tail. Spiderpaw stepped forward, quivering from nose to tail.

"I, Firestar, leader of ThunderClan, call upon my warrior ancestors to look down on this apprentice." Firestar's voice rang out clearly above the sound of the wind and the gentle creak of branches on the rim of the hollow. "He has trained hard to understand the ways of your noble code, and I commend him to you as a warrior in his turn." He fixed his gaze on Spiderpaw and went on, "Spiderpaw, do you promise to uphold the warrior code and to protect and defend this Clan, even at the cost of your life?"

"I do," Spiderpaw replied eagerly.

"Then by the powers of StarClan I give you your warrior name. Spiderpaw, from this moment you will be known as Spiderleg. StarClan honors your courage and your enthusiasm, and we welcome you as a full warrior of ThunderClan."

He took a pace forward and rested his muzzle on the top of Spiderleg's head. The young warrior gave Firestar's shoulder a respectful lick, then stepped back to join the other warriors.

"Spiderleg! Spiderleg!" The Clan raised their voices to greet him by his new name. Dustpelt looked ready to burst with pride, and Ferncloud's eyes were shining with joy to see their eldest son made a warrior at last. Birchkit bounced around his brother's paws, clearly recovered from his scare that morning.

Firestar raised his tail for silence and the noise died away, all the Clan turning curious faces toward him.

"Before we go to our duties, I have another ceremony to perform," Firestar meowed. "Mousefur and I have been talking together, and she has come to a decision. Mousefur, are you still sure that this is what you want?"

The old she-cat dipped her head in assent as she stepped forward.

"Mousefur," Firestar continued, "is it your wish to give up the name of warrior and go to join the elders?"

Brambleclaw thought he heard a tremor in her voice as she mewed, "It is." He guessed it was hard for the proud warrior to accept that she was growing old; the combination of the long journey and her recent illness had proved that she was not as strong as she used to be. Sadness chilled his fur as he remembered her courage and her fighting skills.

"Your Clan honors you and all the service you have given us," Firestar went on. "I call upon StarClan to give you many seasons of rest." He laid his tail upon Mousefur's shoulders and the old cat bowed her head before padding over to stand beside Longtail and Goldenflower.

"I don't need too much rest, Firestar," she rasped. "I'll still keep my claws sharp, and if trouble comes I'll be ready."

A murmur of amusement and admiration rose from the cats around her, and one or two of them called out, "Mousefur! Mousefur!" as if they were welcoming a new warrior. Goldenflower gave her a friendly lick around the ears.

The meeting began to break up. Brambleclaw went over to congratulate Spiderleg and noticed Firestar beckoning him.

"I heard Whitepaw telling Cloudtail about that squirrel

you caught this morning," his leader meowed.

Brambleclaw's pelt bristled. He'd deliberately avoided ShadowClan territory by taking the patrol in the opposite direction; was Firestar going to blame him for invading WindClan now? "Onewhisker said we could have that stretch of woodland," he pointed out, trying not to let his anger show in his voice.

"I know." Firestar's voice was mild. "You haven't done anything wrong. But go easy on that patch of territory just for now. We'll sort it out eventually, but until we do I don't want to take advantage of Onewhisker's good nature."

"I didn't intend to," Brambleclaw replied, relieved. "But it's his responsibility to fight for WindClan's boundaries. Or does he expect us to defend his territory as well as our own, just because we've been traveling together for the past moon?"

Firestar narrowed his eyes. "Don't worry, Brambleclaw," he meowed. "The time will come when every Clan will defend themselves with teeth and claws, and fight for their territories as fiercely as we ever did. But that time is not now." He turned to go, then paused and glanced over his shoulder. "Get some rest, Brambleclaw," he advised. "You'll be coming to the Gathering tonight."

Brambleclaw blinked, hoping his leader couldn't see the anticipation that surged through him, making his fur stand on end. *I'll see Hawkfrost again! I can ask him about the dream!* He burned with curiosity to know whether his half brother had met with Tigerstar too. Did kin share dreams? Not always—

but his dream of the old camp had been so real, almost more real than finding their new home. If Tigerstar was really watching over his sons, surely he would want to visit them both?

He caught his breath, suddenly choking with guilt. Hawkfrost belonged to a rival Clan. The fact that he and Brambleclaw were kin meant nothing compared to their loyalty to their Clanmates and their leaders. It was ridiculous to think that he and Hawkfrost might have shared a dream.

Yet as he padded across to the warriors' den to catch a nap before leaving for the Gathering, Brambleclaw's paws tingled with the thought that he would soon see his half brother again.

CHAPTER 15

The sun had gone down but the horizon still blazed with scarlet when the ThunderClan cats set out. While he was waiting for Brackenfur to go through the tunnel in the barrier of thorns, Brambleclaw realized that Squirrelflight had slipped up to his side.

"Hi, there," she meowed. She sounded friendly but uncertain, as if she weren't sure what his reaction would be. "Are you okay? You've been in a dream all day."

Brambleclaw winced; the memory of his meeting with Tigerstar and Hawkfrost filled his mind so strongly that when he shut his eyes, he could almost feel the brush of his half brother's fur against his flank. He longed to respond to the affection in Squirrelflight's green gaze, but she was the last cat he could tell about his dream, given her feelings about the RiverClan warrior.

He scuffed his paws on the earth. "I didn't sleep well last night; that's all."

Squirrelflight narrowed her eyes, clearly guessing there was something he wasn't telling her. "Keep secrets if you want." She sighed. "See if I care."

Whisking around, she pushed through the tunnel behind Brackenfur.

"Squirrelflight, wait!" Brambleclaw raced after her, furious with himself for seeming to reject her attempt to be friends again. When he burst out at the other end of the tunnel she was padding away with Leafpaw, their heads bent close together. Though he called her name again she didn't turn to look at him.

Sorreltail was the last of the warriors to emerge from the tunnel. Brackenfur had been waiting to check that they had all the cats who were meant to be coming to the Gathering. As she went past, Brackenfur stretched out his muzzle to touch her ear-tip. "Hey, Sorreltail," he murmured. "I'm glad you're coming."

The young tortoiseshell warrior blinked at him and let out a purr.

Firestar led his Clan uphill to the place where they could cross the stream by the stepping-stones, then followed the stream down to the lakeshore. "If we go on Gathering near the horseplace," he meowed, "we must make sure WindClan understands we'll have to cross their territory every full moon."

"That shouldn't be too difficult," Cloudtail muttered to Dustpelt.

The brown tabby warrior grunted. "True. We could probably charge straight through the WindClan camp without any of the warriors lifting a paw."

"That's not fair!" Sorreltail protested. "Onewhisker would

defend his camp as fiercely as any warrior."

Dustpelt and Cloudtail exchanged a glance; Brambleclaw could tell they weren't convinced.

The cats padded along the edge of the lake; the water grew darker as the scarlet faded from the horizon and the first stars appeared. Brambleclaw found his gaze dragged back more than once to where Squirrelflight and Leafpaw walked side by side at the back of the group. He was comforted by the fact that at least she wasn't with Ashfur, who was talking to Rainwhisker and Cinderpelt. Brambleclaw thought that the young gray warrior paid far too much attention to Squirrel-flight.

By the time they were nearing the Twoleg horseplace, the full moon had floated away from the trailing wisps of cloud and was flooding the lake and its shore with pale silver light. Just before they reached the fence, Onewhisker appeared on the brow of the hill above them, flanked by several of his Clanmates. Brambleclaw was surprised to see that Mudclaw was with him, but there was no sign of the new deputy, Ashfoot.

Firestar stopped and waited for the WindClan cats to catch up, greeting Onewhisker with a friendly purr. Although the two leaders walked on side by side, the warriors behind them stayed with their own Clanmates. Brambleclaw spotted Crowfeather and waved his tail to catch his attention, but instead of padding over to greet him, Crowfeather just acknowledged him with a brief nod.

Suddenly Firestar raised his tail for them to halt.

Brambleclaw padded quietly forward to find out what was going on. He paused to taste the air and his neck fur began to rise when he made out the scent of strange cats.

"More kittypets?" he muttered to Crowfeather.

The WindClan warrior bristled, his ears pricked. Brambleclaw followed his gaze and spotted a tiny movement in the grass on the other side of the Twoleg fence. A moment later two cats emerged. The first was a muscular gray-and-white tom; he glared at them through the fence with his lips drawn back in a snarl.

"Who are you and what do you want?" he demanded.

Mudclaw and Cloudtail both sprang forward, ready for battle, but Firestar waved them back with his tail. "We're not looking for trouble," he meowed. "We have come to live near here."

"There are so many of you!" the second cat, a queen with long, creamy fur, exclaimed, her eyes wide with surprise. Her heavy round belly showed that she was expecting kits.

"Actually, there are more than this," Onewhisker told her. "But Firestar's right: we won't bother you."

"Provided you don't bother us," Mudclaw snarled.

The strange tom fluffed up his neck fur. "Set one paw inside this fence . . ."

"Why would we do that?" Squirrelflight asked, pushing forward with a gleam of curiosity in her green eyes. "We don't live with Twolegs."

"Twolegs?" The long-furred queen looked bewildered.

"The pink creatures who walk on their hindlegs,"

Brambleclaw explained. On their journey to meet Midnight they had discovered that not all cats used the same words. "They live in red stone nests like the one over there," he added, gesturing with his tail to the Twoleg nest on the other side of the horseplace.

"Oh, you mean Nofurs," mewed the queen. "We don't live with them either. We live in the stable with the horses."

Brambleclaw tipped his head to one side, puzzled. It sounded as if these two cats were loners, like Barley and Ravenpaw, who lived in a barn near the old territory. But he couldn't imagine any cats wanting to live this close to a Twoleg nest unless they were kittypets, let alone make their home where they could be crushed under the horses' huge feet.

The gray-and-white tom twitched the tip of his tail. "Move on," he ordered. "We don't want you here."

"There's no need to be unfriendly," Squirrelflight protested, while Mudclaw unsheathed his claws and sank them into the grass. Brambleclaw flexed his shoulders and sank his weight onto his haunches. If the strange tom insisted on being this aggressive, there would be a fight.

A small white WindClan queen flicked out her tail to bar Mudclaw's way. "Calm down," she mewed. "Can't you scent the kits? He's only defending his nursery."

Brambleclaw drew a long breath over his scent glands. Whitetail was right; there were more cats here than the two they could see, including kits.

The creamy brown she-cat looked impressed. "There is

another cat living here," she meowed. "Floss had her kits yesterday. These cats are okay," she added, butting her companion in the shoulder. "I don't think we need to worry about them."

"None of us would hurt kits," Firestar promised.

The tomcat took a step back, his neck fur beginning to lie flat. "Make sure you don't," he rasped. He half turned away, then glanced back. "I'm Smoky, and this is Daisy. And you might want to know that there's a dog in the nest with the Nofurs. Small, black-and-white, very yappy. They usually keep it inside, but sometimes it gets loose."

"Thanks," Firestar replied. "We'll keep a lookout."

Smoky nodded curtly and padded off, jerking his head for Daisy to follow him. She hesitated a moment longer before going after him. Her pale fur faded quickly into the darkness.

"Good-bye!" Squirrelflight called. "See you again sometime!"

The Clan cats set off again, skirting the fence and following the line of the shore until they reached the clump of trees where they had made their temporary camp. ShadowClan and RiverClan were already there, and almost the first cat Brambleclaw spotted was his sister, Tawnypelt. As he headed over to see her, Rainwhisker bounded past him to greet a young warrior from RiverClan.

"Hi, Swallowtail! How's the prey running?"

The dark tabby she-cat flicked an awkward glance toward her Clan leader, Leopardstar, who was sitting a couple of taillengths away. "Fine," she murmured.

Rainwhisker bent down to lick her ears in greeting, then jerked his head back. Embarrassed, he licked his own paw instead and swiped it over his face. "Sorry," he muttered. "I keep forgetting things are different now."

Tawnypelt came up, but after that abrupt reminder of Clan differences Brambleclaw stayed a tail-length away from her and formally dipped his head. "It's good to see you," he meowed.

"And you, mousebrain." Tawnypelt stepped forward to press her muzzle against Brambleclaw's. "This is ridiculous! We've been through far too much together to forget about the past. Sharing memories, and liking each other because of it, doesn't make us traitors to our Clans!"

Brambleclaw blinked. She was right, but he knew that other cats didn't feel the same. A little way off, a group of ShadowClan cats was glaring at them, including Rowanclaw, the one who had attacked him when he accidentally crossed the other Clan's scent markings. As Brambleclaw met his furious gaze, Rowanclaw turned to make a sneering remark to one of his Clanmates. Brambleclaw was too far away to hear, but he could guess it was a long way from being complimentary.

He headed for the tree stump, wanting to find a good place to listen to the leaders. He had gone only a few pawsteps when Hawkfrost appeared. The broad-shouldered tabby warrior looked expectantly at Brambleclaw as if he were waiting for him to speak first.

"Er, hi," Brambleclaw meowed. Moonlight dappled

Hawkfrost's pelt, reminding Brambleclaw sharply of his dream. "How are you settling in?"

Hawkfrost dipped his head. "Fine, thank you." His voice was cool, and Brambleclaw backed away, feeling his pelt prickle. Did Hawkfrost think he was being disloyal to ThunderClan by talking to him?

"Sorry," he muttered. "I just thought—"

Hawkfrost tilted his head with a knowing look in his ice-blue eyes. "Don't worry; I'm not one of the cats who thinks cats from different Clans shouldn't have anything to do with one another. I saw what happened with Tawnypelt," he meowed sympathetically. "It's tough to have loyalties divided. We all have friends in other Clans now, and yet we have to act as if being rivals is the only thing that matters."

Part of Brambleclaw wanted to yowl, *Yes! That's just how I feel.* But he could sense curious gazes burning into him from all sides, so he just mewed quietly, "It's hard to forget what we've been through."

Hawkfrost twitched his tail. "I was just saying the same thing to Mudclaw, actually. He's been telling me about the problems in WindClan."

Brambleclaw stiffened. "What problems?"

"Don't you know?" Hawkfrost's eyes glinted with surprise. "The way Onewhisker won't establish firm boundaries, for starters. According to Mudclaw, he gave a whole slice of territory to ThunderClan in return for some healing herbs."

Brambleclaw narrowed his eyes. It looked like Mudclaw was using anything he could to suggest that Onewhisker wasn't fit to be Clan leader.

"Perhaps Tallstar made a mistake when he chose Onewhisker to follow him," Hawkfrost went on. "It would be a pity for WindClan if their leader wasn't strong enough. Not the best start for their new life."

"I'm sure Onewhisker can be a great leader," Brambleclaw argued, pushing away the memory of Tallstar faltering over the ceremony with his last breath. "There's no reason why WindClan can't be as strong as any Clan in their new home."

"It takes a strong leader to make a strong Clan," meowed Hawkfrost. "Onewhisker hasn't received his name or his nine lives yet. Could that be a sign that he doesn't have StarClan's approval?"

His voice was level, mildly curious rather than hostile, and it was impossible for Brambleclaw to disagree. What if StarClan refused to recognize Onewhisker as WindClan's leader? It was certainly true that they hadn't sent any signs to tell him how to receive his nine lives.

"Mudclaw feels the same," Hawkfrost went on. "He knows his Clanmates need strong leadership now more than any other time. Every cat knows it's hard to fix new boundaries when we've all been living so close together, but if we don't, how will the Clans support themselves? What we decide now will affect every cat for many seasons to come. WindClan could end up starving if Onewhisker doesn't claim enough territory."

This new view of Mudclaw burst on Brambleclaw like a ray of sunlight penetrating the forest canopy. He had started to think that the former deputy cared only about his own ambitions. But Mudclaw had shown as much courage and determination as any cat on the journey. Would he really make a more effective leader than Onewhisker?

"Mudclaw was a very good deputy," Brambleclaw began thoughtfully.

Hawkfrost narrowed his eyes. "Speaking of deputies, when's Firestar going to make you his?"

Brambleclaw scuffed his forepaws among the dead leaves. "There are more experienced warriors—"

Hawkfrost flicked his tail dismissively. "*Older* warriors," he corrected, "but more experienced? I think not. How many of them could have made your journey to the sun-drown-place, and then led us here? You're strong and skillful and you uphold the warrior code. Why shouldn't you be deputy?"

"Firestar has good reasons for not appointing a new deputy," Brambleclaw dodged.

"Are you talking about Graystripe?" Hawkfrost blinked. "Every cat *knows* Graystripe is dead. He'd go down fighting rather than let Twolegs turn him into a kittypet. There's only one reason Firestar won't appoint you deputy, and you know it as well as I do. It's because of who your father was. Because of who *our* father was."

Brambleclaw stared at Hawkfrost, and the sense that he was looking at his reflection swept over him once more: they had the same dark tabby pelt, the same powerful shoulders, the same intensity in their eyes, which differed only in color—ice blue and amber.

"Do you have the same problem in RiverClan?" he whispered.

Hawkfrost shook his head. "No. Tigerstar was never such an enemy to RiverClan. Any trouble I have comes from not being Clanborn. It used to bother me, but now I just look at Firestar. If a kittypet can become Clan leader, so can I."

As he spoke, the flicker of a ginger pelt caught Brambleclaw's eye as Squirrelflight hurtled around the stump. Not looking where she was going, she nearly crashed into him and Hawkfrost, skidding to a halt just in time.

"Sorry, I was looking for—" She broke off as her green gaze took in the cats in front of her. "Oh, it's you," she mewed ungraciously to Hawkfrost.

"Greetings, Squirrelflight." The RiverClan warrior dipped his head politely. "Brambleclaw and I were just discussing WindClan. We're afraid there'll be trouble if Onewhisker doesn't receive his nine lives soon."

Brambleclaw was relieved that Hawkfrost hadn't mentioned his speculations about a new deputy for ThunderClan, but his relief didn't last long. Squirrelflight was gazing at his half brother with undisguised hostility, her neck fur beginning to bristle.

"What's that got to do with RiverClan?" she demanded.

Hawkfrost's ice-blue eyes widened, but he said nothing.

"Of course it matters to RiverClan," Brambleclaw meowed to his Clanmate. "Strong leadership is important to every Clan in the forest."

Squirrelflight's only reply was a snort of disgust. Anything more she might have said was interrupted by Mistyfoot, bounding up to join her Clanmate. "Leopardstar wants you, Hawkfrost," she meowed. "We have to discuss what we're going to report at the Gathering."

"Our final decisions about the boundaries," Hawkfrost explained to Brambleclaw.

"Not just that," mewed Mistyfoot. "Leopardstar wants to tell the other Clans how you and Blackclaw drove off that badger."

Hawkfrost shrugged. "Any cat would have done the same," he meowed, but there was an edge of pride in his voice.

The two cats padded away, leaving Brambleclaw staring after them in shock. Hawkfrost had mentioned the badger in his dream! There was no other way he could have known about it before now. That meant his dream was true, and on some mysterious level, all three of them *had* met together. A shiver ran through him from ears to tail-tip.

He wanted to call Hawkfrost back, but a touch on his shoulder distracted him. Squirrelflight was still standing beside him, her eyes filled with a mixture of anger and dismay.

"Are you just trying to cause trouble?" the ginger she-cat hissed. "You took the side of that . . . that mangy furball instead of mine!"

"It's not about taking sides," Brambleclaw meowed crossly. "Hawkfrost seems like a good warrior to me. You're the one who started to cause trouble."

"Only because every time I turn round I find you talking

to him," Squirrelflight snapped.

"And why shouldn't I?" Brambleclaw felt his neck fur begin to rise. "Hawkfrost's my brother. Can't you see that makes me want to get to know him better? And we're here at a Gathering, in case you hadn't noticed. We're *supposed* to discuss things with cats from other Clans. I can't believe you were so rude to Hawkfrost."

"And I can't believe you would criticize Onewhisker's leadership with him," Squirrelflight retorted. "Onewhisker has always been ThunderClan's friend."

"Are you saying Hawkfrost is our enemy?"

For a few heartbeats Squirrelflight did not reply. The anger in her eyes faded, to be replaced by a look of deep sadness. "All right, I give up," she mewed. "It's not going to work, is it? You and me?"

"What do you mean?" Brambleclaw stared at her in dismay. "Why not?"

"Because I can see exactly where I stand in your life. I'm not as important to you as other cats are—as *Hawkfrost* is."

Brambleclaw opened his jaws to argue, but another voice interrupted him.

"Hey, Squirrelflight! I've saved you a place over here." It was Ashfur, signaling from a few fox-lengths away.

Squirrelflight gave Brambleclaw a last, long look, anger and sadness battling in her gaze, then stalked away to join the gray tom.

Brambleclaw leaped after her. "Squirrelflight, wait! I'd *never* choose another cat over you."

But she didn't look back, and there was no way Brambleclaw was going to chase her all the way over to Ashfur. He wasn't about to give the young warrior the satisfaction of watching them fight.

Behind him, Blackstar jumped onto the tree stump and called for attention. As the cats gathered around, Brambleclaw saw Hawkfrost gazing curiously at him. He didn't want to talk about the dream now. Whatever Squirrelflight said, no cat was more important than her, and he couldn't think about anything except the way she was sitting next to Ashfur, the gray warrior bending down to murmur something in her ear.

Brambleclaw stared past Hawkfrost into the shadows at the edge of the clearing, waves of loss and disbelief surging around him like the churning, choking water of sun-drown-place.

CHAPTER 16

❧

Leafpaw stood at the edge of the clearing and watched the four Clans slip back and forth, cautiously greeting old friends and looking for good places to sit. She wanted to ask Crowfeather how Morningflower was getting on, and if she had eaten the herbs Leafpaw had left for her. She knew he was here, because she had seen him with his Clanmates when ThunderClan and WindClan met beside the horseplace. But he had been padding along with his head down, as if he didn't want to talk to her or any other cat. Now he had vanished. *He couldn't be more annoying if he tried!* Leafpaw thought in frustration.

"Leafpaw! Leafpaw, are you dreaming?"

A paw prodded her in the side. Leafpaw jumped as she realized that Cinderpelt was calling to her. At the same moment she spotted Crowfeather across the clearing.

"Sorry, Cinderpelt," she murmured.

"When the Gathering's over," Cinderpelt meowed, "the medicine cats are going to stay behind."

Leafpaw pricked her ears. "Has one of them had a sign about the new Moonstone?"

"I don't know. Maybe." Then she added more briskly,

"Come on, let's find somewhere to sit. The Gathering will start shortly."

Leafpaw glanced at Crowfeather, wondering if she'd have a chance to speak with him first.

Cinderpelt's gaze followed hers. "Take care where your affections fall, Leafpaw," she warned quietly. "Remember that you are a medicine cat."

"I *do* remember," Leafpaw protested. "You don't think I feel any affection for that bad-tempered furball, do you? Every time we see each other he tries to make trouble. I just wanted to know if Barkface had given Morningflower the rest of the water mint; that's all."

Cinderpelt looked at her with the faintest hint of disbelief in her pale blue eyes before leading the way over to the other cats. Leafpaw trailed behind, thinking furious thoughts about the WindClan warrior. Affection? She hated every last hair on his pelt!

Cinderpelt settled down near the tree stump, hitching her injured leg underneath her. Leafpaw was about to sit down as well when she spotted Squirrelflight padding over to Ashfur. Tingling pulses of distress were coming off her; Leafpaw felt them as painfully as if they were her own.

As Blackstar yowled for silence, Leafpaw darted over and sat down on Squirrelflight's other side. "What's the matter?" she whispered. "Have you fallen out with Brambleclaw again?"

"Don't mention his name! It's over between us!"

Leafpaw stared at her. "Tell me what happened," she mewed.

"He was talking to Hawkfrost. He actually stood up for him—a warrior from another Clan! Why won't he listen to me when I tell him that cat can't be trusted?"

"Is that all?"

"What do you mean, is that all?" Squirrelflight lashed her tail. "I've told him you *know* Hawkfrost is untrustworthy, but he won't take any notice. It all comes down to trust, and Brambleclaw obviously trusts Hawkfrost more than me. How can we be together, if that's how he feels?"

Leafpaw felt totally helpless. She was a medicine cat— what did she know about relationships like this? She could understand why Squirrelflight might feel hurt if Brambleclaw preferred spending time with Hawkfrost rather than her, but she was puzzled by the way Squirrelflight seemed so quick to reject Brambleclaw altogether. She pressed her muzzle comfortingly against her sister's. "Don't forget they're half brothers. It's natural for them to enjoy each other's company now and then."

Squirrelflight's green eyes flashed in the moonlight. "This is about *trust*! I don't care that Tigerstar was their father. This is about much more than shared blood!"

Blood . . . The word echoed in Leafpaw's ears, and she recoiled. *Blood will spill blood, and the lake will run red.* She had forgotten about her terrible dream, but now it flooded back into her mind, the water lapping thick and slow like a seeping wound. What did it mean? Whose blood would be spilled?

She looked around for Cinderpelt, desperate to ask her about it, but Firestar, Blackstar, and Leopardstar were standing on the tree stump, ready to begin. Leafpaw had to settle down beside her sister, trying to send wordless comfort to her through the warmth of her fur.

Onewhisker ran over to the stump, but when he tried to leap up his paws slipped and he fell back awkwardly. There wasn't room for four cats to stand up there together. Firestar and Leopardstar exchanged an uncomfortable glance, but Blackstar meowed roughly, "Stay down there, Onewhisker. We must get on with the Gathering."

Onewhisker sat among the roots and bent his head to lick the ruffled fur on his chest.

"It looks as if he isn't a proper leader," Squirrelflight mewed.

"I know," Leafpaw agreed quietly. "The sooner we find another Moonstone the better, so he can receive his nine lives and his name."

Blackstar addressed the Gathering first. "As we agreed before, we have set our boundary markers along the small Thunderpath leading to the lake," he announced. "Leopardstar, I hope that suits you?" His gaze bored into the RiverClan leader as if he were daring her to argue.

Leopardstar dipped her head. "Perfectly, thank you, Blackstar."

Blackstar looked surprised, and for a moment Leafpaw couldn't understand why Leopardstar was being so cooperative. Squirrelflight had told her the small Thunderpath wasn't all that far from RiverClan's camp. The new boundaries had been only roughly agreed upon at the previous meeting, and she thought Leopardstar might have tried to extend her territory. Then she realized that if the Thunderpath were left as the boundary, the Twoleg half-bridge and the little nest Squirrelflight had described to her would be in ShadowClan territory. If the Twolegs caused any trouble it would be ShadowClan's problem.

"Our boundary with ThunderClan has been scent-marked as well," the ShadowClan leader went on. "We have claimed the territory as far as the stream that flows into the lake, and farther away from the lake, as far as the dead tree on the other side of the stream."

"I think it would make more sense to make the stream the boundary all along the border," Firestar meowed calmly.

"It would make more sense to ThunderClan, maybe," Blackstar retorted. "But the stream curves sharply at the end of the clearing, veering deeper into our territory, and there are pine trees on both banks. Scent marks are scent marks, Firestar. If you don't like where we have set them, you should have been quicker with your own."

The ThunderClan leader gave Blackstar a long look. At last he bent his head.

"Very well," he mewed. "But ThunderClan has set scent markers on a line stretching from the dead tree to a tall holly and then to an abandoned fox den under a white rock. Set one pawstep past that boundary, and ThunderClan will have something to say."

"That sounds fair," Ashfur mewed. "Firestar certainly knows the new territory!"

"For our other border," Firestar went on, looking down at Onewhisker, "I suggest that we stick to our first idea of using the stream that runs at the bottom of the hill. That way, cats of both Clans will have access to the water."

"Good idea," Leafpaw murmured.

"I don't understand why Firestar's worried about water." Squirrelflight twitched her whiskers. "With the lake right outside our dens, we're hardly going to get thirsty."

"I think you're missing the point," Leafpaw told her. "If Firestar agrees to make the stream our boundary, it means WindClan gets back the stretch of woodland Onewhisker gave to us."

Squirrelflight blinked. "So this is Firestar's way of turning him down, without making it look as if Onewhisker were being too generous in the first place?"

Leafpaw nodded.

"Thanks, Firestar." Onewhisker sounded relieved, although it was impossible to tell whether that was because he wanted to be able to hunt in the trees, or because he knew this would satisfy his more restless warriors. "That's fine by us. And we'll take the fence on the far side of the horseplace as our other border."

"That leaves the rest of the territory for RiverClan," meowed Leopardstar.

"Except for where we are now," Firestar warned. "This place should belong to no Clan, so that we have somewhere to gather."

The RiverClan leader's eyes narrowed. "You're very eager

to give part of my territory away," she rasped.

For once Blackstar supported Firestar. "We have to gather *somewhere*, and there isn't anywhere else with enough room for all of us."

"This is obviously RiverClan territory," Leopardstar insisted. "There are important herbs growing in these marshes."

Firestar touched her shoulder with his tail. "Leopardstar, our medicine cats hope that StarClan will show us a better place to gather. Give up your claim for now, and maybe by next full moon you will be able to treat all this as yours."

Leopardstar hesitated, then responded with a curt nod. "For now, RiverClan will let the four Clans gather here," she meowed. "But if there is no sign from StarClan within two moons, we will have to think again."

Firestar went on to tell the other Clans how ThunderClan was settling in, proudly adding that they had already made a new warrior. "Spiderleg keeps his vigil tonight," he finished.

A shadow fell across the clearing. Leafpaw looked up to see that a cloud had drifted over the moon: not thick enough to hide it completely, but enough to make the night seem dark and eerie. A cold, damp wind swept off the lake, ruffling fur and rattling the branches overhead. Leafpaw noticed some of the cats around her shift uneasily and glance over their shoulders.

"This isn't like Fourtrees," Ashfur muttered. "We felt safe there."

"StarClan is with us, wherever we are," Leafpaw reminded

him, but her words didn't seem to reassure him or the other cats.

"Onewhisker?" Firestar prompted. "Do you have anything to report? Come up here so we can all hear you." He jumped down so Onewhisker could take his place on the stump.

"We are settling into our camp," Onewhisker began.

"Speak up—we can't hear you." The testy interruption came from Heavystep, a RiverClan elder.

"And you won't, if you can't keep quiet." To Leafpaw's surprise it was Mudclaw who sprang up to defend Onewhisker. "Listen to what our leader has to say."

Heavystep shot a baleful glare at Mudclaw but said nothing.

Onewhisker started again. "Two of our elders were ill, but they are making a good recovery. We thank ThunderClan for the help they sent us."

"He shouldn't have mentioned that," Leafpaw whispered in Squirrelflight's ear. "It makes it sound as if WindClan can't cope without ThunderClan."

"Maybe they can't," Squirrelflight muttered dryly.

Over Squirrelflight's shoulder, Leafpaw glimpsed something moving in the shadows under the trees. Her pelt prickled with a sense of danger close by. The other cats noticed it too, and half the cats sprang to their paws with their claws extended as two lithe shapes slid out of the darkness. *Foxes!*

They crept closer, undaunted by the number of cats in the clearing; Leafpaw saw the gleam of their teeth as they drew their lips back in a snarl. With a fierce yowl, Dustpelt hurled himself at one of them. The fox whirled around, snapping at him, but Dustpelt was too fast, clawing its side and darting away out of range of the pointed snout. Rainwhisker, Hawkfrost, and Russetfur raced over to join him, and behind them more cats padded forward in a snarling, bristling line.

Outmatched, the two foxes turned tail and fled, with Dustpelt and a few others hard on their paws. Leafpaw stared into the darkness, her heart pounding, until one by one the cats returned. To her relief, none of them was injured.

Dustpelt padded up to the tree stump, flexing his claws. "They won't be so curious next time."

One or two cats congratulated him, but most were still uneasy, peering around into the shadows as if they expected the foxes to come back. Leafpaw looked up at the sky, clearly visible above the sparse thicket of trees, and wished desperately that they could be back at Fourtrees. They had felt safe there, under the shelter of the four giant oaks, knowing their warrior ancestors had trodden the same ground for uncountable seasons. There was no sign that their ancestors had ever walked in this place.

"Right," Blackstar meowed. "Let's end this Gathering and go home before anything else happens. Unless any other cat wants to speak?"

There was no reply. The cats began dividing into their Clans. There was none of the usual gossip and leave-taking; every cat wanted to be on their way quickly.

"I have to stay behind," Leafpaw told Squirrelflight. "There's a meeting of medicine cats."

"Will you be okay?" Squirrelflight asked. "Those foxes might be back."

"Would you come back if Dustpelt had clawed you?"

Squirrelflight brushed Leafpaw's ear with the tip of her tail. "Fair point, but be careful, all the same."

Ashfur was waiting for her, and the two cats raced off side by side toward the lake. For once, Squirrelflight didn't wait to see where Brambleclaw was. Leafpaw saw the tabby warrior a moment later. He had stopped to watch Hawkfrost gathering some RiverClan cats together. With an icy feeling in her fur, Leafpaw wondered if Squirrelflight was right when she accused him of being obsessed with his kin.

She felt a light touch on her side. Mothwing was standing next to her.

"Come on. We're meeting over there."

Briefly Leafpaw held her back with a wave of her tail. "Are your elders okay?" she asked in a low voice.

Guilt flooded into Mothwing's eyes. "Yes, but I'm so sorry, Leafpaw. I should have checked that water more carefully."

"It wasn't your fault." Leafpaw brushed against her comfortingly. "How could you smell the water when you were covered in mouse bile? Everything's fine now, and it just meant we had to find new supplies of herbs more quickly than we might have done. That's a good thing."

Mothwing didn't look convinced. She led Leafpaw to the brambles where the medicine cats had met before, when they first arrived at the lake. Cinderpelt and Barkface were already crouched on a bed of dead leaves, dry and sheltered by the wind-ruffled branches. Mothwing and Leafpaw crept in to join them, and a moment later Littlecloud appeared.

"If there are any more wandering foxes, they won't find it easy to get at us here," he remarked as he ducked underneath a bramble to sit beside Cinderpelt.

Barkface, as the oldest medicine cat among them, began the meeting. "That incident with the foxes made it clear we need a better place to gather. We also have to find somewhere like the Moonstone where we can share tongues with StarClan. Have any of you had a sign?"

All the cats shook their heads.

"The Moonstone is more urgent," Cinderpelt pointed out. "Unless Leopardstar changes her mind, we don't need to worry about a gathering place for another moon, but Onewhisker needs his name and his nine lives now."

"StarClan *knows* what we need," Littlecloud murmured. "Perhaps they're trying to tell us, and we're not recognizing their signs."

"And perhaps hedgehogs will fly," Barkface retorted. "Do you think we wouldn't know if StarClan had sent us a sign about something as important as this?"

"Well, maybe there isn't a Moonstone place around here," Mothwing meowed.

Leafpaw winced as Barkface gave her friend a withering look. "If there isn't, then this is not the place StarClan intends us to stay. Do you want to tell all the Clans they have to move somewhere else?"

Mothwing looked down at her paws.

"All the same," Cinderpelt meowed, "that might be exactly what we have to do if we don't have a sign soon. The Clans cannot survive without a place to share tongues with Star-Clan."

"Perhaps this isn't where StarClan means us to be after all," Littlecloud ventured quietly.

Barkface curled his lip. "If we tell the Clans they have to leave, many cats will refuse. What would we do then?"

Guilt gnawed at Leafpaw. Her sister had been among the cats who had led the Clans through the mountains to this place, and she had been the one to interpret the starlight reflected in the lake as a sign that StarClan was waiting for them. Had they been wrong all along?

"Perhaps StarClan wants us to go and *look* for signs?" she suggested.

Cinderpelt nodded. "You could be right, Leafpaw. We must keep a careful watch until we meet at the half-moon."

"And ask patrols to keep a lookout for tunnels like Mothermouth," Barkface added. "If they find anything, their medicine cat can send a message to the rest of us."

"Good idea," mewed Cinderpelt.

"If that's all, we might as well go home," Barkface rasped. "I just want to thank Leafpaw for the help she gave our elders when they were sick. They're doing fine now."

Leafpaw dipped her head.

"Were your elders sick?" Littlecloud asked. "A couple of ours were, too. They must have picked up a bellyache while we were all together. Mothwing, have you had any trouble in RiverClan?"

Mothwing flashed a glance at Leafpaw. "Yes."

"Well, don't give us any details, will you?" Barkface growled. "Are your elders okay or not? What did you treat them with?"

"Juniper berries. And yes, they're fine, thanks, Barkface."

Barkface nodded and got up to leave. When the medicine cats wriggled out of the brambles, Mothwing flicked her tail to draw Leafpaw a little way from the others.

"Thanks for not telling them, Leafpaw," she mewed.

"That's okay." Leafpaw could imagine how Mousefur would react if she found out she had been ill because another cat had fed her tainted water.

Mothwing gave her a long look from troubled blue eyes. "Leafpaw, we are friends, aren't we?"

"Of course we are," Leafpaw answered in surprise.

Mothwing hesitated, flexing her claws into the ground. At last she took a deep breath and mewed, "What Cinderpelt said—about watching for signs from StarClan. You do know I won't get any, don't you?"

"What are you talking about? You're the RiverClan medicine cat! Who else is StarClan going to speak to?"

"Stop pretending, Leafpaw." Mothwing's tail twitched impatiently. "To me, StarClan, our warrior ancestors, these signs we're supposed to interpret—they're nothing but a bunch of stories to keep the Clans happy."

Leafpaw stared at her friend in horror. *How could you be a medicine cat and not believe in StarClan?* "B-but you shared tongues with StarClan at the Moonstone, when you were made a medicine cat!" she stammered.

Mothwing lifted her shoulders in a shrug. "I had a dream, that's all. Don't look so shocked," she added. "It's not the end of the world. I can heal my Clan just as well as any medicine cat. I don't need StarClan to tell me which herb to use."

Leafpaw opened her mouth to tell Mothwing about the signs she had received, and her precious encounters with Spottedleaf, the former ThunderClan medicine cat, while she slept. Then she realized that Mothwing would dismiss those as dreams, too.

"Come on, Leafpaw," Mothwing went on. "You said just now that we have to go out and look for our own signs. Why would we need to do that if StarClan is sending them to us?"

"Well . . . yes. But that's not the *point*. Looking for signs isn't the same as making them up."

Mothwing flicked her ears. "It doesn't sound all that different to me."

Leafpaw felt the ground sway beneath her paws. Mothwing was questioning everything she had believed since she was a kit. But it was impossible to defend, when everything she knew about StarClan, all the encounters she had had with them, were inside her own head.

"It's *not* the same," she insisted. "That's what faith in StarClan means—to go on searching, and believing, even when there aren't any signs. We won't know for certain that they are really there and watching over us until it's our time to go and walk with StarClan."

Mothwing shook her head. "I'm sorry, Leafpaw. It's not like that for me. Maybe it's because my mother was a rogue. I can be a loyal RiverClan cat without believing all the myths about our warrior ancestors."

"But what about your moth's-wing sign?" Leafpaw prompted. At first, Mothwing had struggled to be accepted as a medicine cat because her mother had not been Clanborn. When she was still being considered as an apprentice, Mudfur, the previous RiverClan medicine cat, had found a moth's wing lying outside his den; he had taken it as a sign from StarClan that Mothwing was the right cat to succeed him, and she had begun her apprenticeship. "You can't say that didn't come from StarClan," Leafpaw insisted.

"The moth's wing?" There was a flash of something like fear in Mothwing's eyes. "That was—"

"Leafpaw! Are you coming?" Cinderpelt called.

Leafpaw waved her tail in reply; she wanted to hear what Mothwing was about to tell her.

But the RiverClan cat had turned away. "Cinderpelt wants you," she meowed. "I'll see you at the next half-moon." Before Leafpaw could say anything, she bounded away.

Leafpaw padded over to join her mentor as they made their way back to the lakeshore. Mothwing didn't believe in StarClan! She had always known Mothwing struggled with some parts of being a medicine cat, but she had thought it was just because she found it hard to learn all the different healing herbs. She had never dreamed her friend simply didn't believe in their warrior ancestors.

Every hair on Leafpaw's pelt stood on end. Should she tell Cinderpelt? Would it make any difference? Fear stalked her like a fox as another, even more dreadful thought came to her: had StarClan been silent because they knew that one of the medicine cats didn't believe in them? Was Mothwing's lack of faith putting all four Clans in danger of losing their new home?

Leafpaw let out a long sigh.

"Is everything okay?" Cinderpelt asked.

Leafpaw gulped. She didn't want her mentor to start asking questions about Mothwing. "Yes, fine, thanks," she replied.

"That sigh wasn't anything to do with a certain WindClan warrior, was it?"

Leafpaw blinked. "No, it wasn't," she retorted. "Nothing to do with a certain WindClan warrior at all!"

Cinderpelt's eyes glinted but she said nothing more. Leafpaw gazed at the starshine reflected in the lake and forced herself to see it with Mothwing's eyes, as nothing more than specks of light. A shiver rippled through her from whiskers to tail-tip. *No!* She had to trust that her warrior ancestors had meant the Clans to come to this place.

StarClan, show us we are meant to be here, she prayed, but if any of the shining spirits replied, she did not hear them.

CHAPTER 17

In the days following the Gathering, Leafpaw searched desperately for anything that could be interpreted as a sign from StarClan. She roamed through the woods, finding places by the stream where burdock and marigold grew, and thick clumps of chervil closer to the camp. But even though it was useful to find new stocks of healing herbs, they didn't lead her to a place where the Clans could meet with their warrior ancestors. What would happen if the half moon came and StarClan hadn't sent a sign? Would the Clans really have to think about leaving their new homes, and finding somewhere else?

Two days before the half moon, Leafpaw returned from an herb-gathering expedition with a bunch of strong-scented yarrow. Her eyes were watering, but she recognized Brackenfur coming out of the tunnel through the thorns. He bounded up to Sorreltail, who was on guard.

"Hi, there," he meowed, touching noses with the tortoise-shell warrior. "Do you want to come hunting later—just you and me?"

Sorreltail let out a purr. "Sure. I'm off duty at sunhigh."

"Great! I'll see you then." Brackenfur gave her ears a quick lick and pushed his way back through the tunnel.

Leafpaw padded up to her friend and put down the yarrow stalks. "So that's how the prey's running, is it?"

Sorreltail spun around to face her. "I don't know what you mean!" she protested.

Leafpaw's tail curled up with amusement. "Just because I'm a medicine cat doesn't mean I can't tell Brackenfur likes you."

"Well . . ." Sorreltail's white forepaws kneaded the ground. "He's great, isn't he?" she mewed, her eyes shining with a mixture of pride and embarrassment.

"He certainly is." Leafpaw pressed her muzzle to her friend's side. "I'm really happy for you."

She wished Sorreltail good hunting, then picked up her yarrow and ducked under the thorns that guarded the entrance to the hollow.

"There you are!" Cinderpelt meowed, limping across the clearing to meet her. "Come and look at this."

Leafpaw followed her over to the tallest part of the cliff. Brambles had rooted themselves in a crack a few tail-lengths up the rock, their long tendrils hanging down in a curtain.

"The brambles here were really thorny," Cinderpelt explained. "Far too thick for shelter, so this morning I asked Rainwhisker and Sootfur to shift them. And look what they found."

She slipped behind the prickly curtain, beckoning with her tail. Leafpaw peered carefully around the tendrils and

WARRIORS: THE NEW PROPHECY: STARLIGHT   255

stopped dead in amazement. A deep cleft yawned in front of her, stretching far enough back that the corners were lost in shadow. At one side water dripped down to form a tiny pool. The rest of the floor was covered with broken rock, but in between there were patches of sand that would be cool and dry to lie on.

Cinderpelt's eyes gleamed in the semidarkness. "A perfect medicine cat's den!" she announced. "What do you think?"

Leafpaw gazed around. This was much better than the spot under the overhang where she and Cinderpelt had been sleeping until now. The little pool meant sick cats could drink easily, and there were plenty of cracks in the rock where they could store herbs. She could sleep just outside in the shelter of the remaining brambles, so Cinderpelt had some privacy at night.

"It's great!" she mewed excitedly. "I'll clear out the broken rocks and bring some moss for a nest."

Cinderpelt called Firestar to see her discovery, and the Clan leader summoned Cloudtail and Brightheart to help clear out the den. By the time daylight faded everything was ready, with comfortable nests of moss and bracken for both the medicine cats.

Leafpaw curled up in her new nest and tucked her nose under her tail. She was warm and sheltered beneath the tangle of brambles, and the cleft was barely a tail-length away, so she could be with a sick cat in less than two heartbeats if they called out during the night. Worn out from moving rocks all afternoon, she shut her eyes.

Almost at once she found herself padding along the shore

of the lake with starlight washing around her paws. A few tail-lengths ahead, a lean, gray-black shape was standing on a rock, gazing down into the glittering water. It was Crowfeather.

"Feathertail?" Leafpaw heard him murmur as she approached. "Feathertail, where are you?"

Leafpaw jumped onto the rock beside him, gently brushing her fur against his. When he turned to look at her, his eyes were brimming with sorrow.

"Feathertail is here, among the stars," she told him gently. "She's always with you, Crowfeather, watching over you."

"Why did she have to die?" he whispered. His eyes burned into hers, and Leafpaw felt as if a thorn had pierced her heart.

"I don't know," she admitted.

A beautiful sweet scent swept over her, and she looked back to see Spottedleaf waiting for her.

"I must go," she mewed, turning away from the gray warrior.

Crowfeather didn't reply. He was staring down at the water again, as if he could find the one star among all of them that was Feathertail's endlessly shining spirit.

Leafpaw bounded along the shore toward the medicine cat. "Spottedleaf!" she cried. She stopped, sending pebbles rolling away from her paws, and gazed at Spottedleaf until she felt lost in the medicine cat's shining eyes. "I was afraid I'd never see you again."

"I am here now," Spottedleaf murmured. She ran her muzzle, soft as cobweb, over Leafpaw's ears.

Leafpaw closed her eyes and drank in the familiar scent.

Then she stepped back and took a deep, steadying breath. "Why has StarClan been silent?" she asked, struggling with unfamiliar feelings of anger that Spottedleaf had let her go on worrying for so long. "We have searched and searched for another Moonstone, but we haven't found one. What will we do if we don't have somewhere to share tongues with StarClan? Will we have to leave?"

"Peace, little one," Spottedleaf mewed. "Don't forget that StarClan had to travel here too. This is a new place for us as well, and it will take time to explore every part of it. But starlight on water will show you where to go."

"Do you mean the lake?"

"No. You must seek a different path this time."

"Where? Please show me!" Leafpaw begged.

Spottedleaf turned and bounded away. "Wait!" Leafpaw called, but the beautiful medicine cat had already been swallowed up by the shadows.

Leafpaw raced after her. Suddenly the lake vanished and she was running uphill beside a starlit stream; even though she couldn't see Spottedleaf, the sweet scent hung in the air, guiding her on. Leafpaw's ears filled with the sound of tumbling, sparkling water, and when she looked down into the stream she felt as if she would drown in starlight.

"Spottedleaf, where are you?"

Her cry echoed around her, bouncing off the rocks and shattering the noise of the waterfall. Leafpaw woke up, gasping and scrabbling in her mossy nest. An owl hooted in the trees overhead, and she let out a hiss of frustration. She had lost Spottedleaf's trail and might never find out what the medicine cat had wanted to show her. Her heart pounded with the urge to keep running, to climb into the hills and find the sparkling stream.

Peering into the cleft she could just see the gray curve of Cinderpelt's back, her flank gently rising and falling as she slept. Leafpaw slipped out of the brambles and paused to shake scraps of moss from her fur. It had rained heavily earlier and the walls of the hollow sparkled with raindrops, but now the clouds had cleared away. The moon floated out from behind the trees, and the sky was filled with stars. A cool wind stirred the branches, and Leafpaw heard Spottedleaf's voice among the gentle rustling: "I am here. Come to me."

I will come, Spottedleaf, she replied silently. *Wait for me.*

She padded quietly toward the camp entrance. When she was halfway across the clearing, a tortoiseshell shape appeared from behind some ferns. Leafpaw caught her breath. "Spottedleaf? Is that you?"

"Leafpaw?" came the surprised reply. It was Sorreltail. "Where are you going?"

"I-I'm not sure," Leafpaw admitted. "I've had a message from StarClan. I have to go and find our new Moonstone place."

"Now? Can't you wait for daylight?"

"No." Leafpaw flexed her claws. "I have to follow a stream filled with starlight."

"What stream?" Sorreltail's tail twitched anxiously. "Is it outside our territory? How do you know where to find it?"

"I just do."

"Then I'm coming with you," Sorreltail mewed.

Leafpaw hesitated. Would StarClan mind if she brought a warrior with her, rather than another medicine cat? Then she remembered that all the cats, including warriors, would go to the Moonstone at least once, and she decided that it would be fine. Besides, she liked the thought of having Sorreltail's company, especially if they ran into any trouble. She didn't know exactly where they were going, after all.

"Come on, then!" Leafpaw led the way to the thorn tunnel, where Brackenfur sat on guard with his tail curled neatly around his paws.

"Where are you two going?" he asked, getting up as the two she-cats approached.

"Just out," Sorreltail replied.

"I've had a sign from StarClan," Leafpaw mewed, knowing that Brackenfur deserved an explanation if he was going to let them leave camp in the middle of the night. "I have to go and find the new Moonstone."

To her dismay Brackenfur still looked uncertain. "It's too dangerous for you to go off before daylight. We hardly know this territory yet."

"Can't you trust us?" Sorreltail pleaded. "Can't you trust *me*? I'll bring Leafpaw home safe, I promise."

She and Brackenfur exchanged a long look, and at last the ginger warrior nodded. "Okay, but be careful."

"Don't you think we can look after ourselves?" Sorreltail mewed, flicking Brackenfur lightly across the ears with her tail.

Brackenfur let out an amused purr. "Sorreltail, if any cat can look after herself, it's you."

Leafpaw took the lead, racing through the forest until she came to the stream that marked the boundary between ThunderClan and WindClan. It ran dark and secret, shadowed by bushes on overhanging banks and looking nothing like the sparkling stream she had run beside in her dream.

Leafpaw bounded up the slope and stopped at the edge of the trees. In her dream she had been running on open hillside, so she knew they had to leave the trees behind.

"Where next?" Sorreltail panted.

"Up," Leafpaw replied.

They padded onward, following the boundary stream out of the woods and up the hill. When Leafpaw closed her eyes, she felt as if two cats flanked her, one on each side: her best friend Sorreltail, and Spottedleaf, invisible but for the faintest brush of fur and a hint of her sweet scent. When Leafpaw opened her eyes, she thought she could hear a third set of pawsteps, just on the edge of sound.

As they followed the stream into the hills, Leafpaw decided to tell Sorreltail about her dream. "I met Spottedleaf at the edge of the lake, and she told me that starlight on water would be the sign. Not in the lake, but in a stream. The next moment I was running uphill beside a stream, and the water was full of stars."

"Did you know where you were?"

"I couldn't see anything I recognized. There were no trees,

and the air felt cold and clear, as if I were somewhere very high."

"We'd better keep climbing, then," Sorreltail meowed.

The stream slid quietly over its stony bed, the water dark and glimmering. Leafpaw's head was still full of the surge and bubbling of the stream Spottedleaf had shown her. As they went on it seemed to grow steadily louder, even when they reached the source of the boundary stream and left it far behind.

"I'm coming, Spottedleaf," murmured Leafpaw.

They came to a cleft in the hills, where the land dipped down as if sliced by a giant claw. The valley was lined with gorse and bracken, and it grew steeper and narrower as they went on, the ground littered with broken rocks. Leafpaw reached the end of the valley first, where it led to a sheer, rocky slope. She stopped to wait for Sorreltail, whose tail was beginning to droop with weariness, though she still padded on determinedly. But Leafpaw felt as though she could run forever. The sound in her head roared and tumbled like the waterfall in the mountains where the Tribe of Rushing Water lived. She had grown so used to hearing it echo in her mind that for several heartbeats she didn't realize she could hear it in the waking world too.

"Come on!" she cried to Sorreltail. "We're almost there!"

She launched herself upward, scrabbling and slipping on the damp rock. The peak above her was outlined by the first faint signs of dawn, but stars still shone in the indigo sky.

Wait for me! she begged the glittering warriors. Glancing back at Sorreltail, she called, "Hurry—before the starshine fades!"

She turned to run on, and froze. A cat was standing a few tail-lengths above her, her ears pricked and her tail held high. Had one of the other medicine cats been guided to this place too? Then she realized it was Spottedleaf, waiting patiently for her, trusting her to find this place even though she had lost her in the dream.

When Leafpaw leaped up to join her, she saw that she stood on the bank of a stream pouring down a deep channel in the rock. Starlight glittered on the surface of the water as it spilled over the stones.

"We're here!" Leafpaw breathed. "We've found it!"

"Follow me," Spottedleaf urged.

Leafpaw beckoned Sorreltail with her tail. "Quick! Spottedleaf's here!"

The tortoiseshell warrior joined Leafpaw in a couple of bounds and looked around. "Where?"

"There!" Leafpaw gestured to the starlit shape standing a couple of tail-lengths away on the edge of the stream.

"I can't see her," Sorreltail meowed. She looked worriedly at Leafpaw. "Is that a problem?"

Leafpaw gently drew her tail over Sorreltail's eyes. "No, of course not. She can see that you are here, and that's all that matters. Trust me, she is with us."

Spottedleaf turned away and began to follow the stream upward. Leafpaw scrambled eagerly after her. The ground sloped more steeply than before, and the starlit stream vanished among a barrier of thornbushes that swallowed

Spottedleaf like a fish diving into water.

Leafpaw stopped and put her head to one side as she studied the bushes. She had to follow Spottedleaf, but she'd be clawed to pieces by thorns if she tried to push her way through. Then she spotted a tiny gap and ducked between the prickly stems; there was just enough room to squeeze through without losing half her fur, though the thorns still tugged at her pelt. Behind her she could hear Sorreltail following, her breath rasping with the effort of running up the last stretch of rock.

A heartbeat later Leafpaw emerged on the edge of a steep-sided hollow. The ground fell sharply away on the other side of the thornbushes, and Leafpaw swayed for a moment as she struggled to keep her balance. It was much smaller than the hollow where ThunderClan had made their camp, clear of gorse and bramble and with sides that sloped more gently, lined with moss-covered rocks. Only on the far side did the ground rise into a sheer cliff, shaggy with moss and fern. Water bubbled out from a cleft about halfway up and splashed into a pool in the center of the hollow. The surface of the pool danced and glittered with reflected starlight. It was the most beautiful place Leafpaw had ever seen.

Spottedleaf was standing at the edge of the water. "Come," she meowed, beckoning with her tail.

Just beside Leafpaw's paws a narrow path curved around the side of the hollow, spiraling steadily down until it reached the pool below.

She heard Sorreltail push her way out of the thorns behind

her. "Wow!" she breathed. "Is this it?"

"I think so," Leafpaw replied. "Spottedleaf wants me to go down to the pool."

"Shall I come too?" Sorreltail offered.

Leafpaw shook her head. "I think I should go alone the first time."

Leaving Sorreltail on the edge of the hollow, she stepped carefully down the path. The rock was dimpled with ancient pawprints, too many to count, and with each step she felt her paws slip into the marks left by cats many, many moons before. They were long gone, but Leafpaw's fur tingled just to know they once had been here.

At last she stood beside Spottedleaf at the edge of the pool.

"Look at the water, Leafpaw," the ghostly cat murmured.

Puzzled, Leafpaw looked down, and felt the stone beneath her paws lurch. Instead of stars she saw the reflections of many, many cats, their moonlit pelts shimmering. Countless pairs of eyes gleamed expectantly at her, as if they had known she would come.

Hardly daring to breathe, Leafpaw looked up. All around her sat the shining warriors of StarClan, lining the hollow's sloping sides. Their eyes glowed like tiny moons, and their fur was tipped with the glitter of frost.

"Don't be afraid," Spottedleaf murmured. "We have been waiting for you to find your way to us."

Leafpaw wasn't afraid. She was conscious of nothing but warmth and goodwill in the starry gazes fixed on her. Most of the warriors were unfamiliar to her, but in one of the front rows she saw Dappletail, the ThunderClan elder who had died from eating a rabbit poisoned by the Twolegs. The she-cat looked graceful and beautiful, not thin and desperate as she had been when Leafpaw last saw her. Her eyes glowed with welcome, and she nodded toward two small shapes near the water's edge, tumbling together as they chased a shaft of moonlight. As their play brought them close to her Leafpaw drank in their sweet kit scent. With a stab of joy, she recognized Hollykit and Larchkit, who had starved when Twolegs destroyed the forest. A half-grown cat reached out with a paw to nudge the starry kits away from the water's edge: it was their brother Shrewpaw, the apprentice struck by a Twoleg monster as he tried to hunt for their Clan.

I must tell Ferncloud, thought Leafpaw, knowing how happy their mother would be to know that her three kits were safe in the ranks of StarClan.

Then she realized that one cat was missing. She ran her gaze quickly around the hollow to make sure. There was no sign of Graystripe. Leafpaw's heart leaped. Did that mean that Firestar was right when he insisted that his friend was still alive?

Across the pool, a blue-gray warrior rose to her paws. She reminded Leafpaw of some cat. . . . *Of course, she's the image of Mistyfoot!* This must be Bluestar, Mistyfoot's mother, and ThunderClan's leader before Firestar.

"Welcome, Leafpaw," Bluestar meowed. "We are delighted to welcome you here. This is where medicine cats must come to share tongues with StarClan, and where your leaders will receive their nine lives and their names."

"It's beautiful, Bluestar," Leafpaw whispered. "Thank you for sending Spottedleaf to help me find it."

"You must go back and tell all the Clans," Bluestar continued. "But first there is a friend who wants to speak to you."

A beautiful silver-gray cat left the ranks of cats and padded around the pool toward Leafpaw.

"Feathertail!"

The radiant warrior came to a halt in front of her. She touched noses with her, a caress light as a breeze whispering against Leafpaw's muzzle.

"I thought we left you with the Tribe of Endless Hunting," Leafpaw meowed.

Feathertail shook her head. "I walk in two skies now, with the Tribe's ancestors as well as my own. But wherever I am, I shall never forget the Clans." She hesitated for a moment, then added, "Especially Crowfeather."

"He misses you very much. He chose his warrior name for you."

"Yes, I was watching," Feathertail purred. "I was so proud. He will make a great warrior." She bent close to Leafpaw again, her warm breath stirring the apprentice's fur. "Tell him not to grieve. I will always love him, but there will be many, many moons before we meet again. For now, he must live with his Clanmates in their new home. He cannot be blind to the cats who are around him for all that time."

"I'll tell him," Leafpaw promised.

Feathertail dipped her head and turned away, starlight dappling her silver pelt. The warriors began to fade until they were little more than a starry sheen around the slopes of the hollow, and then they were gone. Leafpaw caught one more breath of Spottedleaf's scent before that faded too.

She looked up and saw that the sky was growing brighter. Sorreltail was standing at the top of the hollow, looking down at her.

Leafpaw ran up the path to join her. "Did you see them?" she asked excitedly.

Sorreltail tipped her head on one side. "See who?"

"StarClan! They were here, all around the hollow! I spoke to Bluestar, and Feathertail!" Leafpaw trailed off when she saw that Sorreltail was looking bewildered, and a little wary.

"I saw a bright mist rising from the pool," she mewed hesitantly.

"That must have been them," Leafpaw told her. She gazed around the hollow with the sound of tumbling starlit water filling her ears. "This is the place."

"Are you sure?"

At that moment the rays of the moon caught the surface of the water, and a pure white light flooded the hollow.

"Yes, I'm sure," Leafpaw mewed. "We no longer have the Moonstone—but we have the Moonpool. This is the place where StarClan will share tongues with us." She turned to Sorreltail, feeling her fur glitter with starlight.

"We've found it! This is where the Clans are meant to be."

CHAPTER 18

Brambleclaw kept his ears pricked for the sound of prey as he slipped through the undergrowth. He could hear Thornclaw and Dustpelt padding close behind him, their bellies close to the ground as they ducked under the bracken. Brambleclaw tried to tell himself he didn't mind that Squirrelflight was not with them. Feeding the Clan and exploring the new territory was more important right now. If Squirrelflight was determined to fight with him, that was her problem. She had never worried about his connection with Tawnypelt, so why was she getting so worked up about Hawkfrost?

The patrol emerged from the bracken and padded along the edge of a broad Twoleg path. This was the farthest a patrol had been from the camp. Until now, they had been busy organizing the dens and barriers in the hollow, and they had found enough prey close by to feed every cat. Now they were beginning to range farther, cautiously exploring the more distant parts of the territory.

Something about the path made Brambleclaw uneasy. "I'm not sure I like this," he muttered. "It's too much like a Thunderpath." His belly clenched as he remembered how the

Twoleg monsters had torn through the forest, leaving a swath of devastation wider than this, but just as straight.

Thornclaw carefully tasted the air. "I don't think it can be," he meowed after a moment. "There's no scent of Twolegs or monsters."

Brambleclaw drew in a long breath and realized that the golden-brown warrior was right. There was no sign of Twolegs, not even stale scent. But there was still something very familiar about the path. "It might be an old Thunderpath," he guessed. "Maybe the Twolegs let the grass grow over it."

"Why would they do that?" Thornclaw wondered.

"Because they're mousebrained," Dustpelt retorted sourly. "All Twolegs are mousebrained." He spotted a vole beneath the nearest bush and began to creep toward it.

Watching him, Brambleclaw went on puzzling about the path. If Twolegs had cut rock from the stone hollow, perhaps they had needed a Thunderpath to take it away. He twitched his ears. It wasn't important, as long as there were no Twolegs here now.

When Dustpelt had killed his vole and scraped earth over it, they went on, still keeping to the side of the path. Brambleclaw was reluctant to set paw on something made by Twolegs, even so long ago, and he guessed his Clanmates felt the same.

Suddenly Dustpelt let out a hiss. Brambleclaw froze, his fur bristling as he followed the brown warrior's gaze through the trees. He could just make out the stone walls of a Twoleg nest.

"There's still no scent," Thornclaw mewed. He looked at Brambleclaw. "What do you want to do?"

Part of Brambleclaw wanted to turn and run back to the hollow as fast as he could. He thought of the nest they had discovered in ShadowClan's territory when they made the first patrol around the lake, and the two ferocious kittypets they had disturbed. But the Clan needed to know everything about their new territory. "Let's take a look," he decided.

Another, narrower path led to the nest from the path they were traveling along, but Brambleclaw took a more direct course through the trees, creeping up on the nest with his belly flattened to the ground.

It was very different from the nests in Twolegplace. There was a door made from flat wooden strips, but they were broken and rotten and hung crookedly from one side. The big square holes in the walls were empty, so wind and rain could blow straight in. The nest looked dark and silent, full of shadows and confusing scents.

A shiver went through Brambleclaw, raising every hair on his pelt. He wanted to leave without going one pawstep nearer, but he knew what Squirrelflight would say: *You never went inside! Are you a mouse or what?*

"Wait here," he ordered his companions, and stalked up to the doorway.

Thornclaw and Dustpelt did not obey his order: *No reason why they should,* thought Brambleclaw, reminding himself that he wasn't deputy yet. They were hard on his paws as he climbed the steps and slipped inside the Twoleg nest.

The weak shaft of light slanting through the door revealed rough gray walls and floors made from splintered strips of wood, with weeds pushing up through the gaps. Straight ahead, a slope of jutting blocks led up to another level.

There was no Twoleg scent, just a powerful aroma of prey. The cracks in the stone walls and the spaces under the floorboards would make good hiding places for mice and voles. Brambleclaw heard Thornclaw's paws thump on the wood, and glanced back to see his Clanmate with a mouse dangling from his jaws.

"Well done!" he whispered.

Dustpelt looked impressed. "This could be a useful place," he meowed. "Provided the Twolegs don't come back."

Brambleclaw agreed—the prey was certainly plentiful and easy to catch—but he didn't like the feeling the place gave him. It was as desolate and hollow as an empty den, and he wondered why the Twolegs had abandoned it.

"Do you want to go up there?" Thornclaw twitched his ears toward the steeply sloping blocks.

"Not if StarClan themselves came and begged me," Dustpelt mewed. "That doesn't look safe at all."

"I'll take a quick look," Brambleclaw meowed, Squirrelflight's imagined scorn ringing in his ears.

He ran swiftly up the blocks before he could spend too long worrying what he might find at the top. As he burst onto the next level, which was made of strips of wood like the floor below, a loud squawking and the rattle of wings set his heart thudding. A moment later he realized it was only a pigeon, disturbed by his sudden appearance. Scattering gray and white feathers, it fluttered up through the space where the roof had broken away.

Brambleclaw padded cautiously forward, peering around until he was sure the place was empty. When he scrambled down to ground level again he found that Dustpelt had caught another mouse, and Thornclaw was crouched in front of a crack in the wall with his ears pricked.

"We don't have time to hunt now," Brambleclaw warned them. He was feeling trapped inside the Twoleg walls, and his paws itched to be out in the open again. "We can find prey outside, and we need to report this to Firestar. Let's go."

Reluctantly Thornclaw followed him out again, and the three cats headed back along the abandoned Thunderpath.

Dustpelt and Thornclaw went straight to the heap of fresh-kill, but Brambleclaw padded over to his Clan leader, who was sitting with Sandstorm and Squirrelflight. "Firestar, I think you should know what we found today," he meowed, and described the empty Twoleg nest.

"And there was no scent of Twolegs at all?" Firestar asked when he'd finished.

Brambleclaw shook his head. "It seems to be a good place for prey, and I suppose it might be useful in the future."

"Maybe shelter," Sandstorm suggested, "if the weather gets very bad. Or if there was another fire . . ." She shivered, and Brambleclaw knew how she felt. He could just remember the flames that had swept through the old ThunderClan camp, devouring everything in their way. He wasn't sure that even the stone walls of the Twoleg nest would protect them from that sort of forest fire.

"Perhaps. Well done, all of you," Firestar meowed.

"I'm going out again," Brambleclaw told him. "We need more fresh-kill." He felt as if a lump of tough starling had lodged in his throat, but he managed to add, "Squirrelflight, do you want to come with me?"

The ginger warrior gave him a long look, and for a moment Brambleclaw was sure she would say yes. Then she rose to her paws and flicked her tail. "Sorry. I said I'd go hunting with Ashfur and Spiderleg."

"Okay." Brambleclaw swallowed his hurt, determined not to let her see how disappointed he was.

"Don't go out again just yet, Brambleclaw," Firestar meowed. "You've been working your paws off ever since the Gathering, and you need to rest. And that's an order," he added, as Brambleclaw opened his mouth to protest. "The sun's hardly up, and you've already done one patrol. Go eat, and then take a nap until sunhigh. Do you think I want one of my best warriors falling sick with exhaustion?"

Brambleclaw dipped his head and turned away.

Thornclaw had been watching, and when Brambleclaw sat beside him with a vole he had taken from the fresh-kill pile he twitched his ears toward Squirrelflight. "Had a quarrel, have you?" he mewed, a gleam of amusement in his eyes. "What did you do?"

"StarClan knows," Brambleclaw grunted. He didn't want every cat in the Clan taking an interest in his quarrel with

Squirrelflight—and he certainly didn't want them to know why they had fallen out in the first place. He flicked his tail irritably.

Why couldn't she see that he was totally loyal to his Clan, and that he still cared for her as much as ever? Deep down, he was sure he knew the answer. The reason she doubted his loyalty was because every time she looked at him, she was thinking of another cat instead.

Tigerstar.

Brambleclaw woke with a start. The angle of the sunlight piercing the branches of the warriors' den told him it was nearly sunhigh. He heard voices outside, and he sprang to his paws, his fur bristling, before he realized that they were raised in excitement, not fear or anger.

Shaking moss from his pelt, he padded out into the open. Several cats were huddled together in the middle of the clearing; as Brambleclaw drew closer he saw they were clustering around Leafpaw and Sorreltail.

The young she-cats looked exhausted, but very pleased with themselves. Leafpaw was speaking to Firestar, gesturing with her tail as if she were pointing out something.

"What's going on?" Brambleclaw asked.

Brightheart glanced around with a gleam of excitement in her good eye. "Leafpaw and Sorreltail have found the Moonpool!"

"The Moonpool? What's that?"

No cat answered, too eager to listen to what Leafpaw was

saying, so Brambleclaw squeezed forward until he could hear as well.

"We climbed beside the WindClan boundary, into the hills, a long way beyond the edge of our territory. And then we found the stream, and the starlight was so bright, I knew it would show us the way. We followed it until we came to a pool. . . ." Leafpaw's voice dropped to scarcely more than a whisper. "It's where we must go to share tongues with StarClan."

Brambleclaw closed his eyes and sent a prayer of thanks to his warrior ancestors. They had shown them the place that would replace the Moonstone. The Clans really were meant to be here; there would be no need to embark on another long and exhausting journey.

Cinderpelt pressed her muzzle against Leafpaw's shoulder. "You have done something very special today," she told her. "The Clans will remember this for many seasons."

"The vision could have come to any medicine cat," Leafpaw mewed, her eyes wide.

"But it came to you," Firestar put in. "The Clan thanks both of you," he added, with a nod to Sorreltail.

"Tomorrow night is the half-moon," Cinderpelt went on more briskly. "We must send a message at once to the other medicine cats, so that we can meet at the Moonpool."

"I'll go," Leafpaw offered.

"You've traveled far enough for one day," Firestar pointed out gently. "You can't go all the way around the lake as well."

Cinderpelt flicked her ears in agreement. "It's too far for

one cat anyway, if we're to meet in time," she pointed out. "From what Leafpaw says, we'll need to set out by sunset tomorrow at the latest. Let me go to ShadowClan and RiverClan, and Leafpaw can rest before she takes word to WindClan."

"Good idea," meowed Firestar. "But do you have to go, Cinderpelt? I can send a warrior instead."

Cinderpelt shook her head. "No. This is news that must come from a medicine cat."

"Then I want two warriors to go with you. We saw at the Gathering that every Clan is sensitive about their territories right now."

Brambleclaw stepped forward. "I'll go." He wanted to see the message carried to Littlecloud and Mothwing, to prove to their Clans that this was the place they had meant to settle. It felt like the final stage of the journey that began with the dream that sent him to sun-drown-place, in search of a badger called Midnight.

"Thanks, Brambleclaw. Sandstorm, will you go as well?"

"Sure," meowed Sandstorm.

As Brambleclaw followed Cinderpelt and Sandstorm out of the camp, he glanced over his shoulder. Squirrelflight was talking excitedly to Leafpaw. She did not look at him, and he had no time to stop and speak to her.

Brambleclaw would have to make this part of their journey alone.

CHAPTER 19

Leafpaw leaped across the stream by the stepping stones and began to climb the hill toward the WindClan camp. Firestar had offered her an escort, but she didn't think she needed one to visit WindClan. She'd thought of asking Sorreltail to go with her, but when she went to look for her friend she was sharing tongues with Brackenfur, and Leafpaw hadn't wanted to disturb them.

The wind ruffled the short moorland grass, bringing with it a strong scent of rabbits and flattening Leafpaw's fur against her sides. Even though she had slept for only a short time since coming back from the Moonpool, the news she carried sent energy surging through her like the water of the starlit stream.

She was nearly at the camp when she caught the scent of cats, and a patrol appeared from behind a gorse bush. It was Mudclaw and Webfoot with his apprentice, Weaselpaw. Leafpaw tensed. All the Clans were extra-sensitive about their boundaries at the moment, and she hoped the WindClan cats would give her a chance to explain her mission before chasing her out.

"What are you doing here?" Mudclaw growled. "This is our territory."

"I have a message for Barkface."

Mudclaw hesitated, then jerked his head. "Come on, then." He led her over the top of the rise and down into the hollow.

Onewhisker was sitting under a bush near the center of the camp, sharing a tough-looking rabbit with Ashfoot. Leafpaw glanced around, looking for Crowfeather. Barkface wasn't the only cat getting an important message from StarClan.

"Onewhisker, we have a visitor," Mudclaw announced.

The WindClan leader stood up, swiping his tongue around his jaws. "What can we do for you, Leafpaw?"

"I need to speak to Barkface," she mewed.

Onewhisker pricked his ears. "A message from StarClan?" he guessed.

Leafpaw nodded, though she couldn't say anything more. It was Barkface's duty to pass the message on to his Clan.

"That's great news!" Onewhisker's eyes shone. "Weaselpaw, go and ask Barkface to come right away."

Webfoot's apprentice disappeared down a tunnel at the foot of the slope. It looked as if it might once have been a rabbit burrow or a badger set. He reappeared a moment later with the medicine cat behind him.

Leafpaw bounded over to him. Barkface dismissed the apprentice with a flick of his tail and beckoned Leafpaw to sit beside him. "What's all this?" he asked.

Leafpaw's excitement bubbled over, and her words spilled out like water tumbling over the shining starlit stones. "And tomorrow night is the half moon," she finished. "Cinderpelt has gone to tell Mothwing and Littlecloud, so we can all go to the Moonpool together."

Barkface stretched forward and rested his muzzle against the tip of Leafpaw's ear. "This is the best news I've ever heard," he murmured. "Thank you for bringing it to me." He heaved himself up and padded over to Onewhisker and Ashfoot. Others had joined them, guessing there was an important announcement coming.

Quickly Barkface told them about Leafpaw's journey. "Tomorrow night all the medicine cats will meet at the Moonpool," he meowed. "The night after that, Onewhisker, you and I will go together so that you can receive your nine lives and your leader's name."

For a moment Leafpaw thought she saw a flicker of panic flash through Onewhisker's eyes. Surely he should be relieved to know he would finally be able to share tongues with StarClan and have his leadership recognized by his warrior ancestors. What reason could he have for wanting to put it off?

Onewhisker blinked and shook his head. Leafpaw decided she must have imagined the panic in his expression.

"From what Leafpaw tells us, it's a long journey," Onewhisker mewed. "You can't travel there twice in two days; you'll be worn out. I've waited this long for my nine lives and my name. I can wait awhile longer."

Leafpaw was impressed by Onewhisker's thoughtfulness.

Then she looked more closely at him, and wondered if he could possibly be afraid that StarClan would reject him, after he was appointed in such a hurry by the dying Tallstar. She blinked sympathetically. Every cat knew that the deputy of a Clan succeeded the leader when he lost his ninth life—even if they had been deputy for only a few moments. That was part of the warrior code, and whatever else had changed on their long journey from the forest, the warrior code would always remain at the heart of every Clan.

Barkface seemed content to leave some time between his visits to the Moonpool, because he didn't try to change Onewhisker's mind. "I'll see you tomorrow at sunset, Leafpaw," he meowed.

"I'll tell Cinderpelt," she replied. "We can meet by the stream at the edge of the trees."

Barkface nodded. "Go well," he murmured, before heading back to his den.

Onewhisker and Ashfoot began talking quietly together. Mudclaw muttered something to Webfoot, and the pair of them raced for the top of the hollow, disappearing over it in a couple of heartbeats.

Leafpaw felt a light touch on her shoulder. She turned, and was startled to see Crowfeather gazing intensely into her eyes. "Have you really found a place to speak with StarClan?" he asked.

"Yes, really." Leafpaw swallowed. "There's something I have to tell you, Crowfeather. Is there somewhere quiet we can talk?"

"Come over here." Crowfeather led her to the edge of the hollow and sat down under a stunted tree with leafless, twisted branches. He looked expectantly at Leafpaw with his head to one side.

She took a deep breath. "I didn't just dream of the Moonpool last night. I saw Feathertail as well." That was one detail she had left out when she told her story to Barkface.

Crowfeather's eyes opened wide. "Feathertail?"

"Yes. She gave me a message for you." Leafpaw's heart pounded so loud, she was convinced Crowfeather would be able to hear it. Would he be angry with what she had to say? After all, he might want to carry on grieving for Feathertail. Leafpaw told herself that wasn't her problem; Feathertail might be watching them right now, and she had to keep her promise to deliver the message.

"She said, 'Tell him not to grieve.' It will be many moons before you can be together again. She told you not to be blinded to the living."

Crowfeather met Leafpaw's gaze with such a hungry look, it was as if he wanted to devour every scrap of her meeting with the cat he had loved so deeply. Leafpaw blinked. How could he ever stop grieving if he felt this strongly?

At last the WindClan warrior looked down at his paws. "I'll never stop wishing she hadn't died," he whispered. "Does Feathertail think I could *ever* forget about her?"

"That isn't what she meant!" Leafpaw protested.

"There'll never be another cat like Feathertail." Crowfeather whipped up his head, and there was a gleam of anger in his eyes. "I don't care how long I have to wait to see her again. If she can wait, so can I!"

He spun around and bounded across the clearing, with Leafpaw staring helplessly after him.

The half-moon floated high above them, shedding soft gray light over the slope beside the rushing stream. The five medicine cats toiled up the last few tail-lengths that led to the barrier of thornbushes. Cinderpelt looked exhausted, her eyes glazed and her pace increasingly uneven, but she seemed determined to keep going. Mothwing hardly seemed tired by the journey at all. Right from the start she had bounded ahead and doubled back to check which way to go next, as if she couldn't wait to reach the place where she would share tongues with StarClan. Leafpaw thought she couldn't have been more eager if she had really believed in them, and she wondered if Mothwing was looking for a chance to prove that StarClan *didn't* exist. She pushed the thought away—Mothwing was loyal and kindhearted, and Leafpaw knew she'd do anything to keep her lack of faith a secret from the other medicine cats.

Leafpaw showed them the narrow gap that led through the barrier of thorns, and at last they stood at the top of the hollow, gazing down at the Moonpool. The water shone with the same pale light she remembered from before, while the stream tumbling from the crack in the rock glittered with starshine. Its gentle plashing into the pool was the only sound.

"Yes, this is the place," Barkface murmured.

He gestured with his tail for Leafpaw to lead the way down the path, and once again she felt her paws slipping into the pawprints made by those cats of long ago.

"I wonder how we're supposed to share tongues with StarClan?" Littlecloud asked, when all the medicine cats were sitting around the Moonpool.

Leafpaw blinked. She hadn't thought of that. Back at Mothermouth, cats used to lie with their noses touching the Moonstone; she remembered the icy chill that would creep through her fur, pulling her into a deep sleep where she could meet with StarClan.

She looked around, searching for something lit up by StarClan, as radiant as the Moonstone had been. There was nothing to see but the moss-covered rocks and trailing ferns—and the starlit surface of the pool. "Maybe we should touch the water?" she suggested.

The medicine cats glanced at one another. "It's worth a try," Barkface agreed.

Shivering, Leafpaw crept forward and lapped a few drops of water. It was icy cold, and tasted of stars and the wind and the indigo sky. She closed her eyes, breathing the scents as they flooded her mouth.

A chill spread from her ears to the tip of her tail, and she could no longer feel the stone beneath her paws. Instead she was floating in a black void, where everything was dark and silent. There were voices, too faint and shrill at first to hear what they were saying. Then the sound of wind and splashing water died away, and she realized they were calling her name.

"I'm here," she whispered.

She opened her eyes. A vast stretch of water lay in front of her: not the Moonpool, tucked in its sheltering hollow, but the lake. Wind stirred the surface into rippling waves, tipped with curls of froth. The water looked as if it reflected a blazing sunset, with all shades of red lapping thickly at the shore. But when Leafpaw looked up, the sky was dark and starlit. The lake was filled with blood!

The voices called to her again, this time loud enough for her to hear, even though she wished she hadn't almost before they had finished speaking:

Before there is peace, blood will spill blood, and the lake will run red.

Leafpaw sprang up to run away, but her paws slipped in the sticky blood, and the stench of death engulfed her. With a gasp she opened her eyes. She was on the edge of the Moonpool again, her belly pressed flat against the cold stone, and beside her lay the other medicine cats. They were stirring and stretching, waking from their own dreams. The moon was dipping below the hilltop; Leafpaw's legs, stiff from crouching so long in one position, confirmed how much time had passed.

Barkface and Littlecloud both looked very troubled; Leafpaw wondered if they had received warnings like hers. Cinderpelt was studying Leafpaw with concern in her eyes, while Mothwing kept her gaze fixed on her paws.

Leafpaw guessed they would set out for their camps at

once. She wanted to talk to Cinderpelt alone, wary of announcing her vision to the other medicine cats. But instead of leading the way back up the path, Cinderpelt sat down again on the edge of the Moonpool.

"Before we go back to our Clans," she began, "I have one more task to do." She waited until the other cats were sitting too, their faces turned attentively to her.

Leafpaw wondered what this was all about, since Cinderpelt hadn't said anything to her on the way. Mothwing shot her a worried glance, and Leafpaw replied with a tiny shake of the head; she hadn't revealed Mothwing's lack of faith to Cinderpelt or any cat.

"Clan warriors receive their warrior name when their mentor thinks they are ready," Cinderpelt continued. "It is the same for medicine cats." With a glint in her eyes she turned to Leafpaw and asked, "Did you think you would have to wait for me to die before you received your name?"

Leafpaw was so taken aback she didn't reply. She hadn't really thought about it. Maybe she had assumed that, yes. But being an apprentice medicine cat was different from being an apprentice warrior; Leafpaw could use healing herbs and share tongues with StarClan just as much as the other medicine cats. A pulse of excitement went through her as she guessed what might be coming next.

"A medicine cat receives her name when StarClan decides she deserves it," Cinderpelt meowed. "Leafpaw, the fact that our warrior ancestors brought you to the Moonpool first shows how highly they regard you."

"That's true," Barkface rumbled.

Littlecloud let out a purr of agreement; Mothwing's eyes were brilliant and she leaped up to press her muzzle against Leafpaw's side. In the midst of her excitement, Leafpaw realized it was a good thing Mothwing already had her full name; how could StarClan show their approval of a cat who did not believe in them?

"Come forward." Cinderpelt beckoned to Leafpaw with her tail.

Leafpaw hardly knew which paw to move first as she stumbled around the Moonpool until she stood in front of her mentor.

Cinderpelt tipped back her head and gazed at Silverpelt. "I, Cinderpelt, medicine cat of ThunderClan, call upon my warrior ancestors to look down on this apprentice. She has trained hard to understand the way of a medicine cat, and with your help she will serve her Clan for many moons."

The words were familiar to Leafpaw from the warrior ceremonies she had seen for her Clanmates. Her paws tingled, as if starlight scorched her fur.

"Leafpaw, do you promise to uphold the ways of a medicine cat, to stand apart from rivalry between Clan and Clan, and to protect all cats equally, even at the cost of your life?"

"I do."

"Then by the powers of StarClan I give you your true name as a medicine cat. Leafpaw, from this moment you will be known as Leafpool. StarClan honors your courage and your faith. By finding this place, you have proved this is truly our new home."

Just as a Clan leader would do at a warrior ceremony, Cinderpelt rested her muzzle on Leafpool's head. Her head full of stars, Leafpool bent to lick her mentor's shoulder.

"Leafpool! Leafpool!" Mothwing called, and Barkface and Littlecloud joined in.

Leafpool bowed her head. "Thank you—all of you. My paws were guided by StarClan in everything I have done, and I hope they will continue to guide me for the rest of my life."

"May StarClan grant that it is so," murmured Barkface, and the others echoed his prayer.

All except Mothwing, but when Leafpool looked at her, the RiverClan cat's face was filled with such pride and affection that she knew Mothwing was as pleased for her as any cat. Right then, it didn't matter a whisker that she didn't share their beliefs.

As she followed the other cats out of the hollow and down the rocky slope, Leafpool felt so full of energy, so committed all over again to the way of a medicine cat, that she half thought she would be able to fly back to the hollow in the woods if she tried. She let the others go ahead, and padded along with her thoughts full of starlight and herbs and water that tasted of the night sky.

Suddenly she felt something sticky dragging at her legs, and her paws skidded in a slippery, viscous liquid. She looked down; there was nothing but short moorland grass under her paws, but the stench of death rose up around her, and though she knew the slope was clear and dry, she felt as if she were wading through a river of blood, running hot and scarlet from the overflowing, death-scented lake.

CHAPTER 20

Brambleclaw halted at the edge of the lake and gazed across the stream into ShadowClan's territory. The pine forest on the far side of the stream was a blue-black shadow against the heavy gray sky. No cats were in sight, but the damp wind brought a powerful reek toward him: the old, familiar ShadowClan scent, nearly as strong as it had ever been.

It was one more sign that all the cats were settling into their new territories. An even more powerful sign was the discovery of the Moonpool. Early that morning Cinderpelt and the newly named Leafpool had returned from the medicine cats' first meeting with StarClan, and in two nights' time Onewhisker would receive the nine lives of a leader at last.

"Yuck!" exclaimed Rainwhisker. "I'll never get used to the way ShadowClan smells. It's like a fox that's been dead for a moon."

"I don't suppose they're too keen on our scent, either," Brambleclaw pointed out.

A splash and a startled yowl behind him interrupted him. He glanced around to see Spiderleg standing in the lake with water lapping halfway up his legs.

"Great StarClan, what are you doing?"

Spiderleg waded back to the shore, hanging his head in embarrassment. "I saw a fish," he explained, and added unnecessarily, "It got away."

Brambleclaw sighed. "You don't catch fish like that. Remind me sometime to give you a lesson. Feathertail taught us when we were on our journey." The familiar ache tugged at his heart when he remembered the beautiful RiverClan she-cat. "Come on; we'd better finish patrolling this border."

He turned to head upstream, and stopped when he caught sight of something moving on the ShadowClan side. A gray cat had emerged from the trees and was racing along the lakeshore toward him. Brambleclaw's eyes widened in surprise when he recognized Mistyfoot. What was a RiverClan cat doing in ShadowClan territory?

"Brambleclaw, wait!" she yowled. She splashed through the stream as if it weren't there and skidded to a halt in front of him, panting. "I've got to talk to Firestar right away."

Spiderleg stepped forward, his neck fur bristling. "What are you doing on our territory?"

"Yeah, let's chase her off," Rainwhisker growled.

Brambleclaw flicked his tail irritably at the two younger warriors. "We're not chasing her anywhere. This is Mistyfoot—remember? She's been a good friend to ThunderClan."

"Thanks, Brambleclaw." Mistyfoot dipped her head, though there was still a wild look in her eyes, as if she'd seen something that terrified her. "Please take me to Firestar."

"Okay." Brambleclaw couldn't think what might be so urgent, but he knew Mistyfoot wasn't the sort of cat to make a fuss about nothing. "You two carry on with the patrol," he told the others. "Watch out for Twolegs, and when you get as far as the dead tree, make sure the ShadowClan scent marks are where they're supposed to be."

Rainwhisker and Spiderleg exchanged a glance, as if they weren't sure they wanted to leave Brambleclaw and Mistyfoot together, but neither of them said anything. They set off upstream; Rainwhisker kept looking back as if he expected Mistyfoot to attack Brambleclaw as soon as his back was turned.

"What's the problem?" Brambleclaw demanded, as he led Mistyfoot to the camp by the quickest route.

"You'll hear soon enough," Mistyfoot meowed grimly. "Brambleclaw, can we *hurry*?"

Startled, Brambleclaw sped up until the two cats were hurtling through the trees, not slowing their pace until they reached the tunnel that led into the camp. Brambleclaw pushed his way through first, and to his relief spotted Firestar at once, sharing a thrush with Sandstorm near the fresh-kill pile. Beckoning Mistyfoot to stay close to him, Brambleclaw padded over.

Firestar swallowed a bite of fresh-kill and stood up. "Mistyfoot, welcome," he greeted the RiverClan warrior. "What brings you here?"

"Nothing good," Mistyfoot replied.

Firestar's ears twitched, and Sandstorm looked up curiously.

"I'm afraid there's trouble for all the Clans," Mistyfoot went on.

"Wait a moment," Firestar interrupted. "We'd better let Dustpelt and Brackenfur hear this too. Brambleclaw, can you find them?"

Brambleclaw raced to the warriors' den. Thrusting his way in through the outer branches, he found Brackenfur curled up next to Sorreltail and gave the ginger tom a sharp prod.

Brackenfur looked up, blinking. "What's wrong?"

"Firestar wants you," Brambleclaw mewed. "Have you seen Dustpelt?"

Brackenfur shook his head, but Cloudtail, who was sharing tongues with Brightheart a few tail-lengths away, raised his head. "He's in the nursery with Ferncloud."

"Thanks." Brambleclaw backed out and pelted across the hollow to the bramble thicket; Dustpelt emerged just as he was skidding to a halt by the entrance. His ears pricked inquiringly when he saw Brambleclaw.

"Firestar wants you," Brambleclaw explained again. "Mistyfoot's here, and she says there's trouble."

His eyes narrowing, the brown tabby warrior followed him over to the fresh-kill pile, where Brackenfur had just joined the others.

"Now," Firestar meowed, waving his tail at Mistyfoot. "Tell us what's wrong."

She had recovered some of her composure, but her eyes were still anxious. "Three nights ago I was on my way back to camp when I spotted two cats on the shore of the lake opposite the island," she began. "It was raining heavily, so I couldn't think why they wanted to hang about where there was no shelter. I was going to order them back to camp when I realized who they were." She paused, digging her claws into the ground.

"Well?" Firestar prompted.

"One of them was Hawkfrost," Mistyfoot replied. She swallowed painfully, as if a tough bit of fresh-kill were lodged in her throat. "And the other was Mudclaw."

"*What?*" exclaimed Dustpelt.

Brambleclaw's belly lurched. What did Hawkfrost want with the former WindClan deputy?

"Before I reached them, Mudclaw raced back toward his own territory," Mistyfoot continued. "But Hawkfrost hadn't chased him off. They'd been talking together, and I got the impression they knew each other quite well. I've suspected before this that Hawkfrost has been sneaking out of camp at night. To tell you the truth," she added awkwardly to Brambleclaw, "I thought he might have been going to meet you. I saw you talking together at the Gathering, and you *are* kin. . . ." Her voice grew defensive as she went on, "I couldn't see much harm in that, so I never asked Hawkfrost to explain himself. Now I know I made a mistake. It must have been Mudclaw he was meeting."

Brambleclaw looked down at his paws, feeling the gaze of his Clanmates scorching his fur. He wanted to think of a good reason for Mudclaw to be speaking to a RiverClan warrior, but he couldn't.

"Hawkfrost went back to camp—and I let him go," Mistyfoot went on. "He didn't know I'd spotted him, and I thought I'd try to find out what was going on before I tackled him."

"What did you do next?" Sandstorm asked.

"I couldn't believe they'd meet on the lakeshore, where any cat could spot them. I remembered how keen on the island Hawkfrost was when we first came here, so I swam out to see if they'd been meeting there. Sure enough, I found their scent . . . some fresh, and some stale. I guess they've been there three or four times at least."

"Mudclaw swam over to the island?" Dustpelt sounded incredulous. "More than once? I'm surprised he even wanted to get his paws wet. None of the WindClan cats likes to swim."

"Then you tell me how his scent got over there," Mistyfoot retorted.

"What did Leopardstar say when you told her all this?" asked Firestar.

Mistyfoot looked uncomfortable. "I didn't tell her," she admitted. "Hawkfrost is a good warrior, and he's popular, especially with the younger cats. It's no secret that some of them think he should have stayed deputy when I escaped from the Twolegs. I was afraid that if I told Leopardstar, she'd think I was trying to make trouble because I felt he was a threat to me. Besides, I didn't see him do anything wrong, apart from speak to a cat from another Clan. I decided to keep an eye on him until I could work out why he and Mudclaw were meeting."

"And now you have?" Brackenfur guessed.

Firestar narrowed his eyes. "Yes, you didn't come here because of something you saw three nights ago. What's happened?"

"This morning Hawkfrost offered to lead the dawn patrol," Mistyfoot replied. "The three cats he chose to go with him are the ones who yowl loudest about what a good deputy he would make. None of them has come back yet."

Brambleclaw glanced up at the sky; the sun was hidden behind rain-laden clouds, but he guessed that sunset could not be far off. Either the dawn patrol had gotten severely lost—or they hadn't been planning to return when the patrol was finished.

"Maybe they just found a good place to hunt," Firestar suggested.

"And you can't blame him for choosing his friends to go with him on a patrol," Sandstorm added fairly.

"You don't understand," Mistyfoot meowed. "When they hadn't come back by sunhigh, I tried to track them. I mean, it was obvious they hadn't set out to do a regular dawn patrol."

"Did they go to the island?" mewed Dustpelt.

"I thought they might have, but when I picked up the scent trail outside our camp, it led into ShadowClan territory."

Brambleclaw felt every hair on his pelt begin to rise. Could there possibly be an innocent explanation for this?

"I knew ThunderClan wouldn't be involved, so I came straight here," Mistyfoot added. "A ShadowClan patrol nearly spotted me, but I made it to the border without being caught. Firestar, I'm convinced that Hawkfrost is involved in a plot to attack WindClan!"

Firestar's green eyes were thoughtful. "There could be other explanations. . . ."

"Name one!" Mistyfoot snapped. "Every cat knows that Mudclaw was furious when Tallstar chose Onewhisker to succeed him. Do you really think he wouldn't do anything about it?"

"Wait!" Brackenfur leaped to his paws. "Now that Leafpool has found the Moonpool, Onewhisker will soon receive his nine lives from StarClan. Mudclaw *has* to attack before then, if he wants to take over the Clan."

"That means he'll strike tonight," Brambleclaw mewed hoarsely.

"Firestar, you have to do something!" Mistyfoot urged.

Firestar's claws scraped the earth. "Why me? Why not go to your own leader?"

"Leopardstar would just suspect me of trying to make trouble for Hawkfrost. And she would never do anything to help WindClan. But Onewhisker's your friend. . . ."

"He's still a Clan leader, and responsible for the safety of his own Clan. He can't expect ThunderClan to come to the rescue every time there's trouble." Firestar stared down at his feet as his claws sank into the ground. Then he looked up. "But you're right. We can't just sit by and do nothing. We'll send a patrol to the WindClan camp to see what's going on. And I'd better call a meeting to warn the rest of the Clan."

"Is that necessary?" Brambleclaw protested.

Firestar gave him a long look. "We don't know for certain that they're not planning to attack us. I hope as much as any cat that we're wrong, but it's a risk we can't afford to take."

Springing up, he raced across the hollow and up the tumble of broken rock to the Highledge. "Let all cats old enough to catch their own prey join for a Clan meeting," he yowled.

Cloudtail, Brightheart, and Sorreltail emerged from the warriors' den. The elders joined them after a moment, Goldenflower leading Longtail. Cinderpelt appeared from her den with Leafpool just behind her; the young tabby was looking wide-eyed with alarm.

Squirrelflight, Ashfur, and Thornclaw paused as they entered the camp with fresh-kill, then dropped their prey on the pile and raced across to join the others.

"Cats of ThunderClan," Firestar began. "Mistyfoot has brought news that suggests Mudclaw and Hawkfrost are planning to attack WindClan. I'm going to take a patrol over to the WindClan camp, but I want every cat alert in case they come here. It's likely that ShadowClan is involved as well."

Shocked murmurs rose from the listening cats. Brambleclaw stared at his paws as he felt his Clanmates looking at him and whispering, linking him to Hawkfrost over and over because they shared the same father. He could not bring himself to look at Squirrelflight for fear of seeing contempt in her eyes.

"Cloudtail, you and Brightheart are in charge of the camp," Firestar went on. "Thornclaw, take two cats and keep watch on the ShadowClan border. If you spot any of their warriors, track them, but don't attack if you're badly outnumbered."

Thornclaw nodded and beckoned to Squirrelflight and Ashfur. Firestar prepared to leap down from the ledge, but before he could move, Cinderpelt stepped forward.

"Firestar, there's something you ought to know. Leafpool told me about a dream she had. It might have something to do with this."

"Okay." Firestar motioned his daughter forward. "Tell us, Leafpool."

"I saw the lake turn red, and heard a voice," the young she-cat explained. "It said, 'Before there is peace, blood will spill blood, and the lake will run red.'"

"That's all?" Firestar prompted. "Nothing to tell you whose blood, or when?"

Leafpool shook her head.

"It's enough to suggest big trouble is coming," Cinderpelt meowed. "I'd take this attack seriously if I were you. It's Mudclaw's last chance to seize control of WindClan, while Onewhisker still has only one life."

"Right." Firestar jumped down. "Let's go."

Brambleclaw followed his leader past Thornclaw, who was organizing his smaller patrol. He couldn't resist glancing sideways at Squirrelflight. He had expected her to look triumphant now that it looked like she had been right all along about Hawkfrost. Instead he saw pity in her eyes.

Her sad look stayed with him all the way as Firestar cut through the trees and raced for the WindClan border.

CHAPTER 21

Night was falling as the ThunderClan cats crossed the stream and entered WindClan territory. Out of the shelter of the trees, a stiff wind was blowing with an icy sting of rain. Now and then the moon or a star shone fitfully between rags of cloud, but for most of the time thick darkness covered the moor. The cats had to find their way by scent alone, barely able to see their own paws.

"There's no sign of a border patrol," Dustpelt whispered, sniffing.

"That could mean they're defending the camp," Mistyfoot replied.

"Shh!" Firestar's low hiss came out of the darkness. "Stay alert. We don't know what we're getting into."

Soon they reached the stream that flowed down from the WindClan camp. Firestar followed it for a while, then halted to taste the air. Brambleclaw did the same; a strong scent of WindClan cats came from up ahead, but none of the other Clan scents. There was no sound of fighting cats, just the buffeting of the wind and the gurgling stream. A faint hope began to grow inside Brambleclaw that Mistyfoot had made a mistake.

"Nothing," Firestar murmured when the silence had stretched out for many heartbeats.

"We could go and ask Onewhisker if everything's okay," Brackenfur suggested.

"What? Stroll into his camp and tell him we came to fight off his enemies?" Dustpelt meowed. "I don't think so."

Sandstorm murmured agreement, and after a moment's thought Firestar echoed it. "You're right. The best thing we can do is go home."

"But something's wrong; I'm sure of it," Mistyfoot protested. Her eyes gleamed with anxiety. "What about Leafpool's dream?"

"We've no idea what Leafpool's dream means," Firestar pointed out. "Meanwhile, we're here in fighting strength on another Clan's territory. Onewhisker would be well within his rights if he ripped our fur off."

Dustpelt snorted. "I'd like to see him try."

The wind was rising, and a sudden gust almost carried Brambleclaw off his paws. In the distance he heard a faint rumble of thunder. "Let's get back before the storm breaks," Firestar mewed.

All the cats turned to follow him. Bringing up the rear, Brambleclaw cast one last glance toward the WindClan camp, and froze as a wisp of scent drifted between his parted jaws.

Hawkfrost!

"Firestar, wait!" he rasped.

Gazing up the hill, he saw several dark shapes flow over the rise from the opposite direction and launch themselves down into the hollow. For a heartbeat he thought he recognized the outline of Hawkfrost's broad head and powerful shoulders at the head of the cats.

A single screech split the night. Firestar whipped around and raced back up the hill. "Come on!"

Brambleclaw was shoulder-to-shoulder with him as they reached the edge of the hollow. More screeches split the night; in the darkness, Brambleclaw could make out nothing more than a caterwauling tangle of fur. He could scent RiverClan and ShadowClan as well as WindClan, but he couldn't recognize individuals or work out which cats he should be attacking.

He heard Firestar yowl, "Mudclaw!" as his leader hurtled down the slope into the camp. Brambleclaw and the rest of the ThunderClan patrol raced after him. A moment later Brambleclaw lost sight of his Clanmates as he plunged into the struggling mass. Before he had a chance to get his breath, a cat crashed into his side, knocking him off his paws. He twisted around and found himself glaring up into the eyes of Cedarheart from ShadowClan.

"Stay out of this!" spat the dark gray tom. "This is not ThunderClan's fight!"

Not bothering to reply, Brambleclaw kicked out hard with his hindlegs and jabbed his feet into Cedarheart's belly. The

ShadowClan warrior staggered backward and vanished, leaving Brambleclaw to stumble to his paws. *Great StarClan, please, don't let Tawnypelt be here!* he begged silently.

He was buffeted from side to side as cats slammed into him in screeching knots of fur and claws. There was no sign of Hawkfrost, though he spotted another RiverClan warrior hurling himself across the hollow and leaping into a clump of gorse with his claws outstretched. The throng of cats shifted, and Brambleclaw had a clear view of Webfoot and Onewhisker struggling together, Onewhisker's teeth sunk deep in Webfoot's shoulder while the tabby tom clawed lumps of fur from his leader's side.

Brambleclaw leaped forward to help Onewhisker, but at the same moment Mudclaw erupted from the shadows. Onewhisker vanished under a whirl of teeth and claws, but a heartbeat later Firestar appeared, grabbed Mudclaw's scruff in his teeth, and hauled him off.

Mudclaw shook himself free. "Do you think this is your Clan?" he snarled at Firestar. "Think again, kittypet! WindClan will have a new leader now, a strong cat who can make the Clan great again."

"Onewhisker is WindClan's leader," Firestar spat back.

Mudclaw threw himself at the ThunderClan leader. As the two cats went down, Webfoot dashed in from the side and fastened his teeth in Firestar's leg. Brambleclaw leaped toward them but was brought to a jolting stop when a weight landed on top of him, rolling him to the ground. RiverClan scent flooded over him, but his attacker was black, not tabby.

As Brambleclaw raked his claws over the cat's face he felt a stab of relief that he didn't have to fight Hawkfrost—yet.

He felt a sharp pain in his side as his attacker's claws found their mark. *We're losing,* he thought, fighting panic when he pictured Firestar struggling alone against two strong cats. *There are too many of them!*

But fear gave him a new surge of strength, and he forced himself to his paws, driving off his attacker with a swift bite to his tail. Suddenly he heard a distant yowling and recognized Squirrelflight's voice. A gleam of moonlight showed her racing over the top of the hollow with Thornclaw and Ashfur beside her.

Only a flash of Firestar's flame-colored flank was visible beneath Mudclaw and Webfoot. Before Brambleclaw could reach him, Squirrelflight hurtled past and flung herself into the battle with a screech of fury. Webfoot fled, and Mudclaw turned to attack the ginger warrior. Squirrelflight reared up on her hindlegs, claws slashing; Mudclaw tried to plunge his teeth into her throat. Brambleclaw flung himself toward Firestar; relief flooded over him as his leader pulled himself to his paws and leaped back into the battle. One flank dripped with blood, but the injury didn't seem to slow Firestar down.

Brambleclaw whirled around to throw himself into the fight against Mudclaw. But he and Squirrelflight had disappeared among the struggling cats that swayed back and forth across the hollow. Brambleclaw found himself fighting flank-to-flank with Crowfeather, their moves well matched and strong after many moons of journeying together. Mistyfoot and Sandstorm were close by, battling against two RiverClan warriors.

Then Brambleclaw spotted Squirrelflight again, this time locked in combat with Nightcloud. Squirrelflight's flank was bleeding, but her teeth were fastened in Nightcloud's scruff, and she was battering the well-muscled she-cat with her hindpaws.

Brambleclaw leaped in to help; Nightcloud tore herself free and fled. Squirrelflight scrambled up, panting.

"What are you doing here?" Brambleclaw demanded.

"There wasn't a sniff of trouble by the ShadowClan border," Squirrelflight replied. "So we came here, in case we were needed."

"I'm glad you did," Brambleclaw mewed fervently.

"Then why are we wasting time talking about it?" Squirrelflight flicked her ears at a couple of ShadowClan warriors a few tail-lengths away. She and Brambleclaw hurtled into battle side by side. At a twitch of Squirrelflight's tail they split up and confused the ShadowClan cats by attacking on each flank, pinning them together so they clawed each other as they tried to reach their enemies.

"Nice move!" gasped Squirrelflight as she raked her claws down the ginger tom's ear.

A lightning bolt of pure energy slammed through Brambleclaw as he met her shining, breathless gaze. But it did not last. Two other cats, locked in a screeching knot of teeth and claws, pushed between them, and when Brambleclaw dodged around them the ShadowClan cats were fleeing, with Squirrelflight streaking after them. A heartbeat later he lost sight of her.

Breathing hard, he looked around. He had reached the other side of the hollow. Ahead of him the cats parted to reveal a huge tabby tom with powerful shoulders padding toward him. Brambleclaw looked up, eye to eye with his brother. Hawkfrost's expression was unreadable; his ice-blue eyes glittered with moonlight.

Then a gray warrior dashed in from the side, sending Brambleclaw crashing to the ground. He let out a screech and struck out with his claws. Pain stabbed him as teeth met in his shoulder, but he shook the other cat off and staggered up again. He caught a brief glimpse of Hawkfrost raking his claws across a WindClan warrior's flank; then more cats thrust between them and his half brother was gone.

Thornclaw and Dustpelt appeared beside Brambleclaw. Together they thrust the invaders back pawstep by pawstep. Brambleclaw realized that the battle had turned, and they were forcing the attackers up the slope at the far side of the camp. He had almost reached the top when a flash of lightning bathed the moor in eerie yellow light. It showed him Mudclaw and Hawkfrost facing each other on the crest of the hill, outlined against the sky. A heartbeat later thunder crashed out overhead, rolling and echoing around the hill as if it would never stop. Rain hissed across the hillside; within moments Brambleclaw's fur was soaked and plastered to his body.

As if the breaking storm were a signal, Mudclaw let out a yowl and fled, with Hawkfrost hard on his paws. Two ShadowClan warriors broke in the opposite direction, heading toward the ThunderClan camp.

Crowfeather raced up to Brambleclaw, his eyes questioning, as if he were waiting for an order.

"Go after them!" Brambleclaw gasped, jerking his head toward the fleeing ShadowClan warriors. Instinctively used to obeying him, Crowfeather took off into the darkness.

Brambleclaw tore across the grass in pursuit of Mudclaw. The former deputy had betrayed his Clan and tried to kill his leader. Brambleclaw vowed that no other cat but he would know the triumph of sinking his claws and teeth into Mudclaw's throat.

He did not stop to ask himself what he would do if he had to face Hawkfrost.

CHAPTER 22

When the rain started, Leafpool crept into a sheltered spot under the thorns at the top of the hollow. Far above her head, the branches of the trees thrashed together against the stormy sky, but down here everything was quiet, the only sound the patter of raindrops, broken by rolls of thunder coming from the hills.

Cloudtail had posted sentries around the hollow as soon as the other cats left with Firestar. Leafpool had volunteered to come up here and give an early warning if she heard invaders. All medicine cats were trained as warriors too, and she would use every fighting skill she possessed to defend her new home.

So far there had been nothing to disturb the forest apart from the breaking storm, but it felt as if the whole night were tense with waiting. She would have given anything to know what was happening at the WindClan camp. Were Hawkfrost and Mudclaw really plotting to overthrow Onewhisker?

Leafpool let her mind drift back to the discovery of the Moonpool, reliving the moment when she had first looked into it and seen her warrior ancestors reflected there. She felt how amazing it was to be a medicine cat, and didn't know how she could bear to wait for the next half moon, when they would meet again. Her fur tingled with anticipation of the future serving her Clan that seemed to stretch in front of her like a stream filled with starlight.

Suddenly she realized that she could hear cats approaching rapidly through the trees. For a heartbeat she thought it was the ThunderClan patrol on its way back. Then a gust of ShadowClan scent was carried to her on the wind. She sprang up, jaws parted to yowl a warning to the Clan in the hollow below. But before she could utter a sound, two shapes broke out of the undergrowth and hurtled straight at her. Barging into her, they shoved her backward until she crashed into the bushes at the edge of the cliff. Scrabbling with her hindpaws, she felt the thorns give way under her weight.

"No!" she gasped.

Her warning was too late. Terrified yowls split the air as the two intruders crashed past her and fell all the way into the camp. Leafpool thrashed wildly with her claws and managed to clutch the edge of the rock. But she couldn't get a grip with her hindpaws to thrust herself back to safety. There was a noise above her, and she looked up, terrified that she would see another ShadowClan warrior coming to finish her off.

Crowfeather gazed down at her, his eyes wide with horror.

"Crowfeather," Leafpool hissed through gritted teeth, in case the movement sent her plummeting down after the two ShadowClan cats. "Crowfeather, help me!"

The WindClan warrior didn't move. The rock where

Leafpool clung was wet from the rain, and she felt her claws begin to slip. "Crowfeather!" she begged. "I'm going to fall!"

Crowfeather stood as if frozen. A hoarse whisper came from him, but his gaze was blank, and Leafpool realized that he wasn't talking to her at all. "Feathertail, I'm so sorry! It was all my fault. I shouldn't have let you fall."

Leafpool realized he was remembering the cave in the mountains where Feathertail had died. "It wasn't your fault," she mewed. "Help me, Crowfeather, please." She felt her claws slip again and tried to dig them in deeper, but there was nothing to grip on the slick surface of the rock.

Slowly Crowfeather took a pace forward and leaned over. Leafpool gasped as she felt her claws give way, but in the same heartbeat his teeth met in her scruff. For a moment they both teetered on the edge of the cliff, and she felt his weight slide toward her. Then Crowfeather heaved backward, his hind-paws scrabbling in the earth, and hauled Leafpool up over the edge. Both cats collapsed, panting. Leafpool let her cheek rest against the solid ground, knowing she had been a whisker away from falling to her death. Crowfeather lay beside her, his flanks heaving. Their eyes met, and Leafpool found she could not look away.

"Thank you," she mewed.

"I did it," Crowfeather whispered. "I saved you."

The air between them seemed to crackle like lightning. Trying to lighten the atmosphere, Leafpool commented, "I must be the last cat you would want to save."

"Is that what you think?" Crowfeather's gaze burned into

her. "Don't you know how I feel about you? And how much I hate myself for feeling that way about another cat so soon after Feathertail's death? I loved her, I really did! How can I love you too?"

"Me? But—"

"You walk in my dreams, Leafpool," Crowfeather whispered.

"No . . ." Leafpool breathed. "You can't love me. I'm a medicine cat." *And I can't love you,* she thought desperately. But she knew that she did, more than she had ever thought possible. To hear that Crowfeather loved her too was what she wanted more than anything else.

"Leafpool! Are you there, Leafpool?" Two cats were running up the edge of the hollow, and a moment later Cloudtail and Brightheart thrust their way among the thorns.

Leafpool and Crowfeather scrambled to their paws. "I'm over here!" Leafpool called.

Cloudtail rushed over to her, his tail fluffed out. "Are you okay?" he demanded. "Is this cat on our side or theirs?" He flicked his tail at Crowfeather.

Crowfeather began to bristle.

"I'm fine," Leafpool meowed hastily. "And Crowfeather's a friend. He was chasing those two ShadowClan warriors. Don't claw him, Cloudtail, please. He saved me from falling over the edge."

The white warrior's eyes narrowed. "Good."

"What happened to the ShadowClan cats?" Crowfeather asked.

"They're dead." Brightheart ducked under a branch to join her Clanmates. "They broke their necks."

Leafpool shivered, knowing how easily that could have been her neck, snapped in the plunge from the top of the rocks. Crowfeather gave her another searching look, then dipped his head to Cloudtail. "I'll go, then. When I left our camp, the fight was breaking up. Onewhisker is still leader of WindClan."

"What about—" Cloudtail began, but Crowfeather had already vanished among the trees.

Brightheart nudged her mate. "Come on; we must get back to the camp. And let's hope we don't have any more unexpected visitors."

For a moment Leafpool stared at the spot where Crowfeather had disappeared, before she turned and padded slowly after her Clanmates. She had nearly been killed by ShadowClan warriors attacking their camp, but she felt as though her paws walked on the wind, and her head was full of stars.

CHAPTER 23

❧

Brambleclaw hurled himself down the hill in pursuit of Mudclaw and Hawkfrost. Rain filled the air, as if the whole lake had been flung into the sky. It washed away the scent of the fleeing cats, and in the darkness Brambleclaw wasn't even sure he was going the right way. But fury lent speed to his paws and sent energy surging through him from ears to tail-tip until he was hardly aware of being cold and soaked to the skin.

A flash of lightning lit up the hillside, and Brambleclaw spotted his enemies streaking ahead of him: Mudclaw had almost reached the lakeshore, and Hawkfrost was a couple of tail-lengths behind. Two or three other dark shapes ran alongside them. In the chaos of the storm Brambleclaw couldn't be sure if any of his Clanmates had followed him, but he kept going, forcing his paws into an extra burst of speed.

The next flash of lightning showed he had halved the distance between himself and his quarry. He pelted past the horseplace, glimpsing a yellow gleam of light in the Twoleg nest on the far side of the field. He was briefly aware that there were no kittypets nearby as he hurtled along the shore close to the Gathering place.

He was forced to slow down when he came to the marsh, and his paws kept slipping from the rain-soaked tussocks of grass into pools of peaty water. Mud plastered his legs and belly fur. Snarling in frustration, he imagined Mudclaw and Hawkfrost escaping him.

His sense of kinship with Hawkfrost had vanished, and he felt hollow with the sense of betrayal. If his half brother thought he would escape a fight because they were kin, he was wrong!

He heard the sound of another cat splashing ahead of him, and made out a dark shape floundering in mud. Letting out a yowl of triumph, Brambleclaw leaped, but as he took off his hindpaws slipped on the soft ground and his straining forepaws barely grazed the other cat's fur. He landed awkwardly on one side; before he could recover a heavy weight landed on him, driving him into the mud, and he felt claws gouge deeply into his shoulder. Mudclaw's eyes, glaring with hatred, were a mouse-length from his own, and the WindClan cat's scent flooded over him.

"Traitor!" Brambleclaw gasped.

He tried to heave upward and throw his enemy off, but the sodden ground yielded under him, and he felt the icy touch of liquid mud soaking into his pelt. He battered helplessly against Mudclaw's belly with his hindpaws.

Mudclaw let out a snarl, baring his teeth. Brambleclaw braced himself as he waited for the shining fangs to meet in his throat. Then a darker shadow reared up beyond Mudclaw, and a massive tabby paw swatted the WindClan warrior on the side of the head. Mudclaw jerked back, off balance, and Brambleclaw managed to slide out from under him to see him grappling with Hawkfrost in a clump of reeds.

Utterly confused, Brambleclaw staggered to his paws, feeling the drag of wet mud plastered over his pelt. The next flash of lightning showed Hawkfrost standing over Mudclaw with one paw on his belly and the other pinning him by the throat. His pelt was soaked in mud, and his ice-blue eyes blazed.

He and Brambleclaw gazed at each other.

"You saved my life," Brambleclaw's voice shook. "Why, Hawkfrost? Why did you help me and not him?"

Mudclaw writhed under Hawkfrost's paws and spat out an insult, but Hawkfrost's gaze never left Brambleclaw. Even in the darkness the young ThunderClan warrior could not break away from the compelling ice-blue eyes. For a few moments the two of them seemed alone in the world, enclosed by the turmoil of the storm.

"You *helped* Mudclaw," Brambleclaw stammered. "You attacked WindClan, but now . . ."

Hawkfrost bowed his head. "True," he meowed. "I joined with Mudclaw because I believe he is the rightful leader of WindClan. But you're my brother, Brambleclaw. How could I let him kill you?"

His words struck Brambleclaw with the force of a blow. It was as if Hawkfrost had known all along that Onewhisker had not been appointed as deputy in the right way. Brambleclaw felt a strange stab of relief that he was not the only cat to fear StarClan would never approve him as the leader of WindClan.

"Mudclaw persuaded me to join with him," Hawkfrost went on. "He promised to leave RiverClan in peace if I and some of my Clanmates helped him drive out Onewhisker."

"Tell him what else I promised," Mudclaw snarled from beneath Hawkfrost's paws. "Tell him how *you* came to *me* and offered your help if I made you WindClan's deputy . . . and helped you take over RiverClan later."

"What?" Hawkfrost's eyes widened. "Brambleclaw, don't listen to him. Why would I want to leave RiverClan? And why would I need to ask any cat for that kind of help?" He lifted his head; Brambleclaw thought he had never seen a cat look so noble, even bleeding and muddy from the battle. "If I am to lead RiverClan one day, it will be by the warrior code, or not at all."

"Liar!" Mudclaw spat.

Hawkfrost shook his head. "I did only what I thought was right," he meowed to Brambleclaw. "Can you honestly say you never had any doubts about Onewhisker's leadership?"

Brambleclaw could not reply. His half brother's words struck too close to home.

As he hesitated, Mudclaw let out a hiss of triumph and heaved himself up, thrusting Hawkfrost back into a reedy pool. Brambleclaw crouched to fight back as the WindClan warrior leaped at him, but Hawkfrost, recovering rapidly, dived between them and lashed out furiously at Mudclaw with teeth and claws. Mudclaw veered to one side, then turned and fled, his dark shape soon lost in the night.

Without another word, Hawkfrost spun around and splashed off after him, leaving Brambleclaw to follow.

Lightning flashed again, and above the answering roll of thunder Brambleclaw heard a cat calling his name. He glanced back to see Squirrelflight standing behind him, her eyes wide with horror.

"What are you doing?" she gasped. "You're letting him go!"

"No—you don't understand—" Brambleclaw began.

"I heard what Mudclaw said! Hawkfrost helped him so he could be deputy of WindClan, and take over RiverClan. He's dangerous, Brambleclaw!"

"But Mudclaw was lying!" Brambleclaw protested.

A claw of lightning tore the sky from top to bottom. The pulsing blue-white flare lit up a cat standing on the shore opposite the island. It was Mudclaw. In the same heartbeat an earsplitting crack sounded across the water. The lightning crackled down to the topmost branches of one of the trees on the island, outlining it briefly in a spike of flame. The tree began to fall, gathering momentum as it toppled. Too late, Mudclaw turned to flee. His screech of terror was cut off as the tree crashed down on the shore, its branches clattering like bones.

Brambleclaw stumbled forward through the swamp until he reached firmer ground. As if the storm had done its work by destroying the tree, it began to move away; the next flash of lightning was over the hills, and the thunder echoed more distantly. The rain faded to a soft hiss, and ragged gaps began to appear in the clouds, allowing a feeble moonlight to fall over the lake.

By its light, Brambleclaw could see more cats gathering on the shore, among them Firestar, Onewhisker, and his deputy, Ashfoot. The WindClan leader looked exhausted, and blood trickled from a long gash on his shoulder. His eyes were hollow with the knowledge that Mudclaw and other WindClan warriors had been traitors plotting secretly against him.

Brambleclaw splashed his way across to his Clan leader and the WindClan cats. Together they approached the tree. Brambleclaw froze when he spotted movement among the branches. He braced himself, ready to battle to the death if Mudclaw was still alive. Then the branches shifted and a tabby cat backed clumsily out, his hindpaws scrabbling for a grip on the pebbles. Brambleclaw blinked. It was Hawkfrost. His half brother had his teeth fixed in Mudclaw's scruff as he dragged him into the open. The WindClan warrior's head lolled at an awkward angle, and his limbs trailed limply upon the ground.

Hawkfrost dragged him up to Onewhisker and let the body fall at the Clan leader's paws. "The tree crushed him," he rasped. "Your leadership is safe."

Onewhisker bent his head and sniffed at the former deputy. "The Clan will grieve for him," he murmured. "He was a fine warrior once."

Ashfoot let out a faint hiss. "He betrayed you!"

"As did you!" Onewhisker spat, rounding on Hawkfrost.

"You helped him." He unsheathed his claws, ready to spring on the massive tabby.

Hawkfrost bowed his head, and Brambleclaw felt his belly clench in horror at what Onewhisker might do in revenge.

"I admit it," Hawkfrost meowed. "And I ask your forgiveness. I truly believed that Mudclaw was the rightful leader of WindClan, and because of that, at his request, I brought cats from RiverClan and ShadowClan to help him. But StarClan has given us a clear sign by sending the lightning to destroy Mudclaw. Onewhisker, you are WindClan's true leader, chosen by StarClan. Do with me what you will."

Onewhisker glanced at Firestar, but the ThunderClan leader just flicked his ears, indicating that this was Onewhisker's problem to solve. Brambleclaw looked closely at Firestar, trying to read his reaction to the news that StarClan approved of Onewhisker's leadership after all. But Firestar's expression gave nothing away.

Meanwhile Ashfoot padded forward to investigate the branches of the fallen tree. "Hawkfrost is right, Onewhisker. You couldn't hope for a better sign than this. StarClan sent lightning to strike the tree and kill the cat who would have taken your place. There's no doubt now that you're the cat StarClan has chosen to lead WindClan."

Onewhisker raised his head, light growing in his eyes. "Then I shall be honored to accept my nine lives." Turning back to Hawkfrost, he went on, "I can't blame you for having doubts, nor any of the other cats who supported Mudclaw. How can I, when I doubted myself? I forgive you freely, you and all the rest."

Hawkfrost dipped his head again and stood back; Brambleclaw padded to his side and brushed against his sodden fur. "I still have to thank you for saving my life," he murmured.

Hawkfrost glanced at him with a flicker of warmth in his eyes. "At least I did one thing tonight I'm not ashamed of," he mewed.

Brambleclaw touched his half brother's shoulder with the tip of his tail. "You believed you were following the warrior code by helping Mudclaw. You can't feel guilty about that."

More cats had begun to appear along the lakeshore, among them Dustpelt and Brackenfur, Mistyfoot and Tornear. They gathered in a ragged semicircle around the Clan leaders and the body of Mudclaw.

"Look at this!" Brackenfur meowed. He jumped onto the tree and padded a little way across the lake water.

"It's like a Twoleg bridge!" Mistyfoot exclaimed.

Brackenfur turned back, springing down onto the pebbles with a rustle of branches. "We can use the fallen tree to reach the island," he meowed. "It's wide enough for all of us to cross safely. We can use it for Gatherings after all!"

Brambleclaw realized that the last problem with their new home had been solved. Thanks to Leafpool they had the Moonpool where they could share tongues with StarClan, and now the island would give them a safe place to gather that would belong to all the Clans, and none.

Instinctively he looked around for Squirrelflight, and

WARRIORS: THE NEW PROPHECY: STARLIGHT   321

spotted her standing beside Dustpelt. He took a pace toward her, wanting to convince her that Hawkfrost had told the truth about why he helped Mudclaw attack WindClan. But as her gaze met his, her eyes narrowed. Deliberately she turned away and began to stalk along the lakeshore.

Brambleclaw stared after her without moving. Squirrelflight clearly wanted nothing more to do with him. It wasn't hard to guess why—she must have seen him speaking with Hawkfrost. He felt hollow inside. Why did Squirrelflight always have to think the worst of the RiverClan warrior?

His dream of meeting Tigerstar and Hawkfrost flooded back into his mind. Whether Squirrelflight liked it or not, the three of them *were* kin. But he didn't share Tigerstar's bad blood; why couldn't the same be true for Hawkfrost?

Brambleclaw longed to share this victory with Squirrelflight, but he knew that as long as she saw only Tigerstar's worst possible legacy in him and his half brother, they could have no future together. He watched her pad along the shore, getting smaller and smaller, and waited until she had vanished among the shadows before he set out for home.

KEEP WATCH FOR

THE NEW PROPHECY

WARRIORS

BOOK 5:

TWILIGHT

As the clans adjust to the perils of their new home, Leafpool and Squirrelflight face difficult choices. One is torn between loyalty to her calling and a forbidden love, while the other struggles with her best friend's betrayal and her growing mistrust of him. Meanwhile, in the shadows, a terrible and unexpected enemy is lurking, planning vengeance . . . and for one beloved cat, the end is coming all too soon.